I0543836

The
Candy
Shop

S.R.Claridge

GLOBAL PUBLISHING GROUP

Global Publishing Group

Printed in the United States of America

First trade edition: November 2013

10 9 8 7 6 5 4 3 2 1

ISBN 978-0-9898467-7-6

The author would like to offer special thanks to her brilliant team of editors, whose expertise is invaluable: Cash, Jerrye, Gary, Matt and Beth

She would also like to thank her family and friends for their love and encouragement, her children for their ongoing patience and humor, her husband for his strength and constant support, and God for every blessing.

A complete list of books by S.R.Claridge is located at the back of this book.

For previews of upcoming novels, reviews and information about the author, visit AuthorSRClaridge.com or find her on Facebook.

CHAPTER 1

It was close to midnight when Special Detective, Rocco Sterling, squealed the tires of his black Hummer, cutting across traffic and whipping into the strip mall parking lot. At the rear of the mall, he leapt from his vehicle and made a beeline for Lieutenant Barkley and Officer Peters who were standing alongside a rusted out dumpster.

"Is it what I think?" Rocco asked, pulling a small flashlight from the pocket of his black, pleated slacks, while stepping atop a milk crate and shining the light into the dumpster.

"Depends on what you're thinking," Lieutenant Barkley grunted, adjusting his belt and maneuvering his pants up and over his beer gut. Barkley was in his late fifties and both his physique and enthusiasm for the job had seen better days.

Peering into the dumpster, Rocco grimaced. *Not again.* It was exactly as he had feared. There lie an attractive African American woman with her throat slit, her left ring finger severed and a single flower pinned to the front of her shirt.

"Third one this month," Lieutenant Barkley snorted. "So if you're thinking we're dealing with one sick, serial killing SOB, then it IS what you're thinking."

Rocco shook his head, narrowing his dark brows. "Who found the body?"

"Three kids who said they climbed into the dumpster, looking for donuts," Barkley explained with a snort, as if the idea was inconceivable.

"I remember doing that. We used to call them Dumpster Donuts," Office Peters interjected.

"That's gross," Barkley groaned.

"They're still fresh," Peters defended. "They just didn't sell during business hours so as soon as they were thrown away we'd climb into the dumpster and retrieve 'em."

"Yeah, well, you grew up in the ghetto," Barkley sneered. "Out here in the suburbs we bought our donuts like every other upstanding citizen."

Peters bit down on his lip. If he hadn't been the new kid on the force he might have dropped Barkley right then and there.

Climbing down from the crate, Rocco shined the flashlight along the outside of the dumpster and across the pavement. "I want the entire area printed and a DNA analysis on everything you find," he ordered.

"We've done that with every victim and every crime scene," Lieutenant Barkley objected. "We've never been able to find anything other than a trace of Lye used to burn off all of the victim's fingerprints. That is, except for the finger that's missing. This killer is clean and careful."

"Do it again," Rocco demanded.

"But…"

"Do it again!" Rocco seethed, whirling around to face Lieutenant Barkley. "Are you going to be able to follow my orders or should I get someone else for this case?"

Officer Peters' eyes widened as they maneuvered their way from Barkley to Rocco and back to Barkley. It was obvious that he had never witnessed Rocco's rage firsthand, though he had certainly heard the stories. Rocco Sterling had a reputation that superseded all others. He was the best detective in the city; maybe even the country and he had yet to fail at solving a murder case. He was known for becoming so intensely involved in his work that he would occasionally lose touch with reality. "If you want to find a serial killer, you have to think and act like a serial killer," Rocco gritted, taking a step closer to Barkley and leaning into his face. "You have to live and breathe like a serial killer. You get it?"

"Yeah, I got it." Narrowing his eyes, Barkley raised his chin in a slight upward nod.

Rocco headed back to his Hummer in long strides. Stopping just before opening the driver's door, he turned to Peters. "Oh, and I used to eat Dumpster Donuts too," he said, shooting Barkley a sarcastic grin and then directing his attention back to Peters. "Bear Claws were my favorite. Finding a Bear Claw meant it was going to be a great evening."

"Right on," Peters blurted and nodded his head enthusiastically. "I was a Long John man, myself."

Barkley sneered.

CHAPTER 2

Kira Sullivan pulled her dark, shoulder length hair back into a low ponytail and stared at her reflection. It was hard to miss the embedded lines time had drawn on her skin, despite her daily ritualistic attempts to reduce them. Everyone had told her forty was the new thirty, but they lied. Forty felt like forty; like life was suddenly half over. Aging was something Kira had trouble accepting, but it wasn't just because of wrinkles, the occasional sprouting gray hair or hot flashes. It was because everything in her world was changing.

Her twins, Michael and Mallory, left for college, rendering her nest empty for the first time in eighteen years. As a typical, mid-western, suburban housewife, Kira had spent the last eighteen years completely absorbed in her children, while her husband, Frank, finished law school and worked his way up to becoming a partner in one of the most prestigious firms in downtown St. Louis. Frank specialized in criminal law and handled all of the high-profile cases in the mid-western region; which meant his workload and travel were often extensive. His schedule was easier on Kira when the kids were home, because they kept her distracted and busy; but now that they were gone, their million-dollar, Ladue home felt like nothing more than an empty shell, shrouding her loneliness.

Kira washed her face and then applied moisturizer and make-up. Holding the eyeliner pencil close to her lashes, she hesitated, taking in her reflection. She was suddenly struck by the reality that no matter how much make-up she wore, it wouldn't conceal the sadness in the pale, blue eyes staring back at her. If it wasn't for the nagging of her best friend, Audrey, to meet for coffee this morning, Kira wouldn't have washed her face or put on make-up at all. In fact, she probably wouldn't have even gotten out of bed.

Arriving at the Starbucks ten minutes late, Kira scanned the shop. As soon as she saw Audrey sitting in a leather arm chair near the back, a lump formed in her throat. It was like being a little kid who falls down and feigns strength until he sees his mom, and then hurls himself into her arms crying. One look at Audrey and Kira could no longer control the wave of emotion. Approaching her best friend, the dam broke and she burst into sobs.

Audrey set her coffee cup on the table and leapt to her feet. "I knew you weren't okay!" She blurted, throwing her arms around Kira and holding her tightly. "Why didn't you call me?" She scolded. "You know I would have come over."

Kira couldn't answer. The lump in her throat was too thick and she feared if she tried to speak she would collapse into a blubbering heap.

"You're lonely," Audrey surmised, pulling back from their embrace and wiping

10

Kira's face with a tan napkin. Kira nodded. She was lonely, but what she was feeling was deeper than just loneliness. She felt as if a part of her life was over, and it was the only part she knew. Her children didn't need her anymore. Her husband was never home. All of a sudden, she felt completely alone.

"You need a hobby," Audrey said, motioning Kira to sit down and then fetching her a cup of coffee. "If you don't find something to do, you're going to slip into depression." Audrey flipped her long, red hair over her shoulder. "Hell, you might already be in depression."

She didn't want to admit it, but deep down she knew Audrey was right. Kira could feel herself on the edge of the abyss, not wanting to get up in the morning, not wanting to shower or clean the house, or even eat. Some mornings she would just stare at the wall and let the tears roll down her cheeks, not even sure of the nature of her thoughts or how to pull herself out of it.

"Look at you," Audrey spat. "You look like shit."

"I feel like shit," Kira sniveled, taking a sip of her non-fat, no-whip, Marble Macchiato. It was both tasty on her tongue and soothing for her soul.

Audrey dug into her Coach handbag and retrieved a small notepad and a pen. "Okay, let's make a list of things you like to do," she said, and this made Kira smile. It was just so Audrey. Ever since they were children, Audrey made lists. Lists for which

11

outfits they would wear to school, lists for which games they would play after school, lists of boys they liked and movies they wanted to see, lists of baby names and later in life, lists of divorce attorneys. Audrey's lists were endless. "What do you like to do?" She asked, her green eyes sparkling with excitement for the task at hand.

Kira shrugged and wiped away the tears that had run down around her chin. Part of the problem was she didn't know what she liked to do. Her whole life had revolved around her children. At first, it was soccer games and cub scouts and being the best room mother. Then, it was Mallory's gymnastics and cheerleading and Michael's football and baseball. Between the kid's schedules, Kira had no time to herself; no time to discover her own interests. She used to love to snuggle on the couch and watch late night movies with Frank, but that was before he became a partner in the firm. Now, when he was home, it was only to fall into bed exhausted, get up the next morning, shower and leave again.

"Do you like to paint?" Audrey asked. Kira shook her head and scrunched up her nose. "Do you like to sculpt things?" Again, Kira shook her head. "Weird," Audrey remarked. "When we were kids you were always the artistic one."

"That was just a phase," Kira said.

All of a sudden, Audrey's eyes widened and she snapped her fingers and pointed at Kira. "You like to dance!" She announced loudly enough that two ladies at the next table peered over the top of their coffee drinks. "I remember you dancing in college. What was the name of that club?"

"Sshhh," Kira scolded. "That was a long time ago."

"Yeah, so? You loved it, right?" Audrey's eyes were beaming with a naughty gleam.

"Yes, I loved it," Kira blushed. "But I'm too old for that now, and Frank would kill me."

Audrey wrote the word, DANCE, on her piece of paper and circled it. "You're not too old; you just turned forty and look at you." She gave her a once over and then scrunched up her face. "Well, don't look at yourself right now, but when you're all fixed up, you're one hot mama."

"Sshhh!" Kira protested.

"And besides, who says Frank needs to know?" Audrey rolled her eyes. "The man's never home anyway."

This was the problem with Audrey. She had ideas, and once she put those ideas into a person's mind, it was difficult to get rid of them. The bigger dilemma was that Audrey was usually right, though that didn't mean her ideas were good; and it certainly didn't mean they wouldn't backfire. This was one of the reasons Frank and Audrey didn't like each other. Frank was a rule-follower and Audrey, a rule-breaker. Frank was also best friends with Audrey's ex-husband, Leon. No one knew what really caused their divorce. Leon said he caught Audrey in bed with another man, which was why he claimed to have started fraternizing with his assistant. Audrey's story depicted Leon with his assistant first and her infidelity was a mere act of retaliation. Either way, the marriage ended but Audrey and Leon's hatred for one another lived on.

"There's an underground Gentleman's Club, called The Candy Shop, on the Riverfront," Audrey excitedly explained. "I've heard that it has a main level where men come to watch women dance and a lower level which is reserved for high paying customers with private interests." Audrey raised one eyebrow, gleaming. "If you know what I mean."

"I'm not interested in any man's private interests," Kira gawked. "I'm married, remember?"

"Sure, I remember but does Frank?" Audrey mumbled beneath her breath.

Pursing her lips together Kira gave Audrey a look that told her to stop picking on Frank. "So he's not the most attentive husband in the world," she defended. "He loves me and we've built a life together."

Audrey rolled her eyes. "I'll make you a deal. If I can get us interviews at The Candy Shop, you have to go with me and interview for a dancer position." Audrey extended her hand across the table. "Deal?"

"Deal," Kira agreed, with a sigh. What were the chances that Audrey could even get the interviews, much less the chance that a strip club on the Landing in St. Louis would want to hire two forty-something's? Slim-to-none, Kira thought. So, later that afternoon when Audrey called to say she had scheduled interviews for them at The Candy Shop, Kira was shocked; but a deal was a deal. After all, what was the harm in going downtown and taking a look?

After showering and blowing her hair dry, Kira gazed at her reflection in the mirror. Was she still young enough to dance the way she did in college? Could she ever feel that carefree and sexy again? She exhaled. Was she lonely for her husband, her fading youth or the feeling of being wanted and needed? She didn't know, but desperation created a willingness to find out.

Several hours later, when she opened the front door to let Audrey inside, her stomach wrenched into nervous knots. "Are you ready for this?" Audrey beamed.

Ready? No. Kira wasn't even sure if she would be able to go through with it and she was worried about what Frank would say if he ever found out.

"I don't know," Kira mumbled. "What if Frank..."

"He won't find out!" Audrey interrupted. "The only way he could possibly find out is if he kept his ass in town long enough to notice you." Audrey put her hands on her hips and cocked her head to the side. "Sweetie, he hasn't been in your life for the past eighteen years, do you really think he's going to start caring now?"

Her words rang true but that truth hollowed out Kira's stomach. It wasn't that Frank didn't love her. She knew he loved her, but their relationship hadn't been a priority for him in a long time. Besides, Audrey was right. Frank was working late again and Kira knew she could return from the interview well before he came home.

"Is that what you're wearing?" Audrey asked, sliding past Kira and heading toward the kitchen. Kira gazed downward and studied her outfit. She was wearing a navy blue pencil skirt, a white blouse with a navy jacket and navy pumps. "You look like an airline attendant," Audrey blurted. "You'll never get the job wearing that."

"What are you wearing?" Kira chided, and Audrey opened her tan trench coat to reveal a bright red negligée and thigh high black stockings with lace around the top. Kira gasped. "I don't own anything like that."

Audrey pulled a small bag from her purse. "You do now," she winked. "I got you a black one." She said smiling with a cat-that-ate-the-mouse grin. "Go put it on," she ordered. "We don't want to be late."

Kira rushed to the bedroom, slipped on the lingerie and surveyed her reflection in the full-length mirror. She was thankful for all of the Pilates classes that had kept her figure slim and her muscles toned. "I don't actually look half bad," she mumbled to herself, switching the navy pumps for a pair of black, strappy stilettos; and then she pulled on her black trench coat and cinched the belt around her waist.

The Candy Shop was a stand-alone building, sitting right on the cobblestone streets of the St. Louis Riverfront, overlooking the Mississippi River. Valet parking was the only option, unless they wanted to park several blocks away and walk; an idea Kira didn't want to entertain while dressed in lingerie and stilettos. "People will think we're hookers," she told Audrey.

The valet looked more like a night-club bouncer than a person who parked cars. He stood six foot four and Kira guessed he was two hundred and twenty pounds of pure muscle. He was bald, dressed head to toe in black, had a black goatee and wore dark glasses, despite the fact that it was dusk. Opening the passenger side door, he helped Kira step out and then walked around the car, took the keys from Audrey and pulled away in Audrey's black Land Cruiser; never uttering a word.

"I hope he brings it back," Audrey mumbled, watching intently as her car pulled away.

"He will," a voice came from behind them and Kira whirled around to see a man, dressed in a dark gray, silk suit and shiny black wing tipped shoes. He stood five foot, ten inches tall, his black hair was salted with gray and his eyes were dark brown. "Ladies," he said, pulling open the solid steel door and motioning them inside. Butterflies fluttered in Kira's stomach. Part of her wanted to turn around and run, but curiosity begged her to stay.

Through the steel door was another set of doors. They were wooden and oversized, with metal spikes and a large dragon headed knocker that gave a medieval feel. Using the knocker, the man hit the door two times, and then glanced up at a security camera which hung in the corner to the left, and gave a nod. A loud clicking sound let them know they had been granted access and the man pulled the door open and ushered them inside.

The entry way was painted dark red and sensual, black and white photographs, hung in thick black frames to the left above two red velvet arm chairs. The floor was light hardwood and a chandelier with tiny red lamp shades on each bulb hung overhead. Long, jagged shards of mirrored glass hung on the wall to the right and reflected the light from the chandelier. Two oversized, medieval looking doors were straight ahead and Kira swallowed hard as the man led them toward the doors.

"Mr. Coronado is expecting you," he said, pulling open one of the doors so that the ladies could step through. "Wait in here."

"Thank you," Audrey said. Kira wanted to speak, but her throat was suddenly dry. *Coronado. Why does that name ring a bell?*

When the man left, Kira turned to Audrey, grabbing her arms. "What are we doing here?" She wailed. "This is insane."

"We're getting you a hobby, remember?" Audrey snapped. "Besides, look around, it's fascinating."

She wasn't wrong. Kira glanced around the room and it was indeed fascinating. It resembled a living room, with two red velvet couches in the center of the room, atop a red patterned rug and a light wooden coffee table that held a line of candles, all in different colors and sizes. To the left was another set of double, wooden, medieval doors and to the right was a single wooden door. Four large stained glass windows, running from ceiling to floor, covered the far wall, each with one star shaped pane of clear glass. Inching closer, Kira noticed that the star was eye-level for an average height person and looked down into what she could only guess was the nightclub. It had a large stage, adorned with gold dancing poles and two golden, hanging cages on either side. A runway jetted out from the front of the stage and was surrounded by cocktail tables and red, velvet covered chairs. She swallowed hard, as the fact that she was about to audition for The Candy Shop felt surreal.

"Beautiful," he said, entering the room and walking briskly toward Kira. "Absolutely breathtaking." Kira turned from the windows and met eyes with Mr. Coronado, who strode past Audrey as if she wasn't even there, took Kira's hand and kissed the top of it. "Demure," he sighed. "That's what my high paying customers like. Demure."

"Mr. Coronado, my name is Audrey and this is Kira," Audrey spoke, extending her hand to shake his; but he never took his eyes off of Kira, nor did he release her hand, which began to make Kira feel uncomfortable. "We're here for the interview," Audrey said, trying to re-direct his attention.

Mr. Coronado was an unusual looking man. He was in his mid-fifties, stood six feet tall with grayish brown hair and crystal clear blue eyes that were so clear they looked almost white. His chin was pointy and his smile reminded Kira of the Joker from Batman. He was dressed in crisply pleated, black slacks and a black and gray patterned V-neck sweater that revealed a tiny clump of chest hair and a platinum skull chain that hung around his neck. He seemed to slither across the room.

"Yes, the interview," he said. "Come, let's have a seat." He released Kira's hand and motioned them toward the red velvet couches. He sat on one while Kira and Audrey sat on the other, facing him. "Let me ask you, first, why you have come to me today?"

Kira wasn't prepared for the question, but thankfully Audrey didn't miss a beat. "We understand The Candy Shop is a high-class establishment where women like us can do what we enjoy in a safe, upscale environment." Audrey sounded so poised it made Kira wonder if she had rehearsed it.

Mr. Coronado looked amused by her answer, or maybe he was simply amused by her; Kira wasn't sure which. "And, what about you?" He asked Kira directly.

She knotted her fingers together in her lap and swallowed hard. "I used to dance in college," she looked up, sheepishly. "I'm probably too old now, but ..."

"I don't employ trampy twenty-something's," he replied curtly, cutting her off. "I employ high class women, who possess sensual beauty." He leaned back, draping his arms across the back of the couch and crossing his right leg over his left. "I employ women with passion." The word seemed to ooze from his lips as his eyes tore through Kira. "Do you have passion?"

"Yes, we..." Audrey began but he interrupted.

"I was talking to Kira."

Kira's breath caught in her chest. Did she have passion? She didn't know anymore. It had been a long time since she had viewed herself as a sensual creature with passion. She blinked quickly, suddenly feeling as if she might hyperventilate.

"You'll find I'm a very patient man," he said, obviously noticing her struggle to form words. "Why don't I have some of the ladies give you a tour and then we'll meet back here."

As he stepped out of the room, Audrey turned to Kira. "What the hell is wrong with you?" She blurted. "He's totally into you and you're like a deer in the headlights."

"I'm sorry," Kira moaned. "He makes me nervous and he kind of creeps me out."

She leaned forward and buried her face in her hands. "I can't believe we're actually doing this. We shouldn't be here."

Audrey scowled. "Don't blow this. I need this and so do you."

Two women opened the double doors and glided in. One was tall and blonde with cleavage stacked so high that Kira found it distracting. She wore bright red lipstick, too much eye liner and her hair hung almost to her bottom. The other woman was Kira's height, had short, dark brown hair, chocolate brown eyes and a warm smile. Both were scantily dressed.

"I'm Miranda," said the brunette, "and this is Shelby." Shelby gave an overly bubbly wave and giggle. "We'll have to make this short because we open in an hour and we have to finish getting ready."

Miranda led the tour and it was quickly evident to Kira that Miranda was the brains and Shelby was the bobble headed eye-candy. They visited the main stage area, backstage and the dressing room. "Lucas will choose your clothing each night," Miranda explained.

"Lucas?" Kira asked.

"Mr. Coronado," Miranda clarified.

"Once you're hired, you'll get to call him by his first name," Shelby giggled.

"IF you're hired," added Miranda with a condescending smirk.

"Exactly what kind of entertainment do you provide?" Audrey asked, using her fingers to make quotation marks around the word entertainment.

Miranda shot Audrey a glare that said she didn't appreciate the innuendo. "We're not prostitutes or call-girls if that's what you were implying."

"No...I..." Audrey stopped. "What I meant to ask was do you strip?"

Shelby giggled. "Only topless. We're not allowed to show anything from the waist down."

"Lucas will give you his guidelines IF he decides you're Candy Shop material," Miranda remarked. "Let's head back."

"What about the downstairs?" Audrey blurted.

Miranda turned slowly, her eyes narrowing. "How do you know about the downstairs?"

"Just rumors," Audrey said.

"Well, you can discuss those rumors with Lucas," she smirked sarcastically and made quotation marks around the word rumors. "I doubt you're downstairs material."

Kira saw Audrey's jaw tighten at the insult and she reached over and squeezed her arm, willing her to calm down and let it go. Audrey rolled her eyes and wrenched her arm away.

Shelby and Miranda led them back to the living room where they waited for Mr. Coronado to return. Audrey sat on the red velvet couch, with her arms crossed, swinging her leg impatiently; while Kira stood in front of the stained glass windows peering down at the stage. She couldn't deny the fact that she felt drawn to it. Common sense told her this was crazy and wrong; but something deep inside yearned for it.

"What a bitch!" Audrey blurted out of the blue. "That Miranda is on my shit list."

Kira laughed at the thought of Audrey's ever-growing shit list. She kept an actual list entitled 'Shit List' and she added names through the years. "Just ignore her," Kira said. "She obviously has a chip on her shoulder."

"She's not even that pretty. Why would Lucas hire someone like that anyway?" Audrey snapped.

"Because she was requested by one of my highest paying patrons," Mr. Coronado answered, having entered the room without either of them noticing. "You see, my customers, my clientele, are my priority. What they request, I offer. It's a form of customer service to which the majority of the outside world is not accustomed." He slid onto the couch across from Audrey and motioned for Kira to come and sit. "I do something for you and then you do something for me. That's how effective businesses are run. Now, stand up and remove your coats," he ordered.

Audrey rose first, un-tied her trench coat and let it fall to the floor around her ankles. Kira rose, un-cinched her coat and draped it off of her shoulders, but kept it mostly on. Mr. Coronado grinned. "Ah," he sighed. "The bold and the demure." He rose from the couch and gestured toward the doors. "Ian will see you out. Come back tomorrow at six o'clock sharp for your wardrobe and new ID's. We'll do a test run tomorrow evening and see if you have what it takes."

"ID's?" Audrey asked.

"The Candy Shop is a private club, exclusive in its membership. You won't be entertaining Frat parties, ladies, nor will you be dancing in front of your neighbor's beer-gutted husband." He raised his eyebrows. "The exclusivity and privacy of my members is in direct correlation to the exclusivity and private identities of my employees."

"I don't understand," Kira whispered.

"I'll assign you a new name and ensure that no one from your circle of existence is present in the club during your shift," he explained.

"How do you ensure that?" Audrey snorted. "You'd have to background check everybody."

"Yes," he nodded, matter-of-factly. "Now, if you'll excuse me." Mr. Coronado exited the room and Ian, the man in the gray silk suit who had originally escorted them inside, led them back into the lobby to wait for Audrey's car to be brought around.

"Ian," Audrey said. "I hate to be a bother, but do you think I could use the powder room before we leave?"

"Certainly," he nodded, and led Audrey back through the double doors, leaving Kira waiting in the lobby alone. Glancing at her reflection in the shards of glass, excitement began to replace trepidation. She felt young

25

again, and though Mr. Coronado frightened her, she couldn't deny that the attention from a strange man somehow nourished her soul.

It was taking Audrey a long time to use the bathroom, and Kira sank into one of the red velvet chairs, noting the softness of the fabric against her skin. She leapt to her feet when Ian came back through the double doors without Audrey in tow. He appeared startled to see that she was still there, but quickly re-focused his attention on the main door; opening it and gesturing a tall gentleman inside.

"Good evening, sir," Ian said. "May I take your coat?"

Kira met eyes with the gentleman and felt her heart flutter. He was handsome, in a polished, sophisticated sort of way. He wore a black suit with a gray textured tie and long black trench coat, which Ian slid from his body and tucked over his arm. His hair was short and dark brown, his skin was tan and his eyes were an alluring hazel. He nodded at Kira and she quickly lowered her eyes to the floor, unsure of whether she was supposed to acknowledge him. With all the talk about privacy and exclusivity, Kira didn't know if her seeing him and him seeing her was some sort of violation of Mr. Coronado's rules. After all, what would have happened if he was someone she knew? That could have been devastating.

As Ian led him through the double doors and into the living room, Kira sank back into the red velvet chair, feeling a twinge of guilt for the instant attraction she had felt for

this stranger. In her defense, she didn't get
out much, so her sphere of men was small;
and none of them looked anything like him.
Her lustful urges were limited to a few good-
looking actors, so she found it startling when
a real man in real life triggered a flustered,
hormonal surge. Not wanting to endure
endless teasing, she decided not to tell Audrey
about the encounter.

CHAPTER 3

Frank didn't come home until after two o'clock in the morning and then he was up again and gone by six. He kissed Kira on the forehead before leaving and told her he would be working late again that evening. For the first time, this was good news, as she would be working her first shift at The Candy Shop. Later that day, Kira practiced dancing in front of a mirror, hoping she still had the right moves.

Arriving at the club, Audrey and Kira were re-routed to the employee entrance, which sat in a back alley between two big dumpsters. Ian escorted them to the dressing room, where he handed each of them a garment bag with their name on it. "Inside you'll find your outfit for the evening, and your new identification. Please take a moment to review the information and convert it to memory," he explained. "Kira, as soon as you are dressed, Mr. Coronado would like to speak with you in the living room."

"I wonder why he wants to see me?" Kira pondered after Ian had left.

"He probably doesn't think you've got what it takes to be here," Miranda chided, striding passed Kira and Audrey and sitting down in front of one of the make-up mirrors.

"She's got more than what it takes," Audrey defended. "Wait until you see her dance."

"Oh, she won't get to see you," Shelby said, bouncing over and fluffing her long blonde hair. "Miranda only does private meetings downstairs. She's got this one super-duper hot client and all he wants her to do is..."

"Shut up!" Miranda jumped to her feet and barked at Shelby.

Shelby's eyes grew wider. "I'm sorry. I didn't think it was a secret."

"Well, it is, so shut up." Miranda huffed out of the room.

"What's wrong with her?" Audrey asked.

Shelby lowered her voice. "She's in love with her client, like totally ga-ga over him, but he hasn't touched her yet." She shrugged. "I told her maybe he's gay, but she swears he's not."

"Are men allowed to touch us?" Kira asked, alarmed by the prospect. Dancing was one thing, but touching was quite another. Kira had no desire to betray Frank's trust or be unfaithful to their marriage.

"They can't touch you upstairs, but I don't know what the rules are downstairs," Shelby replied. "I know there's a high turnover rate downstairs, though. Most ladies last a week or so and then they're gone. They just never show back up for work. Miranda has stuck around the longest, but it's only because she's in love with this guy. She won't tell me what goes on down there."

Audrey pulled Kira to the side and whispered in her ear. "Yesterday, when I said

I had to use the bathroom, I sneaked downstairs to get a peek."

Kira's eyes widened. "You could have gotten caught," she gasped.

Audrey shrugged and rolled her eyes. "Anyway, it's really dark and there's a bar and individual rooms."

"Bedrooms?" Kira whispered.

"I think so. I couldn't see inside the rooms because all of the doors were shut."

A dancer with long black hair strode passed in a bright blue sequined G-string. "You girls better stop your yappin' and get dressed," she scolded.

"Thanks Cher," Audrey mumbled sarcastically, so only Kira could hear and they both giggled. The woman did have an uncanny resemblance to Cher.

Unzipping her garment bag, Kira looked at the outfit Mr. Coronado had chosen for her first night and breathed a sigh of relief. It was classier than she had expected. It was a black sequined mini-dress with black stiletto heels and thigh-high black hose. She was instantly intrigued by the fact that everything fit perfectly. Before she had time to open the white envelope which contained her new identification, Ian poked his head into the dressing room and motioned for her to follow him.

"Mr. Coronado has been waiting for you," Ian sounded stressed. "He doesn't like waiting."

"I'm sorry," Kira uttered breathlessly, following him out of the dressing room, down the long red hallway, up the staircase and through the double doors into the living room. Ian shook his head disapprovingly as he ushered her into the living room and then closed the doors. She saw Mr. Coronado standing near the windows, staring down at the stage.

Upon hearing the door close, he turned to face Kira. "How do you like the dress I've chosen?" He asked.

Kira glanced down at her outfit, noticing right away that she was still clutching the white envelope. "It's beautiful. Thank you," she blushed.

He turned his attention back to the stage. "Every night I watch my girls perform," he spoke slowly, deliberately. "I see how they work the crowd and I study the demographic to which they most appeal. This helps me know when to schedule each performer."

"That makes sense," Kira said, still standing by the door and twisting her fingers around the envelope.

Turning to face her, Mr. Coronado scowled. "You look nervous. We need to give you something to take the edge off." Kira didn't know what to say, as a prickling sensation of fear crept slowly up the back of her neck. He slithered toward a bar which sat in the far right corner of the room, pulled out a stainless steel martini shaker and began cocktail preparations. Kira thought it odd that she hadn't noticed the bar there yesterday and wondered how she could have missed such a prominent piece of furniture. It was large enough to seat three people, was solid black with a red marble top and had three black velvet stools sitting in front.

His eyes never left her as he shook the stainless steel shaker and poured a vodka martini into a chilled glass, finishing it with a bleu cheese olive. Setting the glass atop the bar, he told Kira to sit in one of the stools. "We're going to Role play," he said and she thought her heart was going to beat right out of her chest.

"Role play?" She repeated with hesitancy.

"Yes," he grinned. "Most of the ladies I employ start on the stage and over time, they develop favorite clients who request them downstairs." He lifted the martini and handed it to Kira. "I believe this is exactly how you like it."

How did he know what drink she liked, not to mention her dress and shoe size? This was getting weirder by the moment. She wanted to ask, but he continued talking.

"You see, I start my girls off slowly." He licked his lips and paused. "Have you ever received a big box of chocolate candy?"

Kira nodded and Lucas lifted her glass indicating she should drink. "You can't eat the box all at once now can you?" He shook his head to indicate no. "You have to take bite size pieces."

This story was making Kira crave chocolate.

"Every once in a while I have a client that will request a lady before she has started her stage training and this concerns me."

"Like Miranda?" Kira asked, the martini helping her find the strength to speak.

"Precisely like Miranda," he smiled and Kira was instantly reminded of the Joker again. "When this happens, I oblige the client by allowing the lady to bypass the stage and escort him downstairs, but I want to make sure that she is not trying to eat the box of chocolate all at once."

Kira's heart started to beat faster. Why was he telling her this? Why hadn't he asked to see Audrey too?

"Now, I see questions in your eyes and trepidation on your face," he said. "Sip your martini and I will explain." Mr. Coronado moved around the bar and stood next to her, with his left hand on the bar and his right hand dangling by his side. Each time Kira set her glass down he picked it up and handed it to her. It was obvious that he wanted her to finish the entire drink. "One of my very best customers has requested a private meeting with you."

"With me?" Kira gasped, choking on her martini and sending herself into a coughing spell. "No one even knows I'm here," she said, once the coughing had subsided.

"The privacy of my clients is my utmost concern. I don't ask questions. I provide services," he replied poignantly. "You will meet with him this evening at 8:00pm sharp in the Lair."

"The Lair?" Kira's head was becoming lighter from the effects of the martini.

"That's what we call the downstairs bar," he clarified. "You will meet him at the bar in the Lair at 8:00pm."

"Mr. Coronado?" Kira slurred, feeling suddenly woozier than she should have after only one martini.

"Lucas," he interrupted. "You may call me Lucas."

"Lucas," she repeated, and then gripped the bar to steady herself on the stool. "I'm feeling dizzy."

"Yes, that's normal; the effect will level out in a few moments."

"The effect of what?" Kira asked, aware that what she was feeling was not the alcohol.

"I gave you a special cocktail," he winked, "to make the night easier and take the edge off."

Under normal circumstances this would have made Kira angry, but suddenly she felt elated, like she was floating peacefully through the sky, hovering far above any negativity. She couldn't stop from smiling as insecurity and inhibition melted away. She was high, wistfully higher than she'd ever been. Sliding her hand inside Lucas's, she grinned, "So, where's my box of chocolate?"

"Good girl," Lucas stroked her fingers. "But before I tell you about your gentleman caller, I have to tell you about you." He took the envelope that was still gripped in her left hand, tore it open and set the paper in front of her atop the bar. "While you are here, this is your name."

Kira squint her eyes at the paper. It read: DAISY. She suddenly felt the urge to giggle. "Daisy? That's a flower not a name," she snorted.

"Yes," Lucas said. "It is a beautiful, simple, demure flower having no thorns. It's a flower that grows freely in the open."

"I'm no Daisy," Kira objected. "Why can't I have a normal name, like Miranda and Shelby?"

Lucas appeared to be amused by her new found courage to speak her mind. "Miranda and Shelby have stage names as well. All of my ladies are named after a flower."

"What's Miranda's name?" Kira blurted.

"Rose. Because she has thorns," Lucas remarked and a flash of anger lit his eyes.

"What about Audrey?" Kira cleared her throat. "What's her name?"

"Camellia, because her hair is the bright, red color of a camellia flower." He said it with an air of pride, as if choosing a name for every woman meant he had somehow contributed to creating them, like each one was his personal masterpiece. Lucas stepped behind Kira and pulled the clip from her hair. "Your gentleman friend prefers dark hair to be worn down," he said and placed the clip atop the bar. "Now, finish freshening up and meet Ian at the door to the Lair at 7:50pm and remember, don't eat the whole box in one sitting."

Upon returning to the dressing room, Kira was shocked to find Audrey in a bright red sequined G-string, bikini with white Go-Go boots. "Where have you been?" Audrey clucked when she saw Kira. "You missed all the excitement!"

"I had to meet with Mr. Corona...I mean, Lucas," she slurred. "What excitement?" Kira couldn't stop staring at Audrey's outfit. She looked very seventies seductive.

"Miranda came rushing in here, screaming at the top of her lungs and threw her heels into the mirror," Audrey explained, her eyes wide with drama.

"Yeah," Shelby added. "She was dropping F-bombs like crazy and the bouncer had to carry her out."

"What happened?" Kira asked, still feeling like she was floating above the ground.

"I don't know," Shelby shrugged.

"What did Mr. Coronado want with you?" Audrey asked, changing the subject.

"He wants me to meet a client in the Lair at 8:00pm, and I'm not supposed to eat all the chocolate," Kira replied with no inhibition.

"Already?" Shelby gasped. "You must have been requested by someone."

"How could someone request her?" Audrey barked. "This is our first night, and what chocolate."

Kira shrugged, unable to stop smiling. "I don't know. Weird, huh?"

Audrey studied her. "What's wrong with you?"

"Nothing. I feel incredible." In fact she felt so incredible that her smile seemed to stretch from one ear to the other.

"That's what I mean." Audrey crossed her arms and narrowed her eyes. "Who are you and what have you done with my best friend?" Kira giggled as Audrey grabbed her by the shoulders and stared intently into her eyes. "You're stoned," she blurted. "You're higher than a frickin' kite!"

Shelby leapt up from the make-up table. "We're not allowed to use drugs," she said, with her mouth agape and her eyes wide. "You'll be in trouble if Lucas catches you with drugs."

"We don't have any drugs," Audrey scowled at Shelby and then looked at Kira. "Do we?"

Still smiling, she shook her head to indicate no. "Lucas made me a martini to take the edge off," she slurred.

"Son of a...." Audrey didn't finish her sentence because Ian opened the door and announced it was time for Kira to head to the Lair. "She'll be right there," Audrey firmly told Ian and gave him such a glare that Ian quickly retreated and closed the door behind him. "Listen, Kira," Audrey leaned closer. "You don't want to do anything you're going to regret."

"Or anyone," Shelby added with a snort and a giggle.

"That's not funny," Audrey scolded. "We were just supposed to come here to dance. That's it."

"Sounds like someone's jealous that they didn't get picked to go to the Lair," Shelby sneered.

"I'm not jealous, I'm concerned," Audrey replied.

"Don't worry," Kira said, "I'm gonna take bite size pieces and not eat the chocolate all at once." Kira spun around and almost fell over from the dizziness and Audrey grabbed her before she crashed into a row of hanging costumes.

"Martini, my ass," Audrey blurted. "He slipped you a Mickey."

Kira giggled and broke into an off-key rendition of "Oh mickey, you're so fine, you're so fine you blow my mind..."

"You're loaded," Audrey moaned while Shelby joined Kira in shouting, "Hey mickey!" She then shrieked, "I love that song!"

Ian opened the door a second time and insisted that Kira follow him to the Lair. "I'll be fine," she assured Audrey and sauntered into the hallway behind Ian.

"I wonder if Lucas is going to give all of us chocolate?" Shelby said excitedly.

They were only a few steps from the entrance of the Lair when Miranda came rushing down the hall with the big, bald valet hot on her trail. Upon seeing Kira, she growled in a low, loud, raspy tone, screamed with fury and dove on top of Kira, grabbing her by the hair and pulling her to the ground.

"You bitch!" Miranda screamed. "You think you can replace me?! I'll kill you for this! I'll kill you!"

Before Kira could utter a sound, the valet ripped Miranda off of her and dragged her down the hall, kicking and thrashing. "I'm going to tell everyone," she screamed. "Everyone!"

Ian bent down and lifted Kira to her feet. "Are you okay?" He asked and then paused to look at her. "Aw, hell, you're bleeding," he blurted with a tone that indicated annoyance more than concern. "This is going to cause a delay." He took what looked like a small walkie-talkie from his pocket and spoke into it. "We need medical attention, ASAP. Meet us in the living room."

By the time Ian and Kira entered the living room, Lucas and two other women were waiting. One woman held a first aid kit and the other a make-up case. They rushed toward Kira and began working on cleansing and covering the deep scratches Miranda had left on her neck and shoulder, while Lucas and Ian stood in the corner speaking quietly.

Fifteen minutes and a new, un-torn pair of stockings later, Kira looked as good as new and was escorted back to the Lair entrance. "Your gentleman will meet you at the bar," Ian said.

"How will I know him?" Kira nervously asked, the effects of her mickey-laced martini beginning to wear off.

"He'll know you," he replied matter-of-factly.

She was suddenly overcome with nerves. This wasn't what she wanted. She had only intended to take the stage and dance again, not become some stranger's sexual fantasy. She wrung her fingers together and fought the tears threatening her make-up. "I don't want to do this," she whispered to Ian. "I've changed my mind. I want to go home."

Ian's jaw tightened. "I'd hate to have to tell one of Mr. Coronado's highest paying customers that he's been denied the services he has so generously paid for in advance."

"I came here to dance, not have sex," Kira rebutted.

Ian opened the door to the Lair. "Then go inside and dance." His eyes flashed with something Kira couldn't identify. Was it anger? Fear? "Either you keep your appointment or we'll inform your husband of where he can come to pick you up."

Kira's mouth went instantly dry and tears stung the back of her eyes. Frank could never know she was here or that she had ever entertained the notion of dancing again. He would see everything as a betrayal and it would crush him. "Okay," Kira mouthed. "I'll meet him but after that I'm leaving and never coming back."

Ian gave a nod, motioned her through the door and closed it behind her. Chills darted up the back of her neck when she heard the click of the lock.

CHAPTER 4

Ian placed a piece of duct tape over Miranda's lips and then injected a syringe into the side of her neck. Her body instantly went limp. "Take her," he told the valet, who then dragged her out the back entrance of The Candy Shop where a black stretch limousine was waiting. When the back door opened, he shoved her inside.

"You know where to take her?" The valet asked.

"Oh, yeah." The man in the backseat uttered sadistically, running his fingertips up the inside of her thigh. "I know exactly where to take her."

Shutting the door, the valet watched as the limousine sped off. "You're one sick son of a bitch," he mumbled under his breath.

CHAPTER 5

Kira stood in the hallway for a few seconds, trying to calm her nerves. Her heart was beating wildly as she inched her way down the dark hallway, lined in red velvet drapes and tiny golden sconces casting a yellowish glow. The hallway emptied into the main bar area of the Lair and it was as Audrey had described. The floor was deep, red, plush carpeting, the kind your feet sunk into. There were cocktail tables and chairs and red, velvet couches lining the walls and spaced sporadically throughout the room. The walls were painted dark red, the lighting was dim yellow and shards of mirrored glass and sensual, black and white, framed photographs were hanging eccentrically in various locations. To the left was a bar with six stools. A large mirror hung behind the bar and in front of the mirror stood a bartender dressed in a black tuxedo. He was steadily shaking an aluminum martini shaker. To the right were six closed doors that Kira guessed led to private bedrooms.

Stepping through the red, velvet curtains that adorned the entrance from the hallway to the Lair, Kira immediately recognized the man sitting at the bar. It was the man she had seen in the lobby yesterday, the strikingly handsome one with the dark hair and the bright, hazel eyes; the one that had made her feel flustered. Could this be the gentleman who requested to meet with her? Inching closer, she studied him, all the while wondering why he would have requested her. Taking another step, Kira was startled by an arm that draped around her waist and pulled her toward an inset booth to the immediate right of the entrance. The booth resembled a small cave, and had a red velvet, u-shaped couch and a small cocktail table. Once inside, a person couldn't be seen by anyone in the room unless they walked directly in front of the cave-like opening. Kira was whisked inside and pushed onto the couch, where she sat face-to-face with her worst nightmare.

"Kira Sullivan, as I live and breathe," he said, his eyes beaming with sadistic delight. "I had no idea you were one of the sweet little bits and pieces that make up the Candy Shop." He ran his fingers down her right arm and Kira instinctively pulled away. "What's the matter? Shy?"

She felt her face flush red and her stomach hollow as if she might vomit. Even if she could have spoken, she had no idea what to say. She was staring into the eyes of Landon Parker, the senior partner in her husband's firm, Parker, Sullivan & Bates. "Landon, I..." she stuttered.

"Ssshhh," he interrupted, placing his fingers over her lips and grinning sadistically. "Don't speak, just listen." Kira's eyes began to tear. "Your secret is safe with me as long as you do whatever Lucas asks."

Kira narrowed her brows, the confusion evident in her expression. "I don't understand," she uttered.

Landon folded his hands atop the table. "The Candy Shop is a very good client of ours, as are many of its high-paying customers. You might say Lucas and our firm have a vested interest in keeping our mutual clientele satisfied."

"Does Frank know about this?" Kira asked and watched a sardonic grin spread across his face. Frank was as conservative as they came and she couldn't believe he would have anything to do with a Gentleman's Club.

"Jealous?" Landon chuckled, stroking down her arm with his left index finger. "Wondering if your hubby has been enjoying some bite size pieces from the Candy Shop?"

Bite size pieces, that's the phrase Lucas had used earlier. Kira pulled away from his touch and tightened her jaw. "Frank wouldn't have anything to do with a place like this," she defended.

Landon inched closer and whispered in her ear. "Maybe and maybe not, but the only thing you need to be worried about is whether Frank will find out that his wife is one of the tasty morsels," he sneered and ran his tongue across the lobe of her right ear. "I don't think he'd like that, do you?"

Kira pushed Landon backwards. "Touch me again and I'll scream," she warned.

Landon chuckled aloud as if he were genuinely amused by her reaction. "You do what you're told and keep your mouth shut

44

and we all stand to make a shit-load of money." He rose from the couch. "Now, you shouldn't keep your gentleman waiting."

Kira scooted from the couch and stood up, feeling her knees wobble beneath her.

"Oh, and Kira," he said, taking her by the shoulders and turning her to face him. "I'd hate for anything bad to happen to the people we love. Sometimes too much information has a way of becoming hazardous to a person's health. You understand?" She dropped her gaze to the floor and he quickly lifted her chin so he could stare directly into her eyes. "Though Parker & Bates does have a nice ring to it. It rolls off the tongue better than Parker, Sullivan & Bates, don't you think?"

She stood motionless. Was he threatening Frank's career?

"How are your kids enjoying their first year of college?" His eyes flashed with an unspoken threat. "College can be a dangerous place. It would be a shame if anything happened to them."

Kira suddenly felt like an elephant was sitting on her chest and she couldn't breathe. She was trapped. She had made the biggest mistake of her life and now there was no way out. He was threatening her, her children and Frank's partnership in the firm. Pulling her out of the inset cave, he released her arm and pointed to the man sitting at the bar. "You keep him happy, he keeps Lucas happy, Lucas keeps me happy and everybody wins."

Landon left her trembling and speechless, trying desperately to regain her composure as she made her way across the room.

Upon seeing her, the hazel-eyed man looked surprised but smiled, stood up, gave the bartender a nod and led Kira across the room to a red, velvet couch that sat in the far corner beneath a large, black and white photograph of a man and a woman whose lips were dangerously close to engaging in what she could only imagine would be a kiss of passion. He extended his hand, motioning for her to sit. The bartender followed and set two martini glasses atop the cocktail table in front of the couch.

Mr. Handsome joined her on the couch, his eyes piercing through her, as if he were reading the darkest secrets of her soul. She squirmed uncomfortably beneath his gaze.

"I saw you yesterday in the foyer. What is your name?" He asked.

"Ki..." she stopped. "Daisy." She felt foolish calling herself by that name, but a smile filled his face.

"I like daisies," he said. "They don't have thorns." Kira twisted her fingers into nervous knots.

"What is your name?"

"I'm not allowed to tell you," he answered matter-of-factly, and then leaned forward and whispered. "They give you fake, flower names but they don't assign clients a name."

Kira smiled at his honesty. "So, what do I call you?"

He angled himself to face her, crossed his right leg over his left and leaned his right arm on the back of the couch. "Hmmm... how about we name each other? Based on something about my appearance, choose a name for me."

Mr. Handsome would have been a fitting title, but Kira was too embarrassed to say it aloud. Despite his handsome appearance and muscular build, she kept coming back to his bright, greenish, hazel eyes. "Mr. Green," she said, "because of your eyes."

"Very well," he nodded. "Mr. Green it is, and you are Ms. White, because of the innocence in your eyes."

Kira dropped her gaze to the floor. *Innocence? I'm sitting in a whorehouse and he thinks I'm a saint. What's wrong with this picture? Everything.* Everything was wrong with this picture. She was a married woman, getting ready to partake in God only knew what with a man she didn't even know, but to whom she felt undeniably attracted. She had put her marriage and family at risk and now there seemed to be no way out.

"I'm not going to touch you," Mr. Green said, interrupting her thoughts.

"What?" Her breath caught.

"I'm not going to ask you to have sex with me," he clarified and Kira was instantly puzzled. Relieved, but confused. If he didn't want to have sex then why was he coming to

The Candy Shop? Or was it simply that he had no interest in having sex with her?

"If I'm not your type, Lucas will assign you someone more along the lines of what you're looking for..." she stuttered and stopped talking when a spark of humor lit his eyes.

"You're exactly what I'm looking for." He smiled.

"But... you just said..."

"What I meant was, I will not request anything that we both don't want to do," he interrupted. "This is a mutual relationship."

A relationship? What kind of a man comes to a place like The Candy Shop for a relationship? Kira narrowed her eyes.

"I don't want to eat all of the chocolate," Kira blurted.

"I'm sorry?" Mr. Green cocked his head to the side. "What chocolate?"

She leaned toward him and quietly spoke. "I'm married."

Mr. Green appeared un-phased by her confession. He picked up both drinks from the table and handed one to Kira. "I know," he winked. "I noticed the tan line from your wedding band."

She looked down at her left hand. *Wow, he's observant.* "So, I don't want to eat all the chocolate at once. I just came here for bite size pieces." Her head was foggy from the drugs and she realized by his facial expression that she wasn't making any sense.

He leaned in closer. "I'll tell you what. Why don't we forget the chocolate altogether and just have a drink and chat?"

They spent the next two hours talking, and to Kira's surprise, he didn't touch her and never even made as much as an inappropriate innuendo. He was a complete gentleman. As they walked down the hallway, toward the entrance to the Lair, Kira heard the distinct sound of the door unlocking, and it gave her chills. Were they being watched? Did the bartender notify Ian that they were heading toward the door or were there surveillance cameras? Kira subtly glanced overhead, searching for a camera.

At the end of the hallway, Mr. Green turned to face her, placing both hands on the outside of her shoulders, he leaned forward, as if to kiss her. She froze, a part of her anticipating a kiss and the other part, fearing it. Instead of kissing her, he put his lips against her right ear and whispered, "They are always watching." He drew back quickly, took her right hand and kissed the top of it. "Until next time, Ms. White," he said with a smile, and then disappeared through the door.

Kira didn't say a word on the ride home, though Audrey was babbling so much she couldn't have gotten a word in edgewise. Besides, her head was pounding and she guessed it was the effects of the drug wearing off.

Audrey loved dancing and all of the attention she got from her male patrons. "I felt hot!" She shrieked with delight. "Hotter than hot!"

Kira smiled, a part of her wishing she could share Audrey's excitement; but Landon's threat was ever present in her mind, dampening any desire to return to The Candy Shop.

"What's the matter?" Audrey asked, pulling the Land Cruiser into Kira's driveway and turning to face her. "You've hardly said two words on the way home."

"I'm just tired," Kira lied, opening the passenger door and climbing out. "Headache."

"I'll pick you up tomorrow?" Audrey asked. "Same time?"

Kira abruptly stopped and spun around. "Tomorrow?" She gasped.

"Yeah, Lucas said he wants us there tomorrow night, same time," Audrey shrugged. "Maybe you'll get to dance on the stage tomorrow. I'm telling you, you'll love it. It's incredible."

Audrey was grinning ear-to-ear and Kira couldn't remember when she had seen her so happy. She forced a smile. "Okay. See you tomorrow."

Kira popped three ibuprofen, crawled into bed and stared at the ceiling. She couldn't tell Frank about Landon and his threat because that would mean admitting that she had been in a whorehouse, albeit an upscale whorehouse. She lay there pondering whether or not Landon was actually capable of inflicting physical harm on someone she loved? Her body sank deep into the feather pillow and goose-down comforter. She was mentally exhausted and emotionally drained. She hadn't technically cheated on Frank, and yet she felt as if she had. Though she had only talked with Mr. Green, her lust for him was of such magnitude that in her heart she had already physically given herself to him. Guilt rushed over her as she berated herself. *What have I done?*

By the time Kira awoke, Frank had already come and gone, leaving behind his usual note stating that he loved her and would check in later to see how her day was going. They were like ships passing in the night. Kira crumbled up the note and threw it into the trash, then sauntered to the kitchen to pour herself a cup of coffee. Several sips later, she mustered up the courage to call The Candy Shop and tell Ian she was sick and wouldn't be coming to work tonight.

Ian didn't sound pleased and disconnected the call without saying goodbye.

Kira breathed a sigh of relief. Now, all she had to do was break the news to Audrey and this nightmare would be over. Her plan was simple. She would call in sick for the next several days. Assuming Lucas would not want to employ such an unreliable woman, he would easily replace her with someone else. Her mind then drifted to Mr. Green. What if Mr. Green didn't want anyone else and stopped frequenting The Candy Shop? Lucas would lose his highest paying customer. As soon as the thought entered her mind, she dismissed it. After all, The Candy Shop was filled with women who were more beautiful than she. Mr. Green would have no trouble finding a suitable replacement, Lucas would keep his highest-paying customer, and since she would have been fired by Lucas, Landon couldn't blame her so Frank would never have to know. Everything would go back to normal.

Audrey wasn't happy about Kira calling in sick, but said she wasn't going to miss another opportunity to take the stage. She said she felt more alive than she'd ever felt before. "Who knew all I had to do was get half naked and dance in front of strangers," she joked. "I wish I would have discovered this years ago. I don't know how you ever quit."

Audrey's comment took Kira back in time to her sophomore year in college when she danced at a seedy little club in mid-Missouri. She took the job because she needed money, but kept it because she fell in love with being on stage. It was a feeling of freedom and control. When she was dancing, she felt sexy, alive and beautiful. Remembering how she felt then, she couldn't fault Audrey for what she was feeling now? Besides, Audrey was single and could do anything she wanted. The truth was, had Kira never met Frank, she would have continued to dance her way through college; but he believed strip clubs were amoral cesspools of sin. There was no way she could ever let him find out about The Candy Shop.

At ten o'clock Kira crawled into bed having spent much of the day waiting for Lucas, Ian or even Landon to contact her and confirm that she was really sick. They must have bought the story because a call never came. *Maybe this nightmare is over.* She drifted to sleep, stirring only once around midnight when she heard Frank come in and slip into bed next to her. He draped his arm over her stomach and she snuggled close to him, glad he was home.

When the phone rang at 5:00am, Kira jumped up, saw that Frank was no longer in bed and dove across his side of the bed to fetch the receiver. She could hear the shower running from the bathroom as she pressed the talk button and said hello.

"Mom?" It was Michael and he sounded upset.

"Michael, what's wrong?" Kira gasped. "Are you all right? Is Mallory all right?" Her heart rate accelerated.

"We're fine, mom, but my car's not."

"Were you in an accident? What happened?" Kira felt frantic with worry.

"No, we weren't in an accident. I came out to get in my car this morning and all four tires are slashed," Michael explained.

"Slashed?" Kira repeated, almost in disbelief.

"Yeah, like totally gouged. They can't be fixed." Michael sounded deflated. "I need money for new tires."

"Do you have any idea who would do this?" Kira asked.

"No. I don't get it. I don't have any enemies here, at least I didn't think I did," Michael huffed. "Obviously I'm not as well-liked as I thought."

Kira heard the shower turn off and she took the phone to the bathroom and handed it to Frank. She listened as Frank issued some choice words about the person who slashed Michael's tires and then assured Michael the money would be in his account right away. "I want you to report this to the police," Frank told Michael. "It's vandalism and we can't just let people get away with it."

Kira whispered to Frank. "Does he want me to drive up and go with him?" Columbia was only a two hour drive from St. Louis. "Tell him I can throw on some clothes and be there before 8:00am."

Frank relayed the message to Michael and then shook his head no. "He says he can handle it. He'll take Mallory with him."

Kira deflated. She wanted to rush to his side, but she knew he was old enough to handle it on his own. He didn't need his mommy anymore.

"Well, you must have pissed somebody off!" Frank barked into the phone. "Tell the police I want your car checked for prints."

By the time Frank left for work, an unsettling thought had popped into Kira's head. What if Michael's tires being slashed the same night she called in sick to The Candy Shop wasn't a coincidence? It sounded ludicrous at first, but each time she pushed the thought away, it inevitably crept back in;

and Landon's comment about college being a dangerous place replayed in her mind.

For the next three nights, Kira called in sick, never hearing a word from Ian, Lucas or Landon. How long would she have to keep this up before they would fire her? At 10:30pm Frank called from the office and told her that he needed to catch the red-eye to Chicago and he'd be back tomorrow.

"Why can't you fly out in the morning?" Kira asked.

"Landon thinks we need to meet with the client tonight to make sure all of our ducks are in a row before we set things in motion tomorrow," he explained. "Sorry."

It wasn't the first apology and it wouldn't be the last. Such was the life of being married to a workaholic.

Kira climbed into bed and text Audrey: HOW'S THE DANCING?

Audrey text back: AWESOME! WISH YOU'D COME BACK. LUCAS WANTS YOU BACK AND SO DOES YOUR CLIENT.

"Mr. Green," Kira sighed to herself, and then text Audrey: I CAN'T. SORRY. HAVE FUN.

Setting her cell phone atop the nightstand, Kira turned off the bedside lamp and lay down. She had just closed her eyes when her phone buzzed with an incoming text. It was from Audrey and it read: LUCAS ISN'T HAPPY. YOU NEED TO COME NOW.

Propping herself up against the headboard, Kira text back: NO. JUST CALL ME WHEN YOU'RE ON YOUR WAY HOME.

She hit send and then stared at the phone, waiting for a response. Finally, after several minutes, the phone buzzed and the text read: NO. WE'RE DONE.

"We're done?" Kira said aloud. "What does she mean, 'we're done?'" Kira huffed and stared at her phone. Why would Audrey say that? What difference did it make if Kira was there working downstairs while Audrey was dancing upstairs? It wasn't as if they even got to see each other or work together. She set the phone back onto the night stand, scrunched down into the sheets and closed her eyes. She'd call Audrey first thing in the morning.

At 3:00am the home phone startled her awake. Sliding to Frank's side of the bed, she grabbed the phone, pressed talk and mumbled a half-coherent hello into the receiver.

The voice was automated and robot sounding. It said, "First a terrible awful wreck, then the tires, then the neck." Then silence.

A bolt of fear jolted Kira into a sitting position. With the receiver clutched tightly in her grip, she hollered into the phone. "Lucas? Ian? Landon? Who is this?" She pressed the phone against her ear and could hear faint sobs. She couldn't make out who was crying, but it sounded like a woman. She was sniveling and begging and all Kira could make out were sobs of, "No. No. Please. No."

"Who is this?" Kira yelled into the phone. "What do you want?" But it was too late. They had hung up. Kira's hands trembled as she dialed Mallory's phone, praying that the woman she had heard in the background wasn't her daughter. All she could think about was the mention of the tires and how Michael's tires had been slashed. And what if Mallory was the woman sobbing in the background? Darts of fear prickled up her neck and a wave of nausea hit her stomach when Mallory's voicemail came on. Kira hung up and immediately dialed Michael.

"Yeah?" Michael groggily answered.

"Michael!" Kira exclaimed. "Where is your sister? She's not answering her phone."

"Mom, it's like three something in the morning," Michael moaned.

"I need to talk to your sister," Kira wailed, failing miserably at masking her panic.

"What's wrong? Where's dad? Are you okay?" She could hear fear rising in Michael's voice.

"Your father and I are fine. I just need to talk to Mallory. Do you know where she is?" Tears poured down Kira's face and her hands trembled.

"Relax, mom. She's here. She fell asleep on the couch and I didn't want to wake her to send her home. Hold on a sec, I'll get her."

Kira could hear Michael shuffling around and she pictured him getting out of bed and going to find his sister. The next voice she heard was like an angel speaking. It was Mallory, half-asleep and mumbling into the phone. "Mom?" Mallory slurred. "Are you okay?"

Kira could barely utter words, as relief filled her soul. "Mallory, baby," she cried. "I'm sorry I woke you." Her voice was shaky with emotion.

"It's okay. It's weird, but okay."

Kira smiled, amid the tears. "Put your brother back on and go back to sleep. I love you."

"I love you too, mom."

"Mom?" Michael spoke into the phone. "Everything okay?"

Kira took a deep breath. "I want you to do me a favor. Keep your sister there tonight and for the next several nights. Don't let each other out of sight. Walk to classes together, eat together, stay in groups of people, don't go anywhere by yourself. Can you promise me that?"

"What's going on, mom?" There was genuine concern in Michael's voice.

"It's probably nothing, but I've received some harassing phone calls and with your tires being slashed..." her voice faded. "I just want us all alert and safe."

"Is this related to one of dad's cases?" Michael asked, prompting Kira to remember that they had received prank phone calls and threats one time when Frank was working on a murder case that involved several mobsters from Chicago.

"It might be," Kira lied. "Just promise me you and Mallory will stay together."

"I promise."

After Michael hung up, Kira dialed Audrey and left her a voicemail asking her to call as soon as she left The Candy Shop. Just as she hung up, the phone rang and she quickly answered.

"Hello? Audrey?" Kira blurted.

"I'm monitoring your phone. If you call anyone else, your husband will never come home." It was the same robotic voice and Kira hit the off button. With her whole body shaking she jumped out of bed, rushed to Frank's closet and retrieved a small, metal case from the top shelf. It held a 357 Magnum.

CHAPTER 6

At midnight Rocco shined his flashlight into the dumpster that sat behind Charlie Gitto's Italian restaurant on the Hill. This wasn't the first body found in a dumpster on the Hill but Rocco was certain it was the first one not linked to a Mob killing. Peering inside, he gazed down at an all-too-familiar scene. There lie the body of another woman, with her throat slit, her left ring finger severed and a rose pinned to the front of her blouse. Despite how he wanted, Rocco couldn't bring himself to look away, as anger surged through his veins.

CHAPTER 7

Audrey never returned Kira's calls nor responded to her text messages, and Kira was beginning to worry. It was out of character and something felt very wrong about the entire situation. At 7:00am, after trying her cell phone and home phone again, Kira decided to drive to Audrey's house and confront her in person. She intended to demand an explanation as to why Audrey was so angry about her quitting The Candy Shop, and to guilt her into an apology for ignoring her calls. After all, surely even Audrey could understand that Kira was a married woman and had no desire to cheat on Frank.

Backing her white Lexus out of the garage, she noticed immediately that a large, green trashcan was sitting on the street, just to the right of the driveway. Today was Monday and trash pick-up was every Friday. As of last night her trashcan had been inside of the garage because she remembered placing the kitchen trash bag into the garage container shortly before going to bed. Fear rushed over Kira as she stared at the empty corner of the garage where the trashcan normally sat. This meant that someone had come into her garage while she was sleeping and had taken her trashcan to the street. The question was, why?

Kira left the car running while she stepped out and hesitantly approached the trashcan. Neighborhood covenants forbid having trash receptacles cluttering the street except on the day of pick-up, so regardless of why it was outside and who placed it there, Kira needed to put it back in the garage. As she approached the trashcan, she immediately noticed that it was facing in the wrong direction. The black handle was toward the street instead of toward the driveway which would cause the lid to open away from the trash truck instead of toward it. Gripping the handle, Kira gave the can a tug, but it didn't budge. She pulled harder, causing the bottom to scrape against the pavement, but it barely moved. Unable to remember throwing away anything that was heavy enough to render the trashcan immobile; Kira lifted the lid and peered inside.

Horrified by what she saw, she gasped and instinctively leapt backwards, releasing the lid and letting it slam against the back of the trashcan. Taking a second to muster the courage to take another look, she slowly stepped forward. The trashcan was filled with cement blocks and a note was fastened to the top block with duct tape. Taped to the note was a severed finger. Fighting her gag reflex, Kira dug her cell phone from her jacket pocket and took a picture of the contents of the can. She dialed 9-1-1 and then carefully balanced on her tippy toes so she could read what was written on the note: ONE OVER MONEY. TWO QUIT THE SHOW. THREE WANTED MORE. FOUR, A THORNED ROSE. THE

FIFTH IS REVENGE SERVED HOT AND RED.
YOU CONTROL IF SHE ENDS UP DEAD.

Kira felt as if she might vomit and faint simultaneously. She rocked backwards, wedging the heel of her shoe into a sidewalk crack and stumbling onto the grass.

"Mrs. Sullivan, are you okay?" Carter's voice came from two driveways down. He was ten years old with blonde hair and bright blue eyes, and he spent almost every morning out on his driveway, trying to master his free throw shot. It was an extra-challenge because his driveway sloped, forcing Carter to throw the basketball a little harder and higher to get it through the hoop. Carter rushed toward Kira, his basketball clutched tightly in his grasp. "I saw you fall over." He tossed the basketball onto the grass and extended both arms toward her. Taking his hands, Kira leaned forward and let Carter pull her to her feet.

"I'm okay," she said, forcing a smile and nonchalantly closing the lid to the trashcan. After all, a bloody severed finger was nothing a ten year old boy should see. "My heel got caught in the sidewalk crack and I fell over. Thanks for the help up."

Carter leaned down and retrieved his ball. "You scared me. I thought you passed out."

"Nope, just clumsy." Kira said.

Dribbling his basketball back up the sidewalk, he stopped abruptly and turned to face Kira. "Are you leaving town or something?"

Kira shook her head to indicate she wasn't.

"Oh," Carter shrugged. "I just wondered why Mr. Sullivan had put your trash out early. You know trash day isn't until Friday. I know because it's my job to wheel our trash out to the street every Friday morning. I get paid a whole two bucks to do it." He smiled and then dribbled back to his drive way and shot at the hoop, banking it off the backboard and sending it rebounding into his yard.

While waiting for the police to arrive, Kira pulled her Lexus back into the garage and sat in the driver's seat with the door propped open. She had no idea what she was going to tell the police. Should she mention The Candy Shop and Landon's threats? Her hands were trembling as she text Frank: CALL ASAP. Then she dialed Michael and Mallory to make sure they were both still okay.

It wasn't long before two police cars pulled onto the street and parked in front of the Sullivan home. Upon seeing them, Kira immediately leapt from her seat and raced down the driveway. An African-American officer named Reginald Peters stepped out of his car first and headed up the driveway in long, leggy strides, while Lieutenant Barkley maneuvered himself slowly from his vehicle. Extending his hand toward Kira, Officer Peters introduced himself and Kira felt instantly at ease. She guessed him to be in his mid-twenties, just a few years older than Michael and Mallory, and his smile radiated the enthusiasm and excitement of youth. He stood six feet tall, had dark hair which was cut so short he was almost bald in appearance and light brown eyes that sparkled when he grinned. Lieutenant Barkley sauntered up, seemingly winded from the short walk, and gave Kira a nod.

"What do we got?" Barkley grunted.

Kira explained how the trashcan was mysteriously removed from her garage and placed in the street and then led them to it. This time she stood back while Peters opened the lid and they peered inside. Barkley read the note aloud in a gruff tone: ONE OVER MONEY. TWO QUIT THE SHOW. THREE WANTED MORE. FOUR, A THORNED ROSE. THE FIFTH IS REVENGE SERVED HOT AND RED. YOU CONTROL IF SHE ENDS UP DEAD.

Barkley and Peters exchanged a glance. "Better call Rocco," Barkley rasped and Peters immediately returned to his car to make the call. Turning to Kira, Barkley asked, "Do you have any idea what this note means?"

Prickly tentacles of fear climbed up the back of Kira's neck as she shook her head. "I have no idea." As the lie left her lips, it felt as if Barkley's eyes were piercing right through her.

"What does it mean YOU CONTROL IF SHE ENDS UP DEAD?" Barkley questioned.

Kira's mind was a chaotic whirlwind of thought. She couldn't escape the feeling that FOUR, A THORNED ROSE was somehow referring to Miranda from The Candy Shop, since her flower name was Rose and Lucas had stated it was because she had thorns; but she couldn't mention The Candy Shop to Lieutenant Barkley. That would mean admitting she and Audrey worked there and that was something she didn't want Frank to know. Despite the fact that she hadn't been unfaithful, Frank would consider dancing in a gentlemen's club a breach of trust and their marriage would be over. She couldn't let that happen. "I don't know," Kira said, her mouth growing dry as the lie stuck in her throat.

"Mrs. Sullivan, are you aware that four women have been murdered in the past month, and been left in dumpsters throughout the city?" Barkley's tone was laced with accusation.

Was she aware? Of course she was aware. It had been the lead story in the paper and on the news for weeks, though oddly enough the identities of the victims had not been publically released to the media. It had every woman in the city walking on eggshells. "You don't think I had anything to do with that..." Kira's voice faded as a brutal reality hit her. What if all four women were somehow connected to The Candy Shop? Was the note implying that if she didn't return to The Candy Shop, a fifth woman would be killed? If this were true then she needed to warn Audrey. She could be in danger.

All color drained from Kira's face and her heart began to race.

"Is there something you want to tell me?" Barkley grunted.

Kira licked her lips slowly and met eyes with Barkley. "Is there any connection between the four women who were killed?" Barkley squinted at her, as if he thought this were an odd question. "I mean," Kira cleared her throat, "did they all work together or attend the same church or school?"

"That's classified information," Barkley snorted.

Peters rushed back up the driveway. "Rocco said we're to get a forensics team out here on the double and that we should take Mrs. Sullivan into custody."

Barkley rolled his eyes. "Of course he did, because Mr. Hot Shot has no problem wasting the tax payer's money and our time on a forensics analysis that's not going to show diddly-squat."

"Excuse me?" Kira interjected. "What do you mean take me into custody?"

"With all due respect ma'am," Peters said, "a crucial piece of evidence was found on your property and we'd like to ask you some questions down at the station."

She could tell Peters was trying to be as polite and diplomatic as possible, but she also knew the underlying meaning of what he had said. Being married to a high-powered attorney for almost twenty years had taught her a thing or two. Kira tightened her lip. "And if I refuse to come to the station with you?"

"Then we'll place you under arrest for tampering with evidence or suspicion of murder," Barkley interjected forcefully. "A body part was found in your trash. For all we know, you have the rest of the body stashed in your basement or your freezer and you wrote the note and taped the finger to it..."

"You must be out of your mind!" Kira spat. "Why would I do that and then call the police?"

"You'd be surprised what people do ma'am," Peters said.

"We can do this the easy way or the hard way," Barkley added. "Your choice."

CHAPTER 8

Kira sat at a table in a small, white room, waiting to be questioned. She couldn't believe what was happening. On the way to the station she had text Frank three more times, letting him know that it was urgent that she speak with him; but he had not responded. Was Frank okay? Had something happened to him? It was unusual for him not to respond. Thankfully, both Michael and Mallory text her that they were fine, busy with school, that they loved her and would call tonight. This at least gave her some peace of mind. Still, she sat motionless in the chair consumed with worry and fear.

The steel door opened abruptly, startling Kira from her thoughts. In stepped a tall, slender man with gray hair cut short and silver rimmed glasses. His lips were thin, his eyes were green and his jaw line very pronounced. "Mrs. Sullivan, I am detective Connor Downing of the St. Louis Police Department. You're not under arrest so I'm not going to read you your Miranda rights." He pulled out a chair across from Kira and sank into it, setting a recording device in the middle of the table and then folding his hands. "I just want to ask you a few questions and then you'll be free to go." He smiled and Kira noticed the prominent smile lines jetting from the corners of both eyes. She guessed him to be in his mid-fifties.

She licked her lips and nodded.

"This conversation will be recorded," Connor said, reaching over and placing the device into recording mode. He then looked Kira directly in the eyes. "Please state your name, age and occupation."

She cleared her throat and spoke softly. "Kira Sullivan. Forty. Homemaker."

"Have you ever worked outside of the home?" Connor asked and Kira's heart was pounding so hard she felt like she couldn't breathe. It seemed like an odd question unless he knew about The Candy Shop and was just testing her, to see if she would tell the truth. Kira could feel her body temperature rising.

She opened her mouth to answer when the door burst open and Landon Parker strode in arrogantly. *How did he know where to find me? Does Frank know I'm here?* Kira's pulse quickened and she felt like her heart was going to pound right out of her chest.

Landon made a loud clicking sound with his tongue and shook his head. "Detective Downing, you're not questioning my client without her attorney present, are you? Because I'm pretty sure Captain Jameson considers that to be a big no-no." A sinister smile spread across his lips.

Downing stood up. "I was unaware that Mrs. Sullivan had an attorney. As I informed her, she is not under arrest and therefore doesn't need representation."

"Well, then, if there are no charges, we will be going," Landon said and motioned for

Kira to get up. She stood, albeit hesitantly. Leaving with Landon felt like walking into the arms of the enemy, and yet, what choice did she have?

As Landon ushered her through the door, Downing handed her his card. "If you think of anything you want to tell us, give me a call."

Landon snatched the card from her fingers and shoved it back into Downing's hand. "My client has nothing to say."

CHAPTER 9

Rocco Sterling stood in the forensics lab, mulling over detailed reports on each of the four women found dead. Each report read the same. No DNA found at the scene. No fingerprints left anywhere, not even on the victim's body, despite the fact that each of the women showed signs of sexual intercourse. All of the victim's fingerprints had been burned off by the application of a Lye based substance, with the exception of the severed finger which contained the victim's fingerprints. Lubricant residue from a condom was the only evidence left behind. There wasn't even as much as a skin cell or hair follicle. There was no evidence of a struggle, but that was indicative of the fact that each victim had been given a substantial dose of Flunitrazepam, a sedative better known on the street as "Roofies." Each victim was killed by slitting of the throat and their left ring finger severed. The body was then delivered to a dumpster somewhere in the city and a flower pinned to their clothing. Each flower was different.

Exhaling frustration, Rocco shook his head. *Nobody is this clean.* As Rocco continued to study the files he found a perplexing difference in the fourth killing. In the first three, the victim's left ring finger had been severed and left somewhere in the dumpster with the body, but in the fourth killing, the finger was never found, that is, until this morning in Kira Sullivan's trashcan. This was a bold and deliberate act on the part of the killer and the question taunting Rocco was why? Serial killers were by nature thorough and consistent. They didn't alter their plans for fear that any change would defy the rhythm and delicacy of the killing. It was the process they enjoyed. The fulfillment came from the implementation of a detailed plan and then watching like a sadistic voyeur as the police tried to put the broken pieces together, scrambling for tiny clues. It was a game of cat and mouse and Rocco had every intention of winning, but in order to do so he knew he had to think like both the cat and the mouse. If he knew anything about serial killers, he knew these four women weren't random. He knew they shared a connection and he owed it to them to find their killer.

Lieutenant Barkley poked his head into the Forensics lab but before he could speak, Rocco looked up from the files and blurted, "I'm coming. I'll be there in a minute."

"You're too late," Barkley said. "She's already gone."

Rocco's face turned a fiery shade of red as he strode quickly past Barkley and out the door. "What do you mean she's gone? Who let her go? Was she questioned?"

Barkley scurried to try and match stride with Rocco. "Downing questioned her but her attorney showed up and took her away."

Rocco stopped abruptly. "Her attorney?"

"Yeah, and you'll never guess who it is," Barkley sneered. "Landon Parker."

Rocco clenched his hands into tight, white knuckled fists.

CHAPTER 10

"I've arranged for you to stay at a hotel downtown for a couple of days," Landon said, as his driver maneuvered the black Mercedes through highway traffic. "You don't need questioning neighbors hounding you like vultures."

"How am I going to explain that to Frank?" Kira objected.

"Don't you worry about Frank. I'll take care of it." Landon smirked. "It's for your own protection and Frank will certainly understand that. He won't want his wife being harassed by the police and dragged into a very public police investigation." Every word from Landon's lips seemed to mask an underlying threat, like if she didn't cooperate he'd make sure her face was plastered all over the news as a suspect in the serial killings.

"I'll need to pack some things," Kira said quietly.

"Already done. You'll find your hotel room contains everything you'll need," Landon retorted. "You'll also report to work tonight promptly at 7:00pm. Lucas will meet you upstairs and give you instructions."

"I'm not working there," she argued.

"Oh, I think you are," Landon grinned. "Your client has been asking for you. I think you call him, 'Mr. Green'?"

Kira's face flushed at the realization that Landon or someone had been listening to her conversation with Mr. Green that first night. What else did he know? Probably everything. "I don't want to go there," Kira said. "Please, Landon, I don't want any part of that place."

"It's too late for that," Landon seethed. "Once a piece of candy, always a piece of candy; and everybody likes candy." He laughed and Kira fought the lump welling up in her throat.

With the barrel of a .45 digging into her ribs, Landon escorted her to a suite on the top floor of the Adams Mark hotel. "A car will pick you up at 6:30pm. You will be escorted from your room to the car and to your job. At no other time are you to step outside of this room or let anyone inside. Is that clear?"

Kira nodded.

"Good girl," he said and ran his finger down the side of her face. "Keep being a good girl and you might just live through this." Landon walked toward the door, turned on his heels and grinned at Kira. "I've bought out the entire floor and the rooms directly below your suite, so attempting to scream or pound on the walls, ceiling or floor will be a waste of time and energy; energy you will undoubtedly need for your evening with Mr. Green." Landon let his eyes traipse the length of her body. "Do what you're told."

Landon no sooner left, closing the door behind him than Kira rushed to the phone sitting on the desk and dialed 9 for an outside line. There was no dial tone, just dead air. She hung up and then pressed 0 for the front desk. Again, she heard nothing but dead air. She then tried to make a room-to-room call, but it didn't work. Somehow Landon had rendered her hotel phone inoperable. She rushed to the door and tried to pull it open, but it wouldn't budge. It was locked from the outside. She tugged several times and then backed up and sank onto the bed. Landon had taken her purse with her wallet, cell phone and the 357 Magnum she had retrieved from Frank's closet. Turning toward the window, Kira leapt up and tore open the curtains. The windows were the kind that didn't open, not even an inch, and they were painted solid black. She was trapped like a princess in a tower; a prisoner and the only way out was to return to The Candy Shop.

CHAPTER 11

Dressed in a long, black sequined gown and black stiletto heels, Kira stepped from the limousine and into the back entrance of The Candy Shop. Ian was there to escort her to meet Lucas.

"So nice to see you again, Daisy," Ian smirked. "I had a feeling you'd be coming back."

Shelby flitted down the hall toward them, her blonde ponytail bouncing behind her. "Kira!" She exclaimed excitedly and threw her arms around Kira's neck as if they were long lost friends. "I'm glad you're back. It was like everyone just disappeared all at once."

Ian gave her a scowl and a sideways flip of his head, directing her to leave. Shelby took the hint, shutting up and scurrying past them.

"What did she mean everyone disappeared?" Kira asked, but Ian kept his eyes forward and shrugged.

"Take your questions up with Mr. Coronado," Ian said, pulling open the large, medieval looking door and ushering her into the living room. "He'll be with you shortly."

Kira remembered this room all too well. It was where she and Audrey had first met with Lucas. It was also where Lucas gave her the name Daisy and where she was bandaged and changed after Miranda had attacked her.

The red velvet couches, the candles on the coffee table, the large stained glass windows overlooking the stage and the bar that sat in the corner. More than anything she wished she had never stepped foot in this room.

"Welcome back," Lucas strode through the door and headed straight to the bar and began mixing a martini that Kira suspected was for her.

"Are you going to drug me again?" She blurted sarcastically, letting her eyes drift from the glass to his face.

He smiled. "Yes."

"Then I won't drink it." Kira crossed her arms.

"I can have you injected, but that's unnecessarily painful," he said, still shaking the martini.

Kira sank into one of the bar stools. "Why do you need me here?" Her tone was desperate, but she didn't care. She needed to understand what was happening and her involvement in the bigger picture. "I don't want to be here. I don't want to do this. Why are you forcing me to stay? Why are you threatening me and my marriage and my family? Why have you made me a prisoner?"

Lucas paused and stared at Kira as if she were speaking another language. Then he filled her martini glass and placed it in front of her. "Drink and then we will talk."

Tears burned Kira's eyes as she lifted the glass to her lips and sipped it. She felt the cool chill run all the way down her throat. It felt good. A few more sips and Kira began to feel her muscles relax and the worry and fear that had been all-consuming slowly melt away. The drug was working.

Sitting on the stool next to her, Lucas wiped a tear from her cheek and spun her chair so she was facing him. He then placed his knees on the outside of her knees and raised her chin so their eyes met. "You're not a prisoner. You are one of many beautiful flowers that make up my garden." Lucas lifted his hand and brushed her hair back from her face. "I protect my flowers."

"I don't want to be a flower," Kira slurred. "I want to go home."

"I am a business man. I give people what they want and I do it with such exclusivity that the danger of exposure to anyone is miniscule." He stood up and walked behind the bar. Kira followed him with her eyes, trying to force herself to focus. "No one knows this place exists except those that I allow to know."

"But Audrey knew it existed..." Kira slurred.

"Because I allowed Audrey to hear of it and I allowed Audrey to bring you along." Lucas began mixing another martini. "Women don't come to me for employment. I seek out whom it is I shall employ and make certain they come."

"So, you wanted me and Audrey here? You lured us here?" Kira felt like her eyes were beginning to cross.

"I gave permission for Audrey to learn about The Candy Shop and I granted permission for her to bring you along."

"But why?" Kira slurred.

"Because it is my business," he said poignantly, "and this conversation has come full circle."

"Is Audrey working tonight?" Kira blurted.

"No. Audrey has not shown up."

He raised the glass to her lips and Kira took a long sip. "It's so unlike her. She must be really pissed at me."

"Don't worry about Audrey," Lucas said. "I am sure that such a fiery woman can take care of herself."

Kira felt high now. She felt like she was floating above the bar. "I don't understand," she said wearily, as Lucas fed her another sip.

"What don't you understand?"

"What you do, or maybe why you do it," she slurred.

"I rescue people," Lucas answered flatly. "I save them from the dormancy of an unfulfilling existence. I save them from the sadness of an empty nest, from the heartache of a dying marriage, from the despair of fading youth." The way he described it, it sounded almost poetic.

Kira snorted. "And here I thought you just ran a fancy whorehouse."

Lucas grinned. "Have I touched you or asked you to touch anyone?" Kira shook her head. "Have I told you that I expect you to sexually pleasure anyone?" Kira shook her

81

head again. "How then, can I be running a whorehouse if I am not promoting sex?"

It was a good question and had she not been stoned, she might have been able to comeback with a reasonable response, but her brain was struggling to merely string two words together. Lucas raised the martini glass toward Kira's lips again and she sipped. "I provide a safe environment where men and women can relax without the scrutinizing eyes of the outside world. I take care of my girls and I take care of my clients. You are not a prisoner here. That being said, I will take whatever action is necessary to ensure the privacy and protection of all who belong to me." He raised the glass to her lips and Kira sipped again. "If my girls and my clients decide to engage in a form of sexual interaction, that is a private matter between them as consenting adults. I neither discourage nor encourage the goings-on. I am simply paid to arrange the meeting."

Kira could barely focus her eyes now and she couldn't wipe the smile from her face.

"How are you feeling?" Lucas asked, a grin tempting the corners of his mouth.

"Wonderful," Kira slurred.

"Are you ready to meet with your client?"

"Yesssssss," Kira said, her ess trailing off. "I am ready to meet Mr. Green," she mumbled.

"Mr. Green?" Lucas looked surprised. "Is that the nickname you've given him?" He seemed thoroughly amused. "It sounds mysterious, like something from the game of Clue."

CHAPTER 12

Ian led Kira downstairs and opened the door to the Lair, where she found Mr. Green sitting at the bar, with a drink in his hand and a martini sitting on the bar in front of an empty stool.

"Is that for me?" She asked, pointing to the martini glass.

"Yes," he answered, a smile filling his face. "It was what you had the last time we met, but if you'd like something different this time..."

"No, it's perfect." She picked up the glass and moved across the room to the couch where they had sat last time. He followed and sat down next to her, bending one leg under the other so his knee was touching her thigh.

"I intended to bring you a box of chocolate, but the day got away from me," he teased. "Of course, we wouldn't eat it all at once."

Kira grinned. "That's right. Only bite size pieces."

"You seem different," he said, looking deeply into her eyes.

"I'm not," she blurted. "Same me. Same you."

Placing his palm on the side of her face, he studied her. He then leaned in closely and whispered in her left ear, "Have they drugged you?"

Kira pulled back and fought to focus. "Yes, but it's okay. I feel free," she whispered and his eyes flashed with disappointment.

"I need you sober," he said and stood up abruptly. He strode to the bar and talked in low tones with the bartender, who glanced periodically at Kira, and then handed Mr. Green a key. Moments later, Mr. Green unlocked one of the doors and led Kira into a bedroom, closing and locking the door behind him. Kira's heart raced. In front of her sat a king-size bed, covered in red satin and gold pillows. To the right was a shower adorned in gold fixtures with three shower heads and a glass door and next to it was a huge Jacuzzi tub. Candles were lit all around the room. Mr. Green pushed Kira face first against the wall and pressed his body against hers. "I don't want to cheat on my husband," Kira slurred, as reality began to fight the effects of the drug.

Putting his lips against her ear, he whispered, "You're not going to cheat. I promise. They're watching so we've got to make it look good." He gently rotated his pelvis against her. "I'm going to undress you, then myself and we're going to step into the shower and turn on the water."

Kira's hands began to tremble.

"We're not going to do anything that you don't want to do," he uttered.

"I don't want to be naked," she whispered.

"That part is not optional." He moved her hair and unzipped the back of her dress, letting it fall around her ankles. "It will be harder for them to hear us in the shower with the water running," he whispered as he unfastened her bra and then pulled her panties to the floor. Her whole body trembled, as she stood naked, facing the wall and fighting back tears. "You have to trust me now," he said, turning her to face him.

She watched as he unbuttoned his shirt, slid off his slacks and then his boxers and stood naked, his muscles protruding from his arms and rippling across his stomach. He took a step closer and she felt a mixture of excitement, fear and desire grip her all at once. Sliding his hand around the back of her neck, he pulled her toward him and whispered into her ear. "I'm going to kiss you and lead you into the shower. Once the water is on, turn your back toward me and I will talk into your ear."

Butterflies began fluttering in her stomach but before she could process his words, his lips enclosed on hers in a kiss that sent chills darting everywhere. She wasn't supposed to like it, but how could she not? Frank hadn't kissed her like this in years. She hadn't experienced passion in what felt like forever, and despite the fact that it was wrong, in that moment it felt nothing but right. Kira returned his kiss with the fervor of wanting and he reached down, lifted her into his arms and carried her into the shower.

With all three shower heads blasting, Kira leaned back against him, unable to ignore his wanting pressing firmly against her.

He draped his right arm around her stomach and leaned down, placing his lips against her right ear. "This has to appear real, so I'm going to caress your breast with my hand and I need you to move against me, as if you are enjoying yourself."

As his fingertips explored her nipple, Kira thought she might explode from desire. She tried to fight it, but she couldn't. She wanted him. She wanted to be taken.

"Listen carefully," he whispered into her ear, sporadically planting kisses on her neck and stroking her breast. "The only way I can protect you is to keep requesting you and the only way you can stay alive is to keep coming back."

Kira wanted to concentrate on his words, but she was struggling. Her mind was fogged with sensual thoughts and sexual needs that were undoubtedly accentuated by the lingering effects of the drug Lucas had given her. "The women I stop requesting disappear and they end up dead."

"Mmm-hmm," Kira moaned.

Mr. Green forcefully turned her around, took her face in his hands and stared into her eyes. "Do you understand what I'm telling you?" He whispered. "I can't protect you unless you keep coming back here. Someone is killing every woman I touch." He held her against his chest. "I can't explain why it's happening but you need to know that you are in danger and the only way I can keep you safe now is to keep seeing you. Do you understand?"

Everything was blurry. The steamy shower, mixed with the drug, the alcohol and the wanting, left Kira on the verge of unconsciousness. Turning off the shower, Mr. Green wrapped her in a towel and carried her to the bed.

She gazed up at his silhouette, which appeared fuzzy in the candlelight. "Don't you want me?" She slurred.

"Yes. Very much," he answered.

"Then why aren't you taking me?" She tugged open her towel, exposing her nakedness.

Mr. Green crawled on top of her and then the room began to spin and everything spiraled into darkness.

CHAPTER 13

In the damp darkness, Audrey shook. She curled her knees to her chest and pressed her back against the cold, concrete wall. She didn't know how much time had passed since she had been abducted. Hours? Days? She couldn't tell. The only thing she knew was that she needed water. Her tongue was enlarged and pasty and her throat felt like sandpaper. Her hands and ankles were bound tightly with duct tape and a piece of duct tape sealed her eyes shut, though at the crevice of her nose, she was able to see a glimmer of light. Complaining that she had to go to the bathroom had resulted in her captor planting a swift kick to her abdomen, knocking her to the ground; so now Audrey sat quietly in the darkness, trying not to whimper. She prayed someone would find her before it was too late.

CHAPTER 14

Kira awoke back in her hotel room, dressed in a pair of white satin pajamas. She had no recollection of how she had gotten there or how long she had been sleeping. The last thing she remembered was Mr. Green crawling on top of her in the Lair. Did they have sex? She tried to force herself to remember, but her mind was completely blank. What was happening? Where was Audrey and why hadn't she shown up for work? Was Frank all right? Would he ever find out what she had done? Were Michael and Mallory still safe or had Landon done something to them? Consumed with fear and riddled with regret, Kira clutched a pillow to her chest, rolled over on her side and wept. She had never felt more helpless.

CHAPTER 15

Striding briskly through the precinct doors, Rocco made a beeline for his office, slamming the door behind him. He dropped the case file atop his desk, flipped it open and began mulling over the facts. He had hunted down numerous serial killers in his career, and each time he was able to get into the guy's head and anticipate his next move; but this time it was different. Most of the serial killers he had encountered were blatant misogynists, and had left clues as to the depth of their distaste for women on the victim's body or at the scene, clues that ultimately led the police to him; but not this time. Serial killers were choosy, selective and patient. They usually sought out women of particular appearance, a la brunettes or blondes. They followed ritualistic patterns of behavior; but this killer was different. Rocco flipped through the file and gnawed on his bottom lip. This killer had no particular preference. His first victim was a Caucasian brunette with long hair. His second was a Caucasian blonde with long hair. His third was an African American brunette and his fourth, a Caucasian brunette with short hair. They were all between the ages of thirty and forty-five years old. The only thing consistently serial about his killings was what he did to the women after they were dead; severing the left ring finger, which Rocco knew undoubtedly had meaning, though it

91

escaped him. Pursing his lips together, he shook his head and tried to force his mind to connect the dots. This was happening for a reason, but why? He owed it to these women and their families to figure it out.   He owed it to them to find this man and stop him.

Leaping to his feet, Rocco ripped open the office door and hollered, "Barkley! Peters! Get in here!"

Peters raced toward Rocco's office while Barkley slowly pushed back from his desk, groaned upon standing up and meandered toward the office where he immediately sank into a chair.

Rocco was visibly irritated by Barkley's lack of enthusiasm. "Do I need to request that someone else be assigned to this case?" He barked.

"No, sir," Peters belted. "I can't speak for him, but cracking this case wide open could be my ticket toward promotion."

Barkley guffawed. "What makes you think I'm not striving for a promotion?"

"Your lethargic work ethic," Rocco chided. Maneuvering around the desk, he sat down and folded his hands. "Do we have any leads? Any leads at all?"

Peters and Barkley exchanged a glance that told Rocco they were at a dead end. Rocco shook his head. "Have you read the case updates this morning?" He asked, and they stared blankly.

"The fourth woman has just been identified as thirty-five year old Miranda Miliken from Milwaukee. It says that according to a statement made by one of Miranda's neighbors, she had followed her boyfriend to St. Louis and after their breakup three months ago, began working at The Candy Shop," Rocco summarized the information.

"The Candy Shop," Peters repeated. "Never heard of it. Is it at one of the malls?"

Barkley snickered. "It's a strip club on the Riverfront. Exclusive. Only high-rollers, from what I've heard."

"From what you've heard?" Rocco glared at Barkley. "Where did you hear that?"

"I don't remember," Barkley muttered and shifted uncomfortably in his chair.

"Have you heard anything else about it?" Rocco asked.

"That's it. Just that it's exclusive, members-only. Nobody who ain't somebody ain't gettin' in."

"So I take it you've never been there," Rocco chided, raising one eyebrow.

"Unlike some people, I don't need to lay with whores," Barkley sneered.

"Whoa, man, I don't think we need to be calling nobody a ho," Peters interjected, his eyes wide. "Some girls didn't grow up in the suburbs and they're doin' what they gotta be doin' to support their families and feed their babies. I'm not sayin' it's right."

"It's wrong," Barkley growled. "Places like The Candy Shop promote adultery and anyone who commits adultery is a whore," Barkley stated matter-of-factly, as if no other opinion mattered.

"That's harsh, man," Peters uttered.

"It's a fact. God said it. If a man lies with a married woman he forces her to commit adultery," Barkley sneered.

"Maybe so, but didn't God also say we're not supposed to judge other people," Peters rebutted and Barkley scowled at him.

"Let's not get into a holy war," Rocco interjected.

"Whatever." Barkley crossed his arms and rolled his eyes.

Ignoring Barkley, Rocco took the opportunity to change the subject. "I want you two to go talk to Miranda's neighbor," he said.

"What for?" Barkley moaned. "You're holding her statement in your hand. What more are we gonna learn from her?"

Rocco glared at him. "You're pushing early retirement with that lazy attitude."

All of a sudden, Barkley leapt to his feet with impressive speed, especially for him. "Listen, Mr. Hot Shot Hummer Driver, you're not my boss. I'm a little sick and tired of you thinking you run the show around here. You don't know anything about being a real cop!" Barkley's face reddened. "You think you're big shit because you've nailed some serial killers, but you've got nothing on this case and no matter how many DNA analysis you run or how many prints you dust for, you're still gonna have squat!"

A mixture of shock and rage flashed in Rocco's eyes but before he could say anything, Barkley continued.

"You waltz around here barking orders like you're some god-damned gift to the precinct when everybody knows you're nothing more than a hot-headed ego maniac who's on the verge of being a psychopathic serial killer yourself!" Barkley gripped his left arm and the red color began to drain from his face. "It wouldn't surprise me if we were to find out that you were the killer!" Barkley appeared to have difficulty drawing in a breath, but he kept going. "You're one of those people who thinks you get to have anything or anyone you want, but you don't," he spewed and then winced in pain. "Not anymore!"

"Barkley, man, calm down. You don't look so good," Peters warned and grabbed Barkley's arm to try to lower him into the chair, but Barkley pushed Peter's hands away.

"I'm fine," he seethed through clenched teeth and then redirected his attention to Rocco. "I'm watching you. Oh, yeah, I'm watching you like a hawk and you know what I've noticed about you, Mr. Special Detective? You never seem surprised to see the face of the women we find dead."

"When hunting a serial killer death is not a surprising outcome," Rocco rebutted.

"Maybe. Maybe not," Barkley gripped his chest and sank into the chair, panting and gasping for air.

Rocco dialed 9-1-1, while Peters unbuttoned Barkley's collar and fanned him with a file folder. "The ambulance is coming.

Hang on, man," Peters said. "Has this happened before?" Peters asked.

"No, not like this. I've had chest pains, but this is different," Barkley groaned.

Rocco could see Peters beginning to panic. "Man, he's having a heart attack," Peters shrieked. "He's having a heart attack!"

"Pull it together Officer Peters," Rocco blurted. "If you can't handle a heart attack then you better prepare for a long career of pushing papers across a desk. Besides, have you seen what he eats? This isn't shocking."

"Screw you," Barkley moaned and Rocco smirked.

As the paramedics loaded Barkley onto the gurney and wheeled it into the hall, Barkley pulled the oxygen mask from his face and grabbed Peter's arm. "Keep your eyes on him," Barkley rasped and looked toward Rocco. "I'm telling you. Watch your back."

Once Barkley was gone, Rocco summoned Peters back to his office. "I'll talk to the Captain about getting someone to take Barkley's place on this case and then I'll go and talk to Miranda's neighbor. In the meantime, I want you to find out everything you can about the other three women."

"Like what specifically?"

"Miranda's neighbor said she followed her boyfriend to the city and then they broke up. I want to know who the boyfriend is. Did he possibly date any or all of the other women as well?" Rocco explained.

"Sir," Peters said quietly. "We've talked to the first three victim's families already. They don't know anything."

"That's because we weren't asking the right questions." Rocco's voice elevated. "I want to know every date these women went on. I want to know where they were at every second of every day for the few weeks prior to their murder. A serial killer chooses his victim. That means he was watching her closely, maybe even involved in her life in some way. Someone had to see something."

"What about the media?" Peters asked.

"What about the media?" Rocco rebutted.

"Well, so far the names of the victims haven't been made public..."

Rocco cut him off. "That's because we don't want to give the killer any satisfaction or recognition. He gets off on seeing the faces of his victims plastered on the news and in the paper. It thrills him to see the families mourning the loss of a woman he killed. He revels in the power of being able to cause pain." Rocco's jaw tightened and his nostrils flared. "I will not give him that satisfaction."

"I get that, but, sir, don't you think if we release the names of the victims to the public it might cause people to remember something? Like maybe they would see a picture of one of the victims and it would jog their memory as to where they saw her before?" Peters explained.

Rocco bit down on his lower lip. Peters made a good point. Opening it up to the public might prove helpful. "I'll think about it," Rocco said.

Peters smiled and turned toward the door; and then pivoted quickly in the doorway. "Sir, can I ask you a question?"

"What?" Rocco exhaled.

"What's with you and Lieutenant Barkley?" He shuffled his feet nervously. "I mean, it's obvious you don't like each other."

Rocco closed his eyes momentarily and exhaled. "I'm surprised you haven't heard the rumors already."

"Nobody around here seems to want to tell me anything. New guy syndrome I guess."

"Me and Barkley go way back. I like him fine but he's not too fond of me. It's a personal matter, not business." He shifted in his chair. "A couple of years ago, I dated his sister."

"And you broke her heart and it pissed off Barkley," Peters added, as if he already knew the details.

"Not exactly," Rocco quipped. "She was married at the time, not happily, but still married; and, no, I didn't break her heart."

"Ouch, man," Peters grimaced. "She dumped you and went back to her husband?"

Rocco's eyes glazed over as if he were traveling back in his mind. "Yeah, something like that."

"I get it. It must be weird now to work so closely with Lieutenant Barkley after you and his sister were bumping nasty's." Peters raised his eyebrows two times rapidly and made a vulgar flitting motion with his tongue. "Seriously, though, do you ever see his sister?"

"Every October." Rocco cleared his throat. "I take her flowers."

"For her birthday?"

"No. October was the month she died." Rocco stared down at the desk. "She loved flowers more than any woman I'd ever met. She was crazy about them." A sparkle lit his eyes as the memory overtook him. "She even used to wear them in her hair." He sighed and then looked up at Peters. "So, every October I go to New Mt Sinai Cemetery and bring her flowers." Rocco's jaw tightened. "Any more questions?"

Peters didn't hide his surprise well. His eyes bulged and his mouth fell open. "No, sir. I'm sorry. I had no idea." He started for the door and then turned around again. "Do you want me to check out The Candy Shop?"

"No. I'll handle it," Rocco answered flatly, without looking up from his desk.

CHAPTER 16

Kira was delivered to The Candy Shop an hour earlier than normal and escorted by Ian to the Living Room to wait for Lucas. When Lucas entered Kira could instantly tell he was not happy. His jaw was tight and his blue eyes were icy.

"You have committed an infraction," he announced upon entering. "You have given a client information that should have remained confidential, and for that I have no choice but to punish you."

Kira felt her stomach hollow out. "I don't know what you're talking about."

"Did you tell your Mr. Green that you had been drugged?" Lucas stared through her and before she could open her lips to answer, he continued speaking. "Mr. Green doesn't like to have his women under the influence of any sedatives. He was quite upset by your passing out on him last night, and when my client gets upset, I get upset."

"I'm sorry," Kira stuttered. "I didn't do it on purpose. It was the hot shower and the …."

Lucas interrupted her by placing his index finger on her lips. "You will be punished and then the matter will be forgotten." Before Kira could ask what it meant to be punished, Ian opened the doors and Lucas gave him a nod. "Ian will escort you to the punishment room."

Following Ian down the hall, Kira's stomach knotted. A million thoughts danced through her mind but in the moment one was most prevalent: What was the punishment room?

At the end of the hall, Ian unlocked a door and led Kira inside. It was a small room, with red plush carpeting and a red velvet couch. "Is this like solitary confinement or something?" Kira sarcastically spewed.

"Not hardly," Ian rebutted, "but you'll wish it was in a few moments."

"What does that mean?" Kira asked.

Ian gave her an exhausted expression. "Just do what you're told and things will be easier on you." He left the room and shut the door, locking it behind him.

Kira sank down onto the couch. Her nerves were on end in anticipation of whatever this punishment might be. Whatever it was, she wanted to get it over with. A few moments later, Lucas entered escorted by the big, bald valet. Lucas's expression appeared less angry and more warm as he sat down on the couch next to Kira and brushed a piece of hair from her face. "I don't like to punish my girls," he said with sincerity. "But, as I have told you, my job is to protect you and sometimes that involves protecting you from making mistakes that could inevitably hurt you or us in the long run."

"Lucas, I was drugged. I don't even remember what happened with..."

"I have taken that into consideration," he interrupted, "and your punishment will be lighter because of this, but you will be disciplined for your actions nonetheless."

Kira glanced at the valet, standing guard at the door. "Is he going to rough me up or something?" She sarcastically quipped.

"No. He will simply assist in restraining you."

"Restraining me?" Kira guffawed.

"My world is simple, Ms. Sullivan. Good girls get rewarded and bad girls get punished."

"This is ridiculous," Kira spewed, but Lucas appeared unaffected by her argument. He looked at the valet and gave a nod, at which time two men, who were equally as large as the valet, entered the room, scooping Kira up as if she were a rag doll. They removed her dress and bound her wrists, fastening them tightly to a looped rope that hung from the ceiling. Standing in nothing more than her bra and panties, she tried to kick as they bound her ankles together, but it was no use. She was no match for even one of them, much less two. She was then blindfolded and left alone for several minutes to anticipate the punishment. Everything felt surreal as fear and anger surged through her body. She wanted to scream and cry at the same time, but more than anything she wanted this entire nightmare to end. She wanted to wake up in her bed next to Frank and realize that the whole thing had been a bad dream. What she wouldn't have given to go back in time and undo it all.

Kira heard the door open and then felt a hand slither across the small of her back. She jumped and tried to maneuver away but it was useless. Another set of hands grabbed her waist, as if to steady her. "I'm going to be whipping you with a leather strap," Lucas's voice came from behind her. "The strap will not leave any long term marks on your body but will sting enough for you to remember that we do not tell our clients we have been drugged nor do we pass out on them. This is your first infraction and so your punishment will be only twenty lashes."

Without further explanation, Kira felt the first stinging slap across her back, followed by another and another, as Lucas struck her. Each lash made her instinctively jump and yelp, and it felt as if each one came harder and faster than the one before. He hit her shoulders, her back, her bottom and the back of her legs; and she cried out in pain. Twenty lashes with a whip was enough to reduce her to a sobbing mess, and as the valet unbound her wrists and ankles she sank onto the couch with no energy or will left to fight.

"I don't like having to punish any of my girls and I hope we will not have to do this again," Lucas said, pulling the blindfold from her eyes. "I want you to remember this and to make sure that Mr. Green has no more complaints about your service. "Do you understand?"

"Yes," Kira answered quietly, blinking as her eyes tried to adjust to the light. "I understand."

CHAPTER 17

As soon as Kira had calmed down from her beating, she was escorted to the dressing room to prepare for her night with Mr. Green. Her eyes were puffy and red and it was obvious to everyone that she had been crying.

"Are you okay?" Shelby asked, prancing over to Kira and plunking down in the chair next to her. "I heard you got taken to the punishment room." Kira buried her face in her hands, trying not to cry again. "Oh, don't feel bad," Shelby consoled. "We've all been there at least once."

Kira peeked through her fingers. "You have?"

Several women gathered around the make-up mirror and began telling of their experience in the punishment room. After hearing their stories, Kira felt a little better, like she had actually gotten off easier than the rest of them.

"It's just Lucas's way of maintaining control," the Cher-look-alike explained. "It doesn't mean anything."

"It's how he protects us," Shelby smiled, and Kira looked at her, wondering how someone could be that naïve. Abuse is not protection.

As the women dispersed, Shelby stayed next to Kira while they both applied their make-up. "So, where's Audrey?" Shelby asked. "I haven't seen her since Sunday night."

"I don't know. I'm worried about her."

"Oh, I wouldn't worry, people leave here all the time without saying goodbye," Shelby quipped.

"Yeah, you said that once before," Kira acknowledged. "My first day here you said that not many girls last very long downstairs."

"They don't," Shelby shrugged.

"I wonder why," Kira uttered, half with sarcasm and half as an attempt to keep Shelby talking, hoping a nugget of useful information would spill out.

"The only ones that have lasted are the ones that are requested by several clients, but the ones who have just one client are usually gone pretty fast." Shelby applied a thick line of black eyeliner and then leaned in closer to Kira and lowered her voice. "This one client has gone through four girls already. It must take something really special to satisfy him," she snorted and raised her eyebrows.

"What's his name?" Kira asked, and as soon as the question left her lips she realized how stupid it was. The Candy Shop didn't operate with real names so there was no way Shelby could know his name.

"I don't know. Miranda never told me," Shelby shrugged.

Miranda. Was it possible that Mr. Green was Miranda's old client and that's why she had attacked Kira in the hall that day? The thought made her shudder. Could it be that all of the girls that left were once requested by Mr. Green? "Do you remember any of the names of the girls who were requested downstairs before me and didn't stay very long?" Kira asked nonchalantly.

Shelby took a tissue and blotted her lips. "Let me think. Before Miranda there was a girl named Christine, and then Misty. She was bright blonde, like me, only hers was real," Shelby said with a pout. "But I think she was only here for one night."

"That's right," the Cher-look-alike interjected, repeating their names as if she were trying to commit them to memory. "Wasn't there a third one?" The Cher-look-alike prompted.

"Yes!" Shelby exclaimed excitedly, as if she'd just won at a bingo match. "Her name was Ilesia and she was super-hot. She had the most beautiful dark skin. Her complexion was perfect, like magazine perfect." Shelby's eyes sparkled as she described Ilesia's beauty. "Everyone wanted her and then after she was requested downstairs she just disappeared." Shelby shrugged. "I don't know what goes on down there, but evidentially it takes someone really special to be able to handle it."

"You ladies better hope Lucas isn't listening in right now, or you're all going to the punishment room," a lanky red-head warned as she cinched a red satin robe around her waist and headed toward the costumes.

"What does she mean?" Kira asked.

Shelby lowered her voice to a whisper and leaned closer to Kira. "We're not supposed to talk about what goes on downstairs. It's one of the rules."

"Lucas considers it a breach of security," the Cher-look-alike added with what Kira thought was a twinge of disgust.

"He says women are prone to be gossips but his ladies are not to gossip," Shelby clarified with a big smile. It was obvious that Shelby bought whatever Lucas was selling, hook, line and sinker.

Kira looked into the mirror and saw the Cher-look-alike staring at her. As soon as their eyes met, the Cher-look-alike quickly diverted her gaze and attention elsewhere, but the interaction made Kira take an eerie pause.

Dressed in a short sequined black, strapless gown and stilettos, Kira was allowed to skip Lucas' drugging this evening. Instead, Ian escorted her directly to the bar in the Lair where she was told to wait for Mr. Green's arrival. While the bartender mixed her a martini, she watched closely to make sure he didn't slip anything into her drink. All the while, her mind churned over the names of the girls that had been downstairs before her; and she wondered if she should casually ask the bartender if he knew any of them. She glanced around the Lair, pondering exactly where the cameras and recording devices were hidden. If she were to speak to the bartender, she knew she had to be careful, as the last thing she wanted to do was end up back in the punishment room.

When the bartender placed the martini in front of her, Kira smiled and said, "Thank you." Lifting the glass, she took a tiny sip. "This is wonderful," she said, trying to strike up a conversation. "You'd be surprised how many bartenders aren't able to make a good martini." The corners of his lips curled slightly and he nodded as if to say thank you, but he didn't speak. Kira took another sip. "You know what it is..." she swallowed nervously. "They put too much Vermouth in. That ruins the whole drink." He looked up and for the first time they made eye contact. His brown eyes to her blue and for a moment she thought she saw softness behind his stare; but as quickly as she saw it, it was gone.

"I am pleased you like it," he said as if it were a formal statement and not a genuine feeling.

"How long have you worked here?" Kira asked, aware by the shock on his face that she might be pushing the envelope.

"Since it opened," he answered quietly.

"So, just a few months," Kira stated matter-of-factly and then picked up her martini and slammed the rest of it in one gulp. "Can I have another one please?"

His eyes widened and Kira could tell that he could not have been more surprised. She took a little bit of pleasure in the fact that she was obviously not what he was used to encountering in the Lair.

"I'm new here," she blurted while he mixed her second martini. "I know you probably knew that, but I just thought I'd put it out there." He didn't respond. "I never got to dance upstairs, which is ironically why I let Audrey drag me here to apply for the job in the first place. I love to dance. Well, I used to, when I was younger." Kira couldn't stop talking. She had suddenly become like a nervous Chatty Cathy doll. "My husband would kill me if he knew I even considered dancing again."

The bartender set the martini in front of Kira and she felt his eyes studying her. "You're still young enough to dance," he said and then began cleaning the shaker.

Kira lifted the glass and took a sip. "You're probably paid to say that," she snorted, beginning to feel a little light headed from the effects of the alcohol.

"Probably not," he rebutted and Kira saw a smile in his eyes.

"How old are you?" She leaned in closer. "Do you have a name? I mean, a name I can use? Because I have a name but no one can use it here. When I'm here I have to be a flower." Her words slurred slightly and she rolled her eyes when she said the word flower. "I'm part of Lucas' garden, ya know, but I'm probably more of a weed than a flower. Yeah, I'm a weed. Hey, do you have any weed? I remember smoking weed in college, that's when I used to dance too. College was so much fun and life was so easy back then, wasn't it? I think I thought coming here and dancing again would make me feel young and everything would be easier, like it used to be."

110

There was no question about it, she was drunk. She couldn't remember the last time she'd eaten and the liquor was going straight to her head. The bartender stared at her as if he were both horrified and intrigued by her babbling.

Ian entered the Lair without Kira noticing, at least until he came up behind her and placed his hand on her shoulder, startling her and causing her to shriek. "You're not Mr. Green," she said with a slurred pout.

"No, I am not," he responded. "Mr. Green is unable to make it this evening. Landon will escort you home."

Kira blew raspberries. "Don't lie," she spat. "Landon isn't taking me home, he's taking me to the Adam's Mark, where he's holding me hostage," she announced while pointing her finger at Ian.

"If you are going to resist leaving, I will have you escorted out," Ian threatened.

"A lady always needs an escort," Kira sarcastically spewed, pushing Ian's hands off of her. The next thing she felt was the tiny prick of a needle in the side of her neck and everything went black.

"Nice work," Ian said to the bartender who was still holding the syringe.

CHAPTER 18

Natalie Wild was the name of Miranda's neighbor in the Central West End. By the time Rocco arrived at the apartment building, Natalie's body had already been bagged and loaded into the ambulance. Ducking under the crime scene tape that blocked the front entrance, Rocco rushed up the staircase, skipping every other step, until he got to the third floor. Officer Peters met him in Natalie's living room.

"What happened?" Rocco demanded.

Peters shrugged. "We got a call early this morning that said there was commotion in apartment B3. Our guys came over and found the door busted open, the place trashed and the girl, strangled."

"Son of a ..." Rocco didn't finish his sentence. Instead, he bit down on his bottom lip. "Who's heading up the investigation?"

"Watts, I think," Peters said and pointed toward the kitchen.

Sliding past Peters, Rocco made a beeline for Watts, who was a forty-nine year old, African American man that stood six foot four inches tall and looked as if he were made of nothing but pure muscle. His stature alone intimidated most and he was known on the force for being a hard ass. He normally worked the drug circuit. "Listen, Watts, I want the entire scene dusted for prints, I want a DNA analysis run on every skin cell and hair follicle you find. I want...."

"Cool your jets, Sterling," Watts barked. "This isn't your case. So pipe down and let me do my job. We find anything funny, you'll be the first to know."

"Natalie Wild might have been the only person to have seen our serial killer, so don't tell me this isn't my case," Rocco seethed. Watts held up his palms to indicate that he wasn't interested in Rocco's plight and walked away, making Rocco even angrier. He pounded his fist atop the kitchen counter and grunted. Every nerve stood on end, agitated by the feeling that he was running out of time.

"Got a minute?" Peters said, poking his head into the kitchen and pulling Rocco from his thoughts. Rocco nodded and Peters slid onto a counter stool next to where Rocco stood. "At first, I was thinking this couldn't be our guy. I mean, Natalie was strangled and our guy slits his victim's throat. There were obvious signs of a struggle and our guy sedates his victims, not to mention the fact that her body was left in her home and not thrown into a dumpster. I'm guessing the forensic report is gonna tell us that she wasn't raped, and we know our guy has sex with his victims..."

"What's your point?" Rocco interrupted.

"I thought it couldn't be him but then I noticed her hand," Peters said.

"What about her hand?" Peters and Rocco locked eyes.

113

"There was a small slice at the base of her left ring finger. It looked like someone was about to sever the finger, you know, like out of habit, and then thought otherwise and stopped," Peters explained.

Rocco's eyebrows lifted. "He got careless," Rocco murmured more to himself than to Peters. Thoughts darted in and out of his mind as he tried to connect the dots. "Natalie wasn't one he previously selected. He killed her because he had to, not out of pleasure." Rocco paced back and forth across the kitchen. "Which means my hunch was right and Natalie did have information or could identify him or somehow connect him to Miranda, so he had to get rid of her."

"Yeah, but why now?" Peters interjected. "I mean, why not kill her the same night he killed Miranda? Why wait and risk her telling someone?"

Rocco snapped his fingers. "Because he didn't know she had any information about him. He just found out and I'd bet anything that the minute he found out, he drove straight here and murdered her."

"Makes sense," Peters said. "But it begs the question how'd he find out?"

Rocco abruptly stopped pacing and spun around to face Peters. "I need to know everyone Natalie spoke to this past week. Co-workers. Family. Neighbors. Friends. I want phone records, surveillance video, whatever you can pull." Rocco turned and walked briskly toward the living room and out of the front door with Peters barely keeping stride. "I want video feed of every vehicle that came within a two-block radius of this apartment building in the past twenty-four hours," Rocco barked.

"Where am I gonna get that?" Peters quipped.

"Call the goddamned FBI for all I care, but get me that feed!" Rocco dashed down the stairs and toward his Hummer.

"Yes, sir," Peters uttered, out of breath from trying to keep up. "Sir?" Peters yelled as Rocco pulled open his driver's door and then turned to face Peters with raised eyebrows and an expression of impatience. "What do you think he's gonna do next?"

Rocco's eyes darkened. "Kill."

CHAPTER 19

Scanning through the police files he had thrown onto his passenger seat, Rocco found the address for Kira Sullivan and headed to her house. Landon had whisked her away before they could question her and Rocco had a sneaking suspicion that, for whatever reason, Kira might have information that would prove helpful. If nothing else, he wanted to ask her about the note that was found in her trashcan that read: ONE FOR THE MONEY, TWO QUIT THE SHOW, THREE WANTED MORE, FOUR A THORNED ROSE. THE FIFTH IS REVENGE SERVED HOT AND RED. YOU DECIDE IF SHE WINDS UP DEAD. It was obvious this note referenced the four women that were found dead, the fourth with a rose pinned to her blouse. He knew it was no coincidence, so did the killer and he had a hunch that Kira Sullivan knew too. Why else would the note and finger have been left for her to find? Rocco needed to understand how she fit into the picture and define her connection to the fifth victim who was yet to be slain. Besides, the name Sullivan rang a bell and not being able to place it was driving him crazy.

Rocco's foot grew heavier on the gas pedal as a sense of urgency overtook him. He was running out of time and he could feel it.

He rang Kira's doorbell several times, but there was no answer. Pulling out his phone and checking the time, he noted that it was only 9:30am. He would wait. From what he surmised of Kira Sullivan, she was a forty year old, wealthy housewife who, he guessed, left the house only to have coffee with girlfriends, shop at Plaza Frontenac or run a quick errand to the local market or dry cleaners. He wanted to be there when she returned and catch her off guard before she could run into the house and call her attorney, Landon Parker. Just the thought of that slime ball made his skin crawl.

Climbing back into his Hummer, Rocco signed in to the internal police server and ran a background check on Kira Sullivan. As the information appeared on the screen, he jotted notes onto the back of a file. Her maiden name was Walker. She was currently married to Frank Sullivan, and had been for twenty years. They had two children. She had no criminal record, not even a parking ticket. No liens. No bankruptcies. Nothing. Whoever Kira Sullivan was, she was squeaky clean. Holding the pen between his teeth, he typed in Frank Sullivan and clicked Search. Relevance immediately struck him as he saw that Frank was the Sullivan in the firm, Parker, Sullivan & Bates. It made sense now why Landon whisked Kira from the station before she could be questioned, though he wondered why her husband hadn't come to get her.

Rocco leaned his head against the headrest and closed his eyes momentarily. Memories flooded his mind. It was almost three years ago. Rocco was following a string of murders that started in Illinois but had links to one of the mafia families in St. Louis. Six deaths and seven months later, Rocco nailed the killer. Tony Coronado was his name, though on the street he was called, "Iceman." As is typical of the rich, the Coronado family hired the best defense team money could buy: Parker,Sullivan & Bates. Frank Sullivan took the case. Arrogant was the word that came to Rocco's mind when he thought of Frank. Arrogant. He was so sure he was going to win that he appeared genuinely shocked when Rocco's testimony dismantled his case. Iceman was convicted and went to prison, and was found dead in his cell several weeks later. Rocco surmised it was because someone in the family was afraid he'd try to cut a deal with the Feds. That's often what happens to mob members who know too much. Knowledge makes one both powerful and a liability.

Rocco took the pen and jotted a quick note: Coronado family.

It was after that trial that his life fell apart. Actually, it was during the trial that things started to unravel. He had made the mistake of falling for Adrianne Barkley Parker, Lieutenant Barkley's sister and Landon Parker's wife. He had known Adrianne in high school and one might say it was a story of unrequited love, at least for him. So when their paths crossed three years ago, Rocco looked at it as fate giving him a second chance. She had filed for divorce prior to her affair with Rocco, citing in the paperwork that

Landon was abusive; but it wasn't until Landon hired a private investigator that all hell broke loose. The investigator acquired intimate photographs that detailed Rocco and Adrianne's romance, and shortly thereafter Adrianne was dead.

Rocco spent the next year of his life focused on trying to prove that Landon was behind her untimely death; but every lead ran dry. He couldn't compete with the deep pockets of Landon Parker nor the backing he had from the defense team at Parker, Sullivan & Bates, so the case was dropped. Rocco threw himself back into work, chasing down serial killers in some feeble attempt to cleanse his own soul; but he often wondered who he was kidding. Nothing would take away the sorrow he felt in losing Adrianne and his rage toward Landon. Lieutenant Barkley blamed him for causing trouble in his sister's marriage and ultimately for her death; and Rocco couldn't fault him. Maybe Barkley was right. Maybe Rocco was a psychopathic ego-maniac on the verge of becoming a killer himself. If he was, he knew who his first victim would be. Landon Parker.

Shaking off the memories, Rocco checked the time, 10:00am. He stepped out of his Hummer and rang the doorbell again. He thought there may have been a chance that she was in the shower and didn't hear him the first time. Walking to the side of the two-car garage, Rocco peered through the small rectangular window in the side door and saw a white Lexus parked inside. He twisted the knob but it was locked. Peering quickly over each shoulder to make sure no one was watching, he retrieved a small tool from his front pocket, pressed it into the lock until it clicked, opened the door and slid inside.

The door from the garage to the house was unlocked and Rocco stepped inside and called out Kira's name. "Mrs. Sullivan?" He hollered throughout the house. "My name is Detective Sterling. I'd like to ask you some questions." He glided through the kitchen, past the dining room, through the living room and toward the rounded staircase that led to the next level. "Mrs. Sullivan?" He called up the stairs, but there was no response. Darting up the staircase, he poked his head in every bedroom just to make sure something hadn't happened to her. After all, a serial killer had left her a note. That was reason enough to suspect that she might already be dead.

As soon as he entered the master bedroom, Rocco froze mid-step, unable to believe his eyes. On the nightstand was a picture of Kira and Frank. Kira was smiling and the sun was reflecting in her blue eyes; eyes Rocco knew well. His breath caught in his chest. "Oh no," he uttered, as a wave of realization washed over him. Now, he understood the connection. Now, he knew why the killer left Kira the note and now he feared he was too late.

Dashing out of the front door, Rocco raced toward his Hummer when Carter caught his attention. "Hey Mister, nice car," Carter said, running his fingertips across the grill.

"Hummers are so cool. I'm gonna drive one when I grow up."

"Do you live close?" Rocco asked.

"Right there," Carter pointed. "I'm the house with the hoop over the garage."

"You don't happen to know where Mrs. Sullivan is, do you?"

"She hasn't been home since the police were here two days ago. They took her away in a police car and I think she's in jail." Carter's eyes widened and he had a very serious expression on his face. "It had something to do with her trashcan being outside. We're not supposed to put the trash out until Friday morning but Mr. Sullivan put it out late Sunday night and I think he got Mrs. Sullivan in trouble with the trash people. They might both be in jail," Carter gasped.

"I'm sure it's just a misunderstanding and that Mrs. Sullivan isn't in jail or in trouble with the trash people," Rocco smirked. He found the untainted outlook of a child both amusing and refreshing.

"I don't know," Carter said, shaking his head. "I haven't seen her since."

"I'll tell you what," Rocco said while digging into his pocket and retrieving a business card. "You take this and if you see her, you give me a call right away, okay?"

Carter took the card and read it. "Special Detective." He gave Rocco the once over. "You don't look like the other cops that took Mrs. Sullivan away."

"I'll take that as a compliment," Rocco said. "Now, get home." Carter ran up the sidewalk toward his house and Rocco backed out of Kira's driveway. There was only one thing left to do, and that was to find Kira before she ended up in a dumpster across town.

CHAPTER 20

It was a torrential downpour when Ian opened the front doors and greeted Mr. Green with a welcoming smile. "Good evening, sir," Ian said. "We weren't expecting you for another hour." A flash of lightening lit up the entrance followed by an immediate crash of thunder. "That's quite a storm," Ian gasped, helping Mr. Green remove his wet trench coat. "I'm afraid Daisy isn't ready. Would you like to wait in the Lair for her or shall I have another companion accompany you?"

"No, I don't mind waiting," he stated curtly. "I don't want another companion."

"Very well."

Once inside the Lair, Mr. Green took a seat at the bar and ordered a Scotch on the rocks. He drank it down in one gulp and ordered another. The thunder was so loud it could be heard even in the depths of the Lair and he noticed the bartender jumped at one of the blasts.

"It's really coming down out there," Mr. Green remarked.

"Yes, sir. I imagine it is."

"Tell me about yourself," Mr. Green said, causing the bartender's eyebrows to raise slightly, as if he were surprised by the question. "I'm stuck here until my friend comes, so I thought we could talk."

"Oo-kaaay," the bartender retorted, acting as if no other client had ever tried to engage him in small talk. "What would you like to talk about?"

"Not politics or religion," Mr. Green joked. "How about we start with your name?"

"I'm Benjamin, but most of my friends call me Ben."

"Have you always been a bartender?" Mr. Green asked.

"On and off," Ben answered while washing a glass in the stainless steel sink and drying it with a white towel he had slung over his shoulder.

"Tell me," Mr. Green rested his elbows on the bar, "how does one go about getting a job here? I mean, they must background check the crap out of you."

"Not really. You kind of have to know somebody to get your foot in the door."

Mr. Green lifted his empty glass to indicate he'd like another Scotch on the rocks and watched the bartender flinch ever so slightly when the thunder crashed overhead. "You don't like storms?" He asked.

Blushing just a little, the bartender shook his head. "My granddad was struck by lightning when I was a kid. I've been jumpy in storms ever since."

"Geeze, that'll do it," Mr. Green grimaced and took a sip of his freshly poured Scotch. "So, how'd you get your foot in the door here? Do you know the owners or something?"

Ben lifted his gaze from the sink and stared at Mr. Green. "No," he said poignantly. "I don't know the owners. Never met them."

"So who hired you?"

"Ian. He interviewed me and offered me the job and here I am." Ben lifted his hands, palms up.

Mr. Green smiled. "Are you allowed to sleep with the women or is that against company policy?"

"Unfortunately, that's a big no-no," Ben chuckled.

"That is unfortunate."

Ian rushed to the back door and opened it into the alley just as the black limo pulled up and the valet escorted Kira through the door. "What took you so long?" Ian snapped at the valet. "Mr. Green has been waiting. You know we don't keep our high paying customers waiting." Grabbing Kira by the arm, he pulled her down the hall and into the dressing room. "Get ready quickly," he barked and then meet me at the entrance to the Lair.

Kira sat down in front of the make-up mirror and stared through her own reflection. She felt hopelessly trapped. Where was Frank? How long was Landon going to keep her locked up? Were Michael and Mallory all right? Landon had promised that as long as she did everything she was told, he would leave her kids alone; so she tried desperately to let that be her motivation toward submission, but it was hard. She wanted to hear their voices. She wanted to talk to Audrey. She wanted to tell Frank she was sorry.

"Why the long face?" Kira looked up and saw the Cher-look-alike standing behind her, staring at her through the mirror. When Kira didn't answer, she slinked over and sat down in the chair next to her. "You in some kind of trouble?"

Kira's throat felt dry and it wasn't that she couldn't speak, it was that she didn't know what to say. "Trapped," was all she managed to get out before her eyes began to tear.

"Listen, if somebody downstairs is mistreating you, you gotta tell Lucas," the Cher-look-alike said, but Kira shook her head.

"That's not it," she said softly, fighting back tears.

The Cher-look-alike leaned in close and hugged Kira tightly, almost too tightly. Kira was about to push away when she felt her lips against her ear and heard the Cher-look-alike whisper, "I've got a Taser for you. Get dressed and meet me by the costumes."

Dressed in a red evening gown, gold stilettos and diamond laced gold earrings, Kira followed Ian down the hall toward the Lair. The lights flickered several times as the thunder roared overhead. "I trust we will have no more episodes like last night," Ian said to her.

"No, we won't," Kira answered quietly. "I'm sorry."

"That's more like it," Ian uttered and then opened the door to the Lair, ushered her inside and locked it behind her.

The moment Mr. Green saw Kira approaching, he requested a key to a private room. Ben handed him a key. "The candles have been lit and there is a chilled bottle of champagne in your room, just as you requested," he said.

Mr. Green took Kira by the hand and led her to the room. "You'll be happy to know I'm completely sober," she uttered sarcastically, stepping inside.

"That's promising," he retorted. "I wish I could say the same."

"I'm guessing you won't get punished if you pass out on me," she spewed.

Mr. Green closed the room door and locked it. "Punished?"

Kira rolled her eyes. "Forget it."

Pulling her close, he whispered in her ear. "Have they hurt you?"

Kira swallowed the lump trying to form in her throat and shook her head. "No," she lied and could feel his scrutinizing eyes upon her.

With his lips pressed against her ear, he whispered, "Don't speak loud. I'm going to turn on some music to try and drown out our voices. Remember, we have to make this look believable."

Landon's words replayed in her mind. *Do what you're told and your family might live through this.* She forced a smile, but she knew it was a thin disguise. She could tell that Mr. Green could see right through her. In fact, something felt different between them. Was it because she was sober?

Thunder crashed overhead and the lights flickered off and then came back on. With soft music playing and a glass of champagne in her hand, Kira tried to force herself to relax. Where was the arousal and desire she felt two nights ago? Why was she here? Why was it so important to Landon that she make Lucas happy?

They sat on the end of the bed and sipped their champagne in silence. The tension in the room felt palatable and Kira began to worry that if she didn't please him, he would complain to Lucas and she would end up in the punishment room again. Mr. Green set his champagne glass on the floor and then brushed her hair away from her neck and planted a tiny kiss just beneath her ear lobe. "We need to talk," he whispered as he drew his lips back.

Kira turned slightly to face him and he quickly grabbed her chin and angled her head the other way, staring at her neck. "Where did you get this mark?" He asked.

"What mark?"

"This dot and tiny bruise."

Kira shrugged. "I don't know what you're talking a..." He pressed on her neck and Kira shot off the bed. "Ouch!" She yelped and grabbed her neck.

Leaping to his feet, he pulled her close, speaking more to himself than to her. "That mark was made by an injection, a syringe. Since you're still sore I'm guessing it was administered within the last twenty-four hours."

Kira's heart was racing as she tried to recall what had happened the night before. The last thing she remembered was copping an attitude with Ian and then waking up in her hotel room.

Mr. Green placed his hands around her face and spoke softly. "You've got to trust me," he said. "Can you do that? Can you trust me?"

Tears filled Kira's eyes and though she tried to feign strength, she knew it was obvious that she was breaking under the pressure. She wanted to go home. She wanted to be with her family. She wanted this nightmare to end. "How can I trust you? I don't even know you."

"But I know you," he mouthed. "I know you."

"You don't know me because if you knew me then you would know that I don't want to be here, but they won't let me leave while you're requesting me," Kira cried. "You've made me a prisoner!" Her voice escalated and she pushed his hands from her face. All of a sudden she was consumed with rage. Hot anger was pulsing through her and without thinking she smacked him across the face as hard as she could.

A moment later someone banged on the door. "Open the door immediately or we will open it for you," Ben demanded.

Mr. Green opened the door. "Is there a problem?" He asked. "Because I have made it very clear that I do not wish to be disturbed."

"My apologies," Ben uttered. "We were under the misconception that your interaction with Daisy had become less than agreeable."

"I assure you, our interaction is quite agreeable," he smirked. "The only thing not agreeable is this interruption," he scowled.

"Again, my apologies. I will make sure you are given the utmost privacy," Ben stammered and Mr. Green closed the door and locked it. He then turned up the music a little louder and pulled Kira into his arms as if to dance.

"I don't know if they heard the slap or if they are watching, but we're going to have to make this look more believable," he said and then whirled her around and unzipped the back of her dress. "We're going to have to get into the shower. It's the only safe place for us to talk." Her dress fell to the floor and a tear trickled down her cheek. The last thing in the world she wanted to do was face the humiliation of being naked in front of Mr. Green again; but what choice did she have? She carefully slid her panties and the Taser to the floor and buried them beneath her crumpled dress.

The three shower heads pounded water against her skin and she couldn't deny that the steamy warmth was soothing. Mr. Green wrapped his right arm around her waist and she leaned back against his chest. "Do you remember what I told you the other night?" He spoke into her ear. "Do you remember that I told you that the only way I can protect you is to keep requesting you?"

Her memory was fuzzy. His words triggered flashes of relevancy from their previous shower experience, but exactly what had been said she couldn't recall. Whirling around to face him, Kira forcefully put her lips against his ear and whispered, "If you want to protect me then let me go. All I want to do is go home and as long as you're requesting me, I can't."

He spun her back around and pulled her against him, draping his arm around her shoulders and moving his lips closer to her ear. "Four women are dead because of me. You're going to be the fifth unless I can figure out how to stop it."

Kira's eyes widened and then she shut them as tightly as she could. None of this was making sense. Had he killed four women? Was he threatening to kill her or was he genuinely concerned about her wellbeing? A part of her wanted to melt into a little ball of sobs and beg to be taken home and the other part was so filled with rage that she envisioned taking a bat and beating everyone in sight. She felt like a caged animal, trapped inside a circumstance she couldn't control and caused by a mistake that was inevitably going to ruin her life.

"Kira, you've got to trust me," he whispered and in that brief moment it felt as if time stood still. She could feel her heart pounding in her chest but everything else felt surreal. Slowly turning to face him, Kira stared into his deep green eyes. How did he know her real name? Before she could open her mouth to speak, he continued. "I know who you are and I know about the note left in your trashcan." He pulled her close and held her head against his chest, leaning his head down and speaking softly into her ear. "If I stop requesting you, they will kill you. This is my fault. Somehow, it's my fault. When Christine was murdered I thought I could find out something if I came back here, so I did and I requested Misty. When she wound up dead, I should have stopped coming but I thought the only way to catch the killer was to keep coming back. I came back and requested Ilesia because she was African American and I thought that if I was dealing with a serial killer who had already murdered two Caucasian women, than the likelihood of him murdering an African American was slim." Mr. Green's voice cracked with emotion. "I was wrong and it cost Ilesia her life." He exhaled. "But how could I find the killer if I stopped coming to the very spot where he was selecting his women? So I came back and requested Miranda."

Kira was breathless with fear as he poured his confession into her ear. She didn't know what to do. Was he sick? Was it possible that he had killed these women and not known it? Was he completely insane or could his story be true?

"Miranda and I were together for weeks and the killing stopped. I kept coming back, searching for clues and decided that the killer must have been satiated by those three. I thought it was over and then Miranda was murdered." His voice shook. "All that time I had been searching for a connection between the women and the connection was me."

"I don't believe you," Kira muttered, her body beginning to tremble. "You killed them didn't you?" Kira stepped away from him and crossed her arms over her body. "You're crazy and you just don't remember killing them..."

Mr. Green neared her. "You have no reason to trust me, but you also have no other option." He angled one of the shower heads so that it splashed against the glass door, making a louder sound and better masking their voices. "I thought the connection was this place, I didn't realize it was me until today." His eyes searched hers. "Kira, you've got to believe me."

Tears streamed down her face. She didn't know what to believe and she didn't know what to do. She could start screaming, knowing the bartender would rush to her rescue, but then what? Landon would drag her back to the Adams Mark where she'd remain a prisoner, and for how long? If Mr. Green stopped requesting her, would Landon and Lucas set her free? Or was Mr. Green telling the truth and she would become the next victim? The sound of thunder crashed overhead and the lights flickered.

"The note left in your trashcan tells of the four women killed and mentions a fifth, stating that you control whether she lives or dies," Mr. Green whispered. "How do you control that?"

"I don't know," Kira uttered. "I don't know what's happening."

The lights flickered again. "We need to talk outside of here," Mr. Green said. "What time do they let you go home?"

Kira stared at him, unsure of whether she should tell him that she was being held captive. She didn't know what to say so she just stared. He must have seen her fear and conflicted emotions because he placed his hands on the sides of her face and brushed his lips lightly against hers. "I won't let them hurt you," he promised. "I'll find the killer and stop him, but I need you to trust me with any information you have. It's the only way I can protect you."

A loud burst of thunder felt as if it shook the building, causing the lights to flicker and then go completely out. The music stopped playing and Mr. Green turned off the shower and handed Kira a towel, which she quickly wrapped around her body.

"Sir?" Ian's voice came through the door, followed by three rapid knocks. "I am sorry to interrupt, but I wanted to let you know that we are having some electrical problems due to the storm. We should have the problem resolved shortly."

"Thank you," Mr. Green hollered through the door. "We quite enjoy the candlelight so take your time."

They listened as Ian walked away from the door and asked Ben to follow him.

Mr. Green immediately turned to Kira with a crazed look in his eyes. "Let's go. Now," he whispered.

"What?" Kira gasped. "Go where?"

"Let's get out of here." He took her by the shoulders. "You don't want to do this anymore, right?" He asked and Kira nodded. "And I can't stop requesting you because someone here…someone linked to this place…murders any woman I stop requesting…" He paused and took a deep breath. "So the only way to ensure your safety is to get you out of here."

Kira studied his eyes and her heart started to race. This was a crucial, life-altering moment. This was the moment when she had to make a life or death decision. Trust a stranger who could very well be a serial killer or trust Lucas, who had drugged her and beaten her, and Landon who had kidnapped her and threatened her family. "Okay," Kira mouthed breathlessly. "I'll go with you."

"Get dressed," he ordered. "Quickly."

They both began putting on their clothes and Kira carefully slid the small Taser into the bustier of her dress without Mr. Green noticing. In those brief moments she had devised a plan. If he was successfully able to sneak her out of The Candy Shop, she would then Taser him, steal his car and go to the police. If he was unsuccessful she would tell Lucas that he had tried to kidnap her, hoping they would blame him and not view her actions as an escape attempt.

The lights were still out when they opened the private room door, slid quietly out and locked the door behind them. They left the candles burning and turned on the shower so it would appear as if they were still inside of the room. Mr. Green took Kira by the hand and led her across the Lair and down the hallway toward the exit. "It's always locked," Kira whispered, but she was wrong. This time the door had been left unlocked, probably because Ben left only momentarily to help Ian with the electrical problems and planned on coming right back.

"Do you know the layout down here?" He asked.

"Yes," Kira whispered. "We need to take the hallway to the right, passed the dressing room and follow it as it curves further to the right. The employee entrance opens into an alley in the back of the building."

As they started down the hall, they heard footsteps coming toward them in the darkness. Kira's breathing quickened and she thought her heart might pound right out of her chest. Mr. Green squeezed her hand.

All of a sudden a bright white light blinded them. "Where are you going?" Ben asked, shining a flashlight into their eyes.

"He wants me to put on something sexy," Kira lied without missing a beat and forcing a seductive smile. "He says my dress covers a little too much."

"That's right," Mr. Green chimed in. "I'd like to see her in some lingerie."

Ben lowered the light to the floor. "Well, you passed the dressing room. It's back this way." He strode passed them with the light out in front when Kira did something she never thought she'd have the courage to do. As if a warrior had taken over her body, she pulled the Taser from her dress and zapped Ben in the back of the neck. He dropped like a wet sack of sand, twitching on the floor.

Mr. Green's mouth fell open with what could only have been sheer disbelief and then he quickly took her by the arm and they raced down the hall toward the back door. The rain was beating the pavement as they ran through the alley, down the cobblestone street and up to the lot where the valet had left Mr. Green's car. She stood shivering in the downpour while he reached his hand beneath the front grill, retrieved a lock box with a spare key and unlocked the driver's door. Climbing across the seat, Kira's foot got caught in her dress and she fell forward, slamming her chin against the dash, but there was no time to stop and cry. Mr. Green pushed her into the passenger seat, jumped in and they sped off.

After a few moments of intently staring through the passenger mirror, in anticipation of Lucas' men coming to chase them down, Kira began to catch her breath and loosen her grip on the Taser.

"I don't think we're being followed," Mr. Green said. "But, just in case, we're going to switch vehicles."

Fifteen minutes later they pulled into a Jiffy Lube, drove around to the back and into an opened garage. The door immediately began to close behind the car. Mr. Green killed the ignition and instructed Kira to get out. She froze. Had she made the worst mistake of her life? Was this where he killed all of the women? Her grip tightened around the Taser. Mr. Green looked down at the weapon clutched in her hand. "I hope you're not planning on using that again," he uttered.

"Only if I need to," Kira rebutted.

Disappointment flashed in his eyes but was quickly replaced by a sense of softness. "That's fair," he said.

She followed him two garage doors down, where there sat a black Chevy Traverse. Pulling open the passenger door, he gave her a small smile. "You're chariot, my lady."

She took a deep breath and climbed in. After all, where else was she going to go? She had no identification, no phone, no wallet or money and no car. What's more, she had left her shoes in the private room back at The Candy Shop, which was a wise decision because she wouldn't have been able to run down the cobblestone streets in stilettos. Still, oddly enough she felt even more vulnerable in bare feet.

Mr. Green started the ignition and the garage door behind the Traverse immediately opened. "Whose car is this?" Kira asked.

"I can't tell you and it's better if you don't know. Let's just say that sometimes it's good to have friends in low places," he answered with a wink.

"Where are we going?"

138

"I've got a place in mind. You'll be safe there until I can find out who's behind this whole thing."

Questions danced through her mind, but Kira felt too exhausted to engage in conversation. She was hungry and wet and cold and tired. She wanted to go home and forget everything that had happened, but that wasn't going to happen. When Mr. Green headed out of the city and toward South County, Kira watched carefully, making note of every turn and every street name. On the off chance that he was a crazed killer and she could Taser him and escape, she needed to know how to find her way back to familiar turf. He took highway 55 passed the city of Arnold and then exited onto what looked like an old country road, leading deep into a wooded area. A few miles down, he turned right onto a gravel road and followed it as it wound through the trees. Kira grew more and more anxious. Was he taking her into the woods to kill her?

Pulling up to a small cabin, Mr. Green killed the ignition. "It's not five-star, but it's a roof overhead," he said and placed his hand on the door handle. "You ready to make a run for it?" He asked.

She gripped her handle and on the count of three they both leapt from the Traverse and dashed through the downpour and onto the front porch. "Wait here," Mr. Green said and then left her standing at the front door as he disappeared around the side of the house. Kira was trembling inside and out. She was as much afraid of him as she was afraid to be there without him.

A moment later, the front door opened and Mr. Green motioned her inside. Flipping a switch on the wall by the door illuminated the room in dim lighting and Kira was able to see that there was a small kitchen to her left, a round, wooden dining table and four chairs to her right, a family room straight ahead and what looked like a bedroom off of the family room to the left. Mr. Green strode quickly across the family room, into the bedroom and reappeared carrying two dark green towels. He handed one to Kira and she wrapped it around her shoulders and began to towel dry her soaked hair. "If you need to use the bathroom, it's through the bedroom," he explained.

Kira shook her head. The truth was she did sort of have to go but she didn't want to take her eyes off of him even for a moment. She wasn't going to give him any advantage.

Mr. Green dried his hair with a towel and then slung it over his shoulder. With a loud exhale, he walked into the family room and behind a small desk which sat in the far right corner next to a stone fireplace. Opening the top desk drawer, he retrieved what looked like a black wallet and then closed the drawer and walked back toward Kira.

Placing the wallet in her palm, he took two steps back and said, "Open it."

Kira stared at him, unsure of what to think.

"Go on," he prodded. "Open it."

She slid the two sides of the wallet apart and flipped it open, shocked by what she found. It was a shiny silver badge that read Special Detective. Her gaze lifted from the badge to Mr. Green. "My real name is Rocco Sterling," he said and Kira could hardly believe this was happening. "Do you know who I am?"

Kira's mouth went completely dry as fear gripped her and she slowly nodded her head up and down.

CHAPTER 21

When the lights came back on, Ian found Ben twitching and moaning in the hallway. "Sh-sh-she Ta-Ta-ser-ed me," he stuttered.

"Where did she get a Taser?" Ian growled. "Which way did she go?"

Ben managed to point down the hallway and Ian leapt over him and made a beeline for the back door. Despite the pouring rain, he threw open the door and stepped outside to make a phone call. "She got away," Ian blurted, "and she's with him."

The man on the other end of the call spewed obscenities.

"I'll call Landon," Ian said. "You use your resources to locate him."

The man paused momentarily. "I'll be over to pick up the next girl. Get me someone that looks like Mrs. Sullivan. I want to send a message."

"What about Audrey?" Ian questioned.

"I'm saving her for something really special," he clucked sadistically.

Disconnecting the call, Ian rushed back inside and helped Ben scramble to his feet; and then they burst into the dressing room, startling all of the women. "Line up!" Ian barked. "Line up!"

The ladies looked at one another with confused expressions and then formed a single file line. Ian paced up and down the line, sizing up each woman. He needed a medium-sized brunette with blue eyes. Shelby wiggled her shoulders as Ian passed by. "What are picking someone for?" She asked excitedly. "Whatever it is, I'm game."

Ian rolled his eyes and continued down the line. The Cher-look-alike scowled as he sized her up. "Perv," she mumbled and Ian narrowed his brows.

Stopping in front of the fifth woman in line, Ian asked her name. "Ginger," she answered shyly.

"What is your flower name?" Ian asked with disgust.

"Oh," Ginger giggled. "I forgot. I'm a Geranium."

"Turn around," Ian ordered and Ginger stepped out of line and spun. Her dark brown hair hung almost to her bottom. That was too long, but could be easily cut. "Take this one," Ian directed Ben, who quickly took Ginger by the arm and escorted her out of the dressing room.

"Aw, shucks," Shelby pouted. "When is someone going to request me?"

"I don't think she got requested," the Cher-look-alike noted. "I've never seen them do that before."

"Me either," quipped a tall, red-head wearing a G-string and pasties. "Somethin' don't seem right about that."

Ben and Ian escorted Ginger down the hall and toward the back door. While Ian spoke with Ginger, distracting her, Ben planted the syringe into her neck and Ian caught her as her body went limp and she crumpled forward. As soon as they heard the limousine pull up outside, Ben carried her to the car and placed her in the back.

"Well, done," commented the man in the backseat, as he rubbed his rubber gloved fingers over her thighs. "This is going to be fun."

Ben closed the limousine door and hurried back inside.

CHAPTER 22

Several tiny drops of water ran across her lips, jolting Audrey awake. She opened her mouth, begging for more, and was met with a ladle full that ran down her throat and the front of her dress. She sputtered to swallow without choking. "Thank you," she uttered. "Thank you so much."

"Don't thank me," he sneered. "If it were up to me you'd be dead already."

"Who is it up to then? Who should I thank?" Audrey pried for information. She didn't understand why this was happening or what her captor wanted from her. At this point she would give anything to be freed. "What do you want?" She begged.

"What do you think?" He chided.

"I don't know," Audrey cried. "I don't know what you want but I'll give you anything you ask, just please let me go."

He chuckled aloud. "Let you go," he repeated. "Whether or not we let you go depends on your friend."

Audrey's mind raced, trying to assign relevance to what he was saying. "I don't understand," she muttered. "Which friend? Kira? Is this because of Kira?"

"You were warned." Though she was still blindfolded, she turned her head, following the sound of his footsteps as he moved back and forth in front of her. She tried desperately to peek through the sides of the tape and see if she could make out even his shoes, but the tape was too tight against her skin. "This is what happens when you can't follow the simplest of instructions." He chuckled a raspy laugh as he ascended the staircase, opened the door and then slammed it shut.

She heard the creaking of footsteps above her and Audrey's whole body began to tremble. This wasn't her fault. She had done everything she was told. Where was Kira? Audrey curled into a ball on the concrete floor and tried to stay warm. She felt weak, hungry and was uncertain if her body was trembling from the cold or fear. Either way, the shaking was uncontrollable.

CHAPTER 23

"I want to call my husband," Kira blurted, scanning the room for a phone.

"There's no landline here," Rocco explained, as he built a fire in the stone fireplace and then sat down on the brown leather couch.

Kira was trying hard not to panic but her mind was racing with panic-inducing thoughts. She knew the name Rocco Sterling from Frank, and she knew that Frank despised him. Frank, who was a man who typically did not curse, had used many obscene terms to describe Rocco Sterling. "Can I use your cell phone?" Kira asked.

"No. I threw it in the trash when we switched vehicles," he told her. "I couldn't risk anyone creating a satellite link and following us here. Come sit down," Rocco said. "We need to talk." Kira moved hesitantly toward him.

Her trepidation must have been obvious because Rocco held up both palms and said, "I won't touch you. I promise."

Kira sank onto the opposite end of the couch, never taking her eyes from his. More than anything she wanted to call Frank and have him come and get her.

"I'll answer your questions and then I'm going to need you to answer mine," he began.

Kira didn't hold back. "You testified for the prosecution and destroyed my husband's defense on that big mob case... that was you, right?"

Rocco nodded. "It was the State versus Tony Coronado."

Kira's eyes widened. "Coronado," she mumbled. *That's why the name was familiar.*

"Yes," Rocco said. "He was called Iceman and he killed six people..."

"Coronado," Kira interrupted.

"Am I missing something?" Rocco tilted his head.

Memories flashed in her mind. When Frank lost the Coronado case, they received death threats and the firm hired body guards for the families of Parker, Sullivan & Bates. "It was your fault Frank lost the case," Kira mumbled.

"That's a matter of perspective," Rocco argued. "I believe locking up a killer like Tony Coronado was a win for everyone..."

Kira shook her head. The pieces were coming together. "Lucas said no one knows about The Candy Shop except the people he allows to know."

"I'm not following. Who's Lucas?"

Swallowing hard, Kira took a deep breath. "Lucas Coronado runs The Candy Shop." Rocco's face contorted with shock and then lit with understanding. "I knew the name Coronado sounded familiar but I didn't make the connection to Frank's old mob case. It never entered my mind," she groaned. "I'm so stupid. That's why Landon was there." Kira felt anger rising in her gut. Why hadn't she made the connection sooner?

"Wait a second," Rocco interjected. "Landon Parker was at The Candy Shop?"

Kira nodded. "The first night in the Lair, he was there and he..." her voice cracked.

"You saw him and you talked with him?"

Kira nodded again. "He threatened my kids and Frank's job." She wrung her fingers together. "He told me I better keep Lucas happy."

Rocco studied her face. "How were you supposed to keep Lucas happy?"

"By keeping you happy," she said quietly. Rocco closed his eyes momentarily as if he were processing the information.

"Let's start at the beginning," he said, opening his eyes. "How did you end up going to The Candy Shop in the first place?"

Taking a deep breath, Kira told him about meeting Audrey for coffee and how Audrey began making a list of things she liked to do, which led them to a conversation about how Kira used to dance in college. "Audrey scheduled job interviews for us at The Candy Shop that evening," Kira explained.

"And that was the night I saw you in the foyer?" Rocco asked and Kira nodded.

"Why did you go to The Candy Shop?" Kira asked and then rolled her eyes. "I mean, I know why men go to those places... I mean, I know it's about sex...I'm just, well, why..."

Rocco cut her rambling short. "How did I find out about the place?" He raised his eyebrows and his lips curled into a slight grin.

He was obviously amused by her nervous rambling. "There was a flyer left on my condo door several weeks in a row." He shrugged. "I threw the first couple of flyers away but when the third one came, I couldn't put it down. On the front was a picture of a woman that looked just like..." he paused. "Suffice to say, I felt drawn to go and see if this woman really existed."

"So you went and requested a bunch of different women? Did you have sex with all of them?" Curiosity got the best of her and the question popped out of her mouth before she could stop it.

"No. That's not what happened." He sighed deeply. "The first couple of nights I watched the dancers upstairs and I didn't do anything but have a drink and go home. The third night, when I saw Christine, the woman from the front of the flyer, I was mesmerized." He got off the couch and moved quickly to the kitchen, retrieving a bottle of red wine and two glasses from the pantry. Kira watched intently as he opened the bottle, poured wine in each glass and then carried them to the coffee table, handing her a glass before sitting down. He took a sip of wine and then continued with his story. "Christine was the spitting image of someone I had loved and lost."

"So, you..." Kira pried.

"I had sex with her, yes, but I was really just making-love to a memory, if that doesn't sound too corny," he quipped.

Kira sipped her wine and leaning forward, she set the Taser down atop the coffee table. "Who was the woman you loved and lost?" She asked, drawing her knees up and snuggling into the corner of the couch. She was still in her wet dress and chilled.

Noticing her shivering, Rocco retrieved a black t-shirt and a pair of boxer shorts from the bedroom. "It's not much, but it's dry," he said as he handed them to Kira. She immediately went to the bathroom, taking the Taser with her, and got out of the wet dress. Returning to the couch, Kira felt much better.

"So, you were going to tell me who Christine resembled," Kira prodded and Rocco seemed to stare right through her, as if he were connecting thoughts as they popped into his mind. Suddenly he set his glass on the table and groaned, tugging his hair with both hands. "Omigod." He uttered. "Omigod, that's it. That's it."

"What's it?" Kira asked.

"I didn't put it together before because I didn't know that The Candy Shop was owned by Coronado nor that Landon Parker had any involvement. He stood up and began pacing in front of the couch. "That's the connection."

"I'm lost," Kira said.

He turned to face her. "Adrienne. Adrianne Parker was the love of my life and Landon wants revenge."

"You were the one that broke up their marriage?" Kira gasped.

"No. Landon broke up their marriage by beating the shit out of her," Rocco chided.

"I loved her. I took care of her. I was there for her." He grabbed his wine glass from the table and slammed it down in one gulp, immediately pouring himself another.

"Landon Parker killed her," Rocco spewed. "I know it. I know it." He clenched his right hand into a fist. "I just could never prove it."

Kira was floored. She had only met Adrianne a couple of times at Parker, Sullivan & Bates social functions, but she remembered hearing rumors about Adrianne filing for divorce and being involved with another man. She also recalled overhearing a late night conversation Frank had on the phone with Landon, where Frank kept saying, "I'll take care of it. I'll take care of it." He left right after the call and when she asked him about it the next morning, Frank told her that Landon had gotten drunk and driven his car into an embankment in East St. Louis. He didn't want to deal with the insurance company so he had Frank corroborate his story that his car had been stolen earlier in the day. Ironically, Adrianne was found dead shortly thereafter. They were told it had been a hit and run and the killer had dumped her body down by the river. Chills shot up the back of Kira's neck. Was it possible that Landon ran down Adrianne and then had Frank cover it up? *Frank would never do that! Would he?* She didn't feel sure of anything at the moment.

Rocco slid back onto the couch. "I've screwed everything up," he exhaled. "It's because of me that Adrianne's dead, and

Christine, and Misty, and Ilesia and Miranda, and..." his voice trailed off.

"I'm still here and that's because of you, too," Kira uttered quietly. "You rescued me tonight."

"I think you and that Taser did a pretty good job of holding your own," he quipped. "The fact is you're in danger because of me. They'll be looking for you. Landon Parker alone has infinite resources, but put him together with Lucas Coronado and we don't stand a chance."

Kira took another sip and then set her glass atop the coffee table. "I have a chance now, which is more than I felt I had the past two days while locked in a room at the Adams Mark." Their eyes met and she smiled. "I trust you," she mouthed and the strange thing was, she really did. She didn't know if it was because he had already seen her naked and vulnerable and hadn't taken advantage of her or if it was the fact that his story rang true; whatever the reason, she trusted him.

Rocco smiled and for a brief moment the sparkle returned to his green eyes. Exhaustion beckoned both of them to sleep and Kira crawled into the king sized bed and laid down. She was ready to close her eyes when she saw him take a pillow and blanket and head for the door. Shooting up into a sitting position, she blurted, "Please don't."

Spinning on his heels, Rocco gazed at her, confusion over her outburst evident on his face.

"I don't want to be alone," Kira admitted, while nervously twisting the edge of the sheet around her fingers.

Rocco nodded and stretched out the blanket on the floor next to the bed, which made her laugh. "Do I have to spell it out for you?"

"That might save time," Rocco teased.

"I want you to... I'm not hitting on you or anything like that...but...," she stammered. "Would you sleep up here? I mean, will you just sleep next to me?"

Rocco gnawed on his bottom lip. She could tell he felt conflicted, but after everything they had been through, why should this be awkward? In the shower at The Candy Shop they had touched in ways that were far more inappropriate, and yet, as he crawled into bed next to her and she snuggled her head against his chest, she had to admit that this felt more intimate. Maybe it was because this time it wasn't her body that was exposed, it was her heart.

CHAPTER 24

Rocco woke Kira at 5:00am and moved her to a small motel just a couple of miles from the precinct. He needed to get to the office and do some research, but he wanted to keep her close; and though no one knew he owned the cabin, it wouldn't have been difficult for someone to find out that it was left to him by his great uncle. If they were up against Landon and Lucas, their resources knew no bounds, and Rocco knew he needed to assume that they had access to every bit of public and private information available. He needed to stay one step ahead of them or he feared the next time he saw Kira it would be shining his light into a dumpster.

On his way into the precinct he stopped and purchased several disposable cell phones. He needed to function now as if they were always listening. He also had to assume that they would be watching the precinct to see if he showed up. That meant he couldn't go directly back to the motel after working or he'd lead them right to Kira.

"Where have you been?" Peters blurted the moment he saw Rocco. "I've been calling your cell nonstop for the past three hours!" Peters was visibly upset.

"I lost my phone," Rocco quipped. "What's up?"

"Body number five is what's up!" Peters belted and it stopped Rocco dead in his tracks.   "Who?" Rocco barked. "Where?"

"We don't know who yet. Forensics is still trying to get a print, but just like all of the others, the acid has burned her fingerprints clean off." Rocco made a beeline for his office with Peters in tow. "She's Caucasian, brunette with blue eyes, that's about all we know."

That fit Kira's description. But it couldn't be her. She was alive and well when he left the motel and that was a little over an hour ago.

"What flower was on her? Rocco asked.

"A geranium, why?" Rocco breathed a sigh of relief. Even though common sense told him Kira was safely hidden, had the flower been a daisy, he might have lost it altogether. Rocco sank into his office chair. "Don't you want to go check out the scene?" Peters asked.

"You handle it and let me know what you find. I've got some leads I need to follow up on," Rocco explained and then dismissed Peters, who walked wearily from the office, obviously puzzled by Rocco's odd behavior.

Jumping up and closing his office door, Rocco returned to his desk and began running searches on the computer. First, he requested phone records for Kira Sullivan's home and cell numbers, as well as the records for all numbers associated with Landon Parker, Frank Sullivan and Lucas Coronado. He wasn't sure about Frank's involvement, but from what Kira had told him, he had to assume that Landon and Lucas were working together. Both men had a reason to hate Rocco; one for putting his son behind bars and the other for sleeping with his wife. The piece of the puzzle that didn't make sense was why Kira Sullivan was dragged into it. There had to be a connection through Frank, but Rocco couldn't fathom what it was. Money? Blackmail? Revenge?   Whatever the reason, Rocco had to find it before they found Kira.

Pulling out the notes he had made from his late night conversation with Kira, he noted that she said Lucas told her that no one finds out about The Candy Shop except for those he allows to know. That implied that Lucas was the puppet master in this great charade. He was pulling all of the strings or so it would seem. Rocco had also jotted down the fact that Kira found out about The Candy Shop from Audrey, which prompted the question how did Audrey find out about The Candy Shop? Was she instructed to take Kira there? If so, by whom? Rocco leaned back in his chair, staring at his notations on the page. Audrey was the obvious starting point.

CHAPTER 25

As the phone records started coming in, Rocco quickly realized he needed more manpower and that meant a visit to the Captain's office to request additional help. Rocco and Captain Jameson had had run-ins before. There was no doubt in anyone's mind that they tolerated one another at best, so Rocco wasn't surprised when his request was curtly denied.

"You've got Peters and Barkley. That's enough," Captain Jameson barked.

"Barkley is in the hospital," Rocco clarified and I need someone to replace him.

"Don't try to pull the wool over my eyes, Sterling. I wasn't promoted to running this shin-dig yesterday," Jameson growled. "Everyone knows you and Barkley don't get along. You screwed his sister and you both need to get over it."

"It isn't about that," Rocco argued.

"Yeah? Then what's it about?"

Rocco squinted at Jameson. "I need someone with a little more enthusiasm for the job, at least until Barkley is released to come back to work."

Jameson's jaw tightened. "You know we've had cutbacks. I'm running a thin operation as it is. I don't have anyone to give you, so do what you have to do to make it work."

Rocco stormed back to his office. As soon as he solved this case he was seriously considering putting in for a transfer. He didn't like the fact that everyone knew about his relationship with Adrianne. He didn't like dealing with the tension between he and Barkley and he didn't like the fact that Jameson would never lift a finger to help him. He needed to move somewhere where nobody knew him and the past could no longer control his life. He needed a fresh start. A do over.

He had promised Kira he would contact Frank first thing and let him know she was okay. Putting in a call to Parker, Sullivan & Bates, Rocco asked to speak with Frank Sullivan. "I'm sorry but Mr. Sullivan isn't in the office right now. Can I put you through to his voicemail?" Asked the snide sounding receptionist.

"No. When do you expect him to return?" Rocco asked.

"I'm not sure sir, but I can connect you to his voicemail where you can leave him a message," the woman said as if she was annoyed by his question. "He checks his messages even when he's out of the office."

Rocco hung up.

Perusing the record of incoming and outgoing numbers listed on Kira Sullivan's cell phone bill, he jotted down reoccurring numbers and plugged them into the department recognition program. He was able to identify Audrey's cell phone number, Frank's cell phone number, and both of their children, Michael and Mallory. He then requested phone records for Audrey's cell. An hour later, he sat analyzing the data from her phone and was intrigued by his findings. There were seventeen calls between Audrey and Frank within the last three weeks. He knew Kira and Audrey were friends, but he didn't realize Audrey and Frank were so close. What could they possibly have been discussing with that frequency?

Rocco dialed Frank's cell and listened to the voicemail message. "You have reached Frank Sullivan of Parker, Sullivan & Bates. I'm sorry to have missed your call. Please leave me your name, number and reason for your call and I will get back to you at my earliest convenience." Beep.

Rocco opened his mouth to speak and then decided against it and hung up. Leaving a message prematurely could bring a barrage of unwanted attention to him and to the department, and he didn't need Jameson breathing down his neck for pissing off high-powered people at Parker, Sullivan & Bates. He needed more information before he contacted Frank directly. He needed to have some kind of leverage, and he had a hunch that Audrey was exactly what he needed.

Peters knocked on Rocco's door and then popped his head in the office. "I gotta talk to you," he said in a hushed tone, scurrying into Rocco's office and shutting the door behind him. "I gotta hunch somethin' ain't right."

"Yeah, ditto," Rocco mumbled, jotting down Audrey's address and heading for the door. "We'll talk on the ride," he said and Peters sped up to keep stride.

"Where are we headed?" Peters asked and Rocco hushed him until they stepped outside and he surveyed the parking lot. Was he paranoid or were his senses so keen that he could feel someone watching them? This was the fine line between crazy and good-at-your-job, and Rocco straddled it.

Rocco immediately turned around and walked back inside the precinct and all the way back to the supply room. He plucked two Kevlar vests from the wall and tossed one to Peters. He then checked the clip on his 9mm Beretta with an eye roll. Rocco's opinion of the 9mm Beretta was well known on the force. In a heated argument with Captain Jameson last year, Rocco had yelled throughout the precinct that Jameson was as weak and pathetic as the puny 9mm he made his officers carry. Rocco was an obvious advocate of arming officers with heavier firepower, like a 40 or 45 caliber firearm, but Captain Jameson would hear none of it.

Peters followed Rocco back to his office, where he slid open his bottom drawer, unlocked and lifted a hidden bottom and retrieved two 45 caliber pistols, a Glock and a Colt. He handed Peters the Colt and noticed his eyes bulging from their sockets.

"Where the hell are we goin', man?" Peters gasped. "If the Captain catches us with these, it's the end. No promotion. No career. It's over, man. Over."

"Then don't let him catch you," Rocco quipped, tucking the Glock into the back of his pants and covering it with his shirt. Peters nervously followed suit, un-tucking his uniform shirt to cover the gun sticking out of the back of his pants.

Peters followed Rocco down the stairs to the underground parking garage that housed all of the squad cars. "We're not taking your Hummer?" Peter's asked.

"Can't," Rocco uttered, taking a set of keys from the lock box and heading toward a random squad car.

"I thought you hated cop cars," Peters said. "At least, that's what I've heard."

Rocco exhaled. "You can't believe everything you hear."

They climbed in and Rocco sped out of the garage, across the lot and into traffic, keeping his eyes on the rearview mirror to see if they had a tail.

Peters gripped the dash. "Whoa, man! What the hell are you doin'?"

Rocco didn't answer. He swerved through traffic, took a few last minute turns and then spun the car to a stop in a Schnucks parking lot. In one fluid motion, Rocco pulled a 38 Smith & Wesson from beneath his pant leg and took aim at Peter's head. "What are you doing?" Peters gasped, throwing both hands into the air.

"Can I trust you?" Rocco blurted and Peters nodded his head rapidly up and down. "Because if I find out you're one of them I'm going to plant a bullet right between your eyes."

"What's the matter with you, man?" Peter's voice shook. "I ain't never done nothin' to betray your trust."

"If I find out you can't be trusted, I'll kill you. Got it?" Rocco gritted.

"Yeah, man, I got it. I got it." Peters slowly put his arms down as Rocco lowered the gun. "Man, you about made me shit myself! You gonna let me in on what's going on?"

Rocco started at the beginning and detailed everything he knew. He told him about Adrianne and his belief that Landon murdered her. He told him about the trial and conviction of Lucas Coronado's son, the Iceman, and his suspicion that Landon and Lucas were working together. He explained how both of these men had reason to hate him and obviously a desire to seek revenge.

"Do you think they're going to frame you for the murders?" Peters questioned.

"Maybe." Rocco hit the steering wheel. "My prints have got to be on every one of those women. I only had sex with Christine, but I talked with and was close to the others. I hugged them goodnight, kissed the top of their hand..." Rocco's voice tapered off. "I'm being set up."

"Okay, man, calm down. We'll get to the bottom of it," Peters encouraged. "So far Forensics hasn't listed your prints on any of the victims."

"I know," Rocco exhaled. "I've been checking every day. I don't get it. There's no way that's possible."

"Well, our killer is clean, super-clean, so maybe he's wiped off your prints while cleaning off his own?" Peters posed, but they both knew that wasn't believable. It would be almost impossible to remove every print, every skin cell and every hair follicle unless you showered the body and went over it with microscopic detail.

"So, how does Kira Sullivan fit in the picture?" Peters questioned and Rocco shrugged.

"That's what we need to find out, and I think her friend Audrey has the answer."

"Let's go talk to Audrey," Peters quipped. "You got the address?"

"Yeah, but I've got a feeling she won't be there." Rocco started the car and pulled back into traffic, heading toward Audrey's home. "According to Kira, Audrey sent her a strange text message several days ago and hasn't responded since. The morning she found the finger and note in her trashcan, she was headed to Audrey's house, and Kira said that one of the dancers at The Candy Shop told her that Audrey hadn't shown up for work."

"You think Landon and Lucas killed her?" Peters asked and Rocco gnawed on his bottom lip.

"I hope not. She might be the only one who can explain Kira's involvement." Rocco sped up. The sooner they talked to Audrey, the safer Kira would be.

"Did you run a trace on her cell phone?" Peters asked.

"Yep. The last place shown is on the Riverfront, but the signal's no longer live. My guess is it's probably at the bottom of the Mississippi river."

Peter's eyes widened. "Do you think it's on her body? Should we get some divers to check it out?"

"Not yet," Rocco uttered. "I got a hunch that would end up being a waste of money and I don't need Jameson breathing down my neck."

Rocco pulled into Audrey's driveway and they knocked on the front door. He wasn't surprised when no one answered. Circling to the back, Rocco pulled out his special lock-picking tool, rammed it into the lock and twisted until the lock popped open. "That's breaking and entering," Peters whispered.

"I didn't break anything," Rocco chided. "I entered but I didn't break." Pushing the door open, Rocco stepped inside Audrey's kitchen with Peters right behind him. "Close the door," he ordered Peters. "And lock it."

"That's ironic," Peters huffed, following his instructions.

A quick scan of Audrey's home rendered the conclusion that Audrey wasn't kidnapped against her will, at least not from her home. There was no evidence of a struggle and nothing to lead them to believe that anyone had broken into the house. "If she was taken, it was probably from The

Candy Shop and not from here," Rocco mumbled.

"You think she got wind of something bad going down and just disappeared on her own? Like she's hiding out somewhere?" Peters questioned.

"I don't think so. If that were the case she'd have tried to contact Kira and warn her..." his voice trailed off as he approached a built in desk off the kitchen, upon which sat a laptop. "Also, she probably would have taken her laptop with her." Rocco ran his fingers across the keyboard. "I wish we could tap into her email," he uttered to himself.

"Why can't we?" Peters said, scooting past Rocco and sliding into the desk chair.

"It's illegal for one, but mainly because I don't know how," Rocco quipped, which made Peters guffaw loudly.

"It ain't no more illegal than breaking and entering," he snipped. "And I just so happen to have super-human hacking skills."

"Really? Well, by all means, impress me," Rocco grinned.

A few clicks across the keyboard and Peters had opened Audrey's email account. "Where do you want to start?" He looked up at Rocco with a smile that spread from ear to ear.

"Look for any emails to or from Frank Sullivan."

Moments later, Peters pulled a flash drive from his shirt pocket and downloaded all of the email correspondence between Frank and Audrey. "Do you always walk around with one of those little drive thingies?" Rocco teased.

"I never leave home without it," Peters answered with an air of pride. "I may look like a badass but beneath all this lies a computer genius."

Rocco smirked. "You don't look like a badass."

Peters continued to copy files from Audrey's laptop, while Rocco searched the rest of the house. "There's a bunch of emails from a guy named Leon," Peters mentioned when Rocco came back into the kitchen. "Do you want me to copy those too?"

"I've got a better idea," Rocco said. "Let's take the laptop."

"That's stealing," Peters scolded with his eyebrows raised.

"It's borrowing," Rocco clarified. "As soon as we find Audrey, we'll give it back to her." Rocco grinned. "Besides, we'll need to clean your grimy prints off of it."

Peters shook his head. "Working with you ain't gonna be boring." He unplugged the laptop, wrapped the cord around it and they left the house the same way they had entered, being careful to close and lock the door behind them.

CHAPTER 26

Rocco's paranoia was rubbing off on Peters. He drove home after work peering out his rearview mirror making sure he wasn't being followed. Upon arriving home, he walked through his apartment with his gun drawn, checking under the bed, behind the shower curtain and in every closet. "I'm losing my cool," he commented to Freddie, his big black Persian cat that was cleaning himself on the sofa. "Totally losing my cool."

Popping a frozen burrito in the microwave, Peters opened a bottle of Bud Light and sat down in front of his computer. He plugged in the flash drive and pulled up the emails he had downloaded from Audrey's computer. It didn't take long for the harsh facts to expose themselves. Frank was the one who told Audrey about The Candy Shop and encouraged her, even pressured her to take Kira on an interview. But that wasn't all. It was obvious by the context of their email correspondence that Audrey and Frank were sexually involved.

"The plot thickens," Peters muttered to himself as he got up and retrieved the burrito from the microwave. "You want some?" He asked Freddie, who sat up, sniffed into the air and then rushed over.

The sound of the explosion made Peters drop the burrito plate. It flipped out of Peters' hand, slammed to the floor and shattered into pieces. Peters grabbed his 9mm from the table and raced to the window. He looked down just as the second explosion erupted, turning his car into an inferno of flames.

CHAPTER 27

Rocco ordered a private car service to pick up Kira at the motel and drive her to the police station. He specifically requested a black Cadillac with tinted windows. He then ordered two more black Cadillacs and instructed the drivers to pull into the underground parking garage and wait amid the squad cars. As soon as the car with Kira arrived, he put her into the trunk of one of the squad cars and ordered the three black Cadillacs to exit the garage simultaneously and head in opposite directions. They were each instructed to drive to a different hotel and remain there for twenty minutes.

A few minutes after the cars left, Rocco slipped behind the wheel of the squad car with Kira in the trunk and pulled out. He hoped his diversion plan worked and that whoever Landon and Lucas had tailing him had mistakenly followed the Cadillacs. If anything, it would buy them some time to get away and find a safe location for the night.

Rocco took highway 40 toward downtown, stopping at the Residence Inn by Marriott on Jefferson Avenue. He had already arranged for a room under an alias, and parking outside of the building, he opened the suite door and then whisked Kira out of the trunk and through the door without uttering a word. "I'm going to unload the car," he said. "Keep the door locked until I get back."

Closing the door behind him, Kira stepped back and surveyed the suite. There was a main level with a kitchen to the left and a living room area to the right. A set of steps led upward to a loft which contained a king sized bed and master bath. When Rocco knocked on the door, Kira peered through the peephole, ensuring it was him, and then opened the door. He rolled in a luggage carrier filled with suitcases, electronic devices and bags of groceries. Kira immediately began unloading the groceries and placing items in the cabinets and refrigerator.

"I want to pay you for this," she said. "I don't expect you to endure the financial burden of taking care of me."

Rocco chuckled. "You are going to pay me," he rebutted. "Who do you think is going to cook all this food?"

Kira smiled. She may not prove very helpful in solving the case, but she could cook and keep him fed while he worked. "That I can do," she said.

Rocco turned the coffee table into a computer work center, setting up a laptop from his office, Audrey's laptop, a laser printer, and several cell phones and recording devices. He set a duffle bag in the corner by the fireplace and then carried two suitcases upstairs and placed them atop the bed. "I bought you some clothing and shoes," he hollered from the loft. "I guessed on the size, so I hope they fit."

Kira was still barefoot and adorned in his black t-shirt, so anything was an improvement. "What size shoes did you get?" She hollered back, curious to see if he was even in the ballpark.

"Eight and a half," he answered, peering over the ledge as if to see her reaction.

Kira grinned. "Impressive. Very impressive. Let's hope your investigative skills are as good as your ability to size up women," she teased.

"Ouch," he muttered. "That was uncalled for."

Kira whipped up some spaghetti and meatballs and a salad, opened a bottle of red wine and set the table. After they ate, he helped her clear the dishes and then they carried their wine glasses to the couch and sat down.

Rocco had a distant look in his eyes and Kira had the feeling that he wasn't telling her something. "Did you talk to Frank?" She finally mustered the nerve to ask.

"No, he wasn't in the office and I didn't feel this was something I should discuss on a voicemail," Rocco answered without making eye contact. "Before we talk about Frank..." he began and then stopped to drag the duffle bag over by his feet. Rocco unzipped it and pulled out several handguns. "Have you ever shot a gun before?" He asked and Kira shook her head to indicate she hadn't.

"Then this will be weapons training 101." He picked up a .45 and handed it to her. It was heavier than Kira imagined it would be. "That's a .45 and it's loaded so don't point it at me or at yourself." Kira swallowed hard as she felt her hands begin to tremble. He took the gun from her hand and replaced it with a 357 magnum. It felt equally as heavy but the shape of the handle fit better in her hand. Since she had held Frank's 357 several times, she was more comfortable with this style of gun. The third gun he gave her was a 9mm Beretta and that was Kira's favorite. "I like this one best. It's lighter," Kira remarked and Rocco rolled his eyes.

"I told the Captain the 9mm is a chick gun," he mumbled.

"What?" Kira asked, not knowing what his comment meant.

"Nothing. Long story," Rocco quipped. "Do you still have your Taser?"

Kira nodded and retrieved it from the kitchen counter.

Over the course of the next hour, Rocco taught Kira how to load cartridges into the 9mm clip, snap it into place and put on and take off the safety. He also instructed her to keep both the gun and the Taser within her reach at all times. "If you go to the bathroom, you take them with you," he emphasized. "Tomorrow I'll take you somewhere and teach you to shoot."

He refilled their wine glasses and then returned to the couch. "I need to ask you some questions and they're not going to be..." he paused as if thinking of the right word. "Comfortable."

Kira took a sip of wine and shifted her body on the couch. Nothing about this entire situation had been comfortable, so how much worse could it get. "I'll answer what I can," she agreed.

She could see the awkwardness in Rocco's face as he scooted closer to her and lifted Audrey's laptop from the table to his knees. He explained that he and Peters went to Audrey's house that afternoon, how Peters managed to hack into her email, and their findings led Rocco to ultimately decide to borrow Audrey's computer. "I wanted you to be able to see this first hand, for yourself," Rocco explained.

"What did you find?" Kira's curiosity peaked.

Rocco slowly licked his lips, hesitancy written across his face. Reaching into the duffle bag he pulled out a copy of Audrey's cell phone record and handed it to Kira. The calls between Audrey and Frank were highlighted. Then he opened Audrey's email and showed Kira the correspondence between Frank and Audrey. Kira shook her head. "I don't understand," she said.

"I think Frank and Audrey may have been having an affair," Rocco said hesitantly.

Kira laughed. "Frank can't stand Audrey. He refers to her as, 'the bitch.' He'd never sleep with her."

"I'm sure he made it appear that way," Rocco consoled, "but seventeen phones calls is a substantial amount of talking with someone he supposedly hates."

"Seventeen phone calls..." her voice faded.

"In the past three weeks," Rocco added. "There aren't any calls between them before that time, well at least not within the prior six months."

She couldn't believe what she was seeing. She couldn't believe Frank would cheat on her, much less with her best friend; and she was equally amazed, if not moreso, that Audrey would betray her. "There has to be a reasonable explanation," Kira remarked.

Rocco put his hand on her knee and gave it a tender squeeze. "I know this is hard for you, but I need to get your insight on some of these emails." He leaned closer and continued. "You said that Audrey was the one who told you about The Candy Shop and you also said that Lucas told you that no one finds out about The Candy Shop except for those he chooses, right?"

Kira nodded.

"This leads me to believe that the person who told Audrey about The Candy Shop has got to be working with Landon and Lucas and probably instructed Audrey to bring you along."

"That would make sense," Kira shrugged. "But why?"

"That's what I'm trying to find out and I'm hoping you can help me." He opened an email thread between Frank and Audrey, dated two weeks prior and handed the laptop to Kira.

Kira read the thread, beginning with Audrey's letter to Frank. It read:

FRANK, I DON'T THINK I CAN DO THIS. WHY DO I HAVE TO BE THE ONE TO TELL HER ABOUT TCS?

"TCS is short for The Candy Shop," Rocco interjected.

"Thanks, Sherlock," Kira teased.

To which Frank had responded:
AUDREY, YOU HAVE TO DO IT OR SHE'LL FIND OUT ABOUT US.

Kira's stomach felt as if it hollowed out completely and she didn't know whether she would burst into sobs or throw up. "You don't have to continue reading," Rocco said quietly.

"Yes I do," Kira whispered and scrolled down to the next email. It was dated last week.

AUDREY, I'LL ARRANGE INTERVIEWS AT TCS BUT YOU'LL HAVE TO TAKE HER. SHE WON'T GO ALONE.

To which Audrey had responded:
WHY IS THIS SO IMPORTANT? IMPORTANT ENOUGH THAT YOU'RE THREATENING TO TELL HER ABOUT WHAT HAPPENED BETWEEN US IF I DON'T DO WHAT YOU ASK? I DON'T GET IT.

To which Frank responded:
I'D BE HAPPY TO GIVE IT TO YOU (NUDGE, NUDGE, WINK, WINK).

To which Audrey wrote:
YOU'RE SO BAD! OKAY, I'LL TAKE HER BUT YOU OWE ME BIG TIME.

To which Frank wrote:
FOR YOU I'M BIG ALL THE TIME. YOU NAME THE TIME AND PLACE.

Kira stopped reading. She couldn't take any more of their playful and flirty banter. It felt surreal. How had she not seen it? How had she been so blind? She had convinced herself that he was just a workaholic, that that was the reason he was always gone and emotionally distant. Was he with Audrey every night that she thought he was working late?

"I'm sorry," Rocco uttered.

"Who does this?" She spat. "Who sleeps with their wife's best friend and then convinces his lover to take his wife to a whore house?"

Rocco shrugged. "It does seem a bit strange," he admitted. "Which is why I think there's more to it than just that." Kira gulped down her wine and extended her glass toward Rocco, in a gesture asking for more. "Why don't I open another bottle?" Rocco raised an eyebrow and headed for the kitchen. "Or two," he mused.

Several glasses of wine later, Kira finished reading all of the emails from that thread and sat staring blankly at the coffee table. She was trying to force herself to look at the situation logically instead of emotionally, which was damn near impossible. One of the temporary cell phones rang, startling Kira from her thoughts. "That's Peters," Rocco said. "He's the only one with this number."

"They blew up my car!" Peters yelled as soon as Rocco answered. "They blew up my mother-f-ing car!" He panted.

"Calm down," Rocco ordered. "Where are you?"

"I'm with Freddie, man. I was scared to stay at my place. Whoever we're dealing with knows where I live!"

"Who's Freddie? Can he be trusted?" Rocco asked.

"Yeah, man, but I need a place to go."

"All right." Rocco gnawed on his bottom lip and paced back and forth. "Call a cab and have him drop you at the Conoco station on Jefferson and Market Street. Call when you're there and I'll pick you up." He hung up the phone and filled Kira in on the details.

"Is he going to be staying here?" Kira asked.

Rocco's lips started to form the word yes and Kira deflated. She wanted to be alone with Rocco, now more than ever. She tried to hide her disappointment, but she knew Rocco had already seen it in her eyes. Sitting back down on the couch next to her, Rocco took both of her hands in his. "If you're uncomfortable with Peters staying her, I'll get him a different room," he said. "Just say the word."

Kira didn't know what to say. How could she ask him to spend more money on a separate room when they had a pull out couch and plenty of room here? It would be silly. Besides, they were probably safer together. "Whatever you think is best," she uttered, looking down and fiddling with her fingers on her lap.

Rocco gently took her chin and guided it upward so that he could look into her eyes. "For reasons outside of our control, you and I were brought together. By all rights you're supposed to be dead and I'm certain that I'm supposed to be framed for your death. I don't know why." He drew in a deep breath. "What I do know is that we were both set up by the same people; me, out of revenge and you..." he paused and narrowed his brows. "I don't really understand why Frank sent you to The Candy Shop. I don't know what he gains from it."

"Maybe he gains Audrey," Kira said quietly, tears forming once again in her eyes. "Maybe I was supposed to be murdered and then he was going to live happily ever after with my best friend."

"Maybe. But he loses you and I can't think of a greater loss." Rocco wiped a tear from her cheek. "I don't understand all of the motives yet, but I can promise you one thing. I will not let anything happen to you."

Without thinking, Kira leaned forward and planted a tender kiss on Rocco's lips. There was something alluring in his honesty. She let her lips linger against his, unsure if she was more afraid to pull them away or lean in. He ran his fingers up the side of her neck and tenderly drew her closer, deepening their kiss.

The phone interrupted their moment of intimacy and Rocco apologized as he took the call. "I have to go get Peters," he explained, heading for the door. "Keep your gun and

Taser close and lock the door the moment I leave."

Kira followed him to the door. "You're coming back, right?" She didn't want to sound desperate but the prospect of being alone in all of this was terrifying.

Rocco smiled. "I promise."

CHAPTER 28

While Rocco was gone, Kira continued to sift through the emails on Audrey's computer. She read one dated the day before she met Audrey for coffee. It read:
AUDREY, YOUR INTERVIEW AT TCS IS TOMORROW EVENING. I CAN'T WAIT TO SEE THE SEXY OUTFITS YOU'LL BE WEARING!

Kira wanted to gag. Tears streamed down her face and she didn't bother to try and stop them or wipe them. She felt the heartbreak and let the emotion flow out of her.

Getting up to retrieve tissues, Kira refilled her wine glass and went back to perusing Audrey's email. She stumbled on one dated a week ago yesterday, on the first night Kira and Audrey worked at The Candy Shop. Judging by the timestamp on the email, Audrey had sent it after she returned home from work. It read:
FRANK, I DROPPED KIRA OFF AT HOME BUT SHE'S NOT HAPPY WITH HOW THINGS WENT TONIGHT AND NEITHER AM I. SHE DIDN'T SAY A WORD ON THE DRIVE HOME AND I HAVE A HUNCH SHE WON'T RETURN TO TCS AGAIN. THEY DRUGGED HER WITH SOMETHING WHICH WASN'T COOL. I'M WORRIED.

Kira scrolled down and read Frank's response:

AUDREY, DON'T WORRY, THERE ARE
OTHER FACTORS AT PLAY. EVERYTHING
WILL BE OK.

Kira buried her face into a couch pillow
and screamed as loud, long and forcefully as
she could. Her body shook from anger and
she swore if Frank were standing in front of
her right now she'd have no problem Tasering
his balls, or worse. *I might even shoot him,*
she thought and then quickly pushed the
thought from her mind. She couldn't kill the
father of her children no matter how much
she hated him in this moment; no matter how
much he deserved it.

Skimming through the last of the
emails, Kira began to sense that there was a
problem. Frank's tone sounded less playful
and more upset. In an email dated last
Sunday, Frank wrote:
AUDREY, KIRA HAS CALLED IN SICK THE
PAST THREE DAYS. YOU HAVE TO GET HER
TO WORK TODAY OR I CAN'T CONTROL
WHAT HAPPENS. WE'LL ALL BE IN DANGER
IF SHE REFUSES TO SHOW UP.

Audrey never answered this email and
Kira sat back and began to form a timeline of
events in her mind. Sunday was the day she
had text Audrey and Audrey text back telling
her that Lucas was upset and that she needed
to come to work. That was when Kira had told
her "no" and Audrey text back, stating: "We're
Done."   If memory served her correctly that
text came around 10:30pm. At 3:00am on
Monday Kira received the automated voice
phone call at her home, saying: "First a

terrible awful wreck, then the tires, then the neck." And then the caller warned her that if she called anyone else Frank would never come home. At 7:00am Monday morning, while leaving to drive to Audrey's house, Kira found the note and finger in her trashcan, which is how she ended up at the Police station, where Landon found her and took her into captivity at the Adams Mark.

Kira felt a surge of adrenaline. Something had gone wrong with their plan, she could feel it. She didn't know what it meant, but Audrey was in trouble and probably Frank, too. Leaping from the couch, Kira searched the room until she finally found a pen and some paper in the kitchen. Returning to the coffee table, she jotted down the timeline, noting anything and everything she could remember. According to Shelby, Audrey hadn't returned to work since Sunday night. Kira didn't believe Frank's tense sounding email and Audrey's same-day disappearance were a mere coincidence.

Using one of the temporary cell phones, Kira dialed Michael's cell. She was overjoyed to hear his voice and to learn that he and Mallory were safe and, as she had requested, were staying together. "Mom, are you okay?" Michael asked. "Dad said you were really shaken up by the case he's been working on and that you guys had received threats so he moved you to an unknown location for a while. He said you wouldn't be able to answer your phone or text or anything until things quieted down. Are things better now?"

Kira was speechless, stunned that Frank had contacted their kids and lied to them in order to make her disappearance believable. This proved that Frank knew Landon had taken her prisoner. This proved that Frank knew Landon had confiscated her cell phone and was holding her against her will. A lump lodged itself in Kira's throat. *How could he have done this to me? Why?*

"Mom? Are you still there?" Michael beckoned. "Are you okay?"

Swallowing hard and struggling to fight back emotion, Kira took a breath. "I'm here, sweetheart, and I'm fine." Her voice shook and she cleared her throat to mask it. "Your father's right, I'm a little shaken up by this case but everything's going to be okay. I need you to take care of your sister, all right?"

"You know I will," Michael said. "Do you want us to come home and stay with you while dad's gone?"

"No!" Kira blurted and then tried to soften her tone. "No, I'm fine. I want you two to stay where you are and stay together. If you need me, you can reach me at this number, but don't give this number to anyone else. You understand? It isn't safe."

"Mom, what's going on?"

Michael was sharp, always had been, and Kira knew he wasn't buying the story, but she didn't know enough about the truth to tell him. "I promise I'll tell you everything, but I can't right now. I love you and Mallory so much," Kira's voice cracked with emotion. "We'll talk soon."

"Love you, mom," Michael said and then disconnected the call.

It felt as if her whole world was caving in around her and Kira curled into a ball on the couch and wept.

CHAPTER 29

Audrey lifted herself from the concrete floor and leaned against the wall. Her side ached from lying on the hard, cold floor for so long, and she was thirsty. She didn't know how long it had been since her captor had dribbled tiny droplets of water on her tongue, but she needed more. "Hello?" She called out. "Is anybody up there?"

A moment later she heard the door creak open and footsteps descending the staircase. "What do you want?" Her captor's voice barked.

"Water," Audrey uttered. "Please may I have water?"

"If I give you too much water, then you'll have to urinate, and that would be a hassle," he groaned. "Besides, aren't you ready to give up and die?"

If there had been any moisture left in her body, Audrey would have cried, but there were no tears left. "What do you want from me?" She asked. "I'll do whatever you want."

"You don't get it, do you?" He scoffed. "You're the back-up plan. See, somebody's gotta pay. An eye-for-an-eye. If it ain't your friend, then it'll be you."

"You mean Kira? My friend, Kira?" Audrey sat up a little straighter. "Where is she? What have you done to her?"

CHAPTER 30

Kira had cried herself to sleep on the couch and was startled awake by a pounding on the hotel door. Fumbling for her gun, she leapt up and rushed to the door, peering through the peep hole. Upon seeing Rocco, she opened the door. "Where's Peters?" She asked.

"I got him a room next door," Rocco answered, gliding inside and locking the door behind him. "Freddie is a damn cat and I can't stand cats," Rocco said. "No way I was going to be able to sleep with that cat roaming the room. I told Peters if that damn cat got on me in the middle of the night I was going to shoot it, so he opted to get his own room."

Kira grinned. It was amusing to see a big, strong man afraid of a little cat. "What took you so long? I thought he was being dropped off right up the street."

"We had to make sure we weren't followed," Rocco explained, and then sat down on the couch and exhaled a big sigh. He looked exhausted.

Sliding onto the couch next to him, Kira held up her timeline. "Do you feel like going through some things or do you want to go to bed?"

Rocco rubbed his eyes. "I won't be able to sleep anyway, so show me what you've got."

Kira told him about the emails she had read and showed him the timeline she made and also about Frank's phone call to their son, Michael. "That call proves that Frank is working with Landon or at least knew Landon was kidnapping me," she said.

"That's not surprising," Rocco uttered. "I get the feeling Frank is working more than one angle here."

"What do you mean?" Kira studied his face.

"I don't know, but it seems to me that Frank's motive in this isn't to live happily ever after with Audrey. I get the feeling he's trying to save his own ass, but from who? That's the question."

"I don't know," Kira chided. "It sounds like he can't wait to get rid of me and spend his life with her. He can't wait to see the sexy things she'll be wearing."

Rocco leaned forward and took a sip of his wine and then licked his lips. "Frank's correspondence with Audrey came on strong three weeks ago. Something had to have happened to drive that interaction." Rocco explained.

"I think we both know what happened," Kira sarcastically quipped. "He screwed her."

Rocco squeezed her knee. He knew better than anyone how difficult it was to learn that the person you loved hadn't been faithful. He was a mere three days from the alter when he found out his fiancée had slept with one of his close friends. He had been devastated. Over time he learned to view it as a blessing, but regardless of the spin he put on it, it left a scar. "I think this is about something greater than sex," Rocco said.

"Love?" Kira mouthed. "Do you think he loves her?"

"That's not what I meant," Rocco clarified. "You told me that Frank couldn't stand Audrey…"

"He couldn't," Kira interrupted. "Or at least he acted like he couldn't."

"So, what changed? And why did it change all of a sudden?" Rocco gnawed on his bottom lip. "Or did it really change?"

A pounding on the door made Kira jump and Rocco placed his hand on her knee, as if silently telling her to stay put. Drawing his gun, he approached the door and peered through the peephole. "It's Peters," he said and pulled open the door.

"Sorry to bug you man, but I found something interesting," Peters said, walking briskly into the room, carrying a laptop. He set it down at the kitchen table and Kira and Rocco gathered around. "Nice to see you again, Mrs. Sullivan," Peters said with a nod.

"What do you got?" Rocco asked.

"After Miranda's neighbor was murdered, you told me to get the surveillance feed from outside her apartment building," Peters began.

"Right," Rocco acknowledged.

"Well, here's the feed." He clicked a few keys and brought up a video feed of the street in front of the apartment building. "This is the view from the highway department cameras located here," he pointed at the

189

screen, "and here." They all stared at the screen. "Forensics estimates that Natalie Wild's TOD was around 5:00am Wednesday morning."

"TOD?" Kira interrupted.

"Time of death," Rocco and Peters answered simultaneously.

"There aren't many vehicles in this area in the wee hours, but at 4:28am we show one car passing the building, turning left and parking directly behind it." Peters pulled up surveillance feed from another camera angle. "See, you can see the car pull in on this feed and then turn and go behind the building on this feed."

"That's a squad car," Rocco said.

Peters zoomed the feed. "I think that's squad car number twenty-seven."

"It's probably just someone making a routine check. That's not exactly the best neighborhood. I'm sure the city precinct has a lot more check points and random drive bys than we do out in the suburbs."

Peters looked up and stared at Rocco. "What if it's not a routine check?" Peters' eyes lit with excitement. "What if the killer is one of us?"

"One of you?" Kira gasped.

"Not one of us," Peters pointed at himself and Rocco. "But one of us as in a cop."

Rocco shook his head. "I'd say it's highly unlikely and you're grasping at straws."

"Fine," Peters uttered, "but no one else shows up in a car or on foot." Rocco exhaled and walked into the living room. Peters followed. "Okay, explain this to me," Peters taunted. "Miranda's body is found Sunday night. It takes Forensics a couple of days to identify her and on Tuesday our guys get a statement from Natalie Wild, who mentions that Miranda worked at The Candy Shop. Wednesday morning Natalie is killed. Are you telling me that's a random coincidence?" Peters was gawking at Rocco.

"No, I'm just saying I think the idea that one of our guys did it is a stretch."

"Then who else knew what Natalie told the cops?" Peters blurted. "No one knew except those with access to the police report." Peters jumped up and down in front of Rocco. "I'm telling you, man, there's an insider and he's one of ours."

Kira sat on the couch, quietly listening to their banter. "That's how Landon knew to find me at the station," she mumbled softly.

Rocco leaned forward. "I thought you called Landon because Frank was out of town."

Kira shook her head. "He just showed up, claimed to be my attorney, and took me out of there."

Rocco was on his feet now, pacing back and forth. "Okay, let's go with your theory even though it's a stretch," he said to Peters. "Who would be working with Landon and Lucas, and better yet, why?"

"What about Captain Jameson?" Peters posed. "Everyone knows he can't stand you and all he talks about is how funds have been cut. Maybe he's cut a deal with Coronado in return for a substantial donation?"

"Unlikely," Rocco grunted. "He may be an asshole but he isn't a criminal."

"Well, what about Barkley? He has reason to hate you and would probably love to help set you up to look like a killer," Peters said.

"Barkley was the one who took me to the station," Kira added.

"Yeah, but Barkley had a heart attack in my office on Tuesday, remember?" Rocco raised his eyebrows at Peters. "He's in the hospital and couldn't have murdered Natalie Wild early Wednesday morning. Besides, I don't think Barkley has the stamina to run around murdering women and throwing them into dumpsters."

Rocco plunked back down onto the couch. "The fact is, the squad car in the video feed could have been driven by anyone, and anyone could have followed Kira from her house to the station and reported it to Landon."

Kira could see Peters deflate.

"We can't discount the possibility that the killer could live in Natalie Wild's apartment building as well," Rocco added. "Let's get some rest and reconvene in the morning." He unlocked the door and ushered Peters out. "I think we need to go back to the very beginning and start with the relationship between the firm of Parker, Sullivan & Bates and Lucas Coronado."

CHAPTER 31

Rocco offered to sleep on the pull out couch, but Kira once again asked him to sleep next to her. He knew she was afraid and he wanted to make her feel safe, but at the same time, it was not easy to control his desire. While she showered and got ready for bed, he laid atop the comforter with his fingers interlocked behind his head, trying to connect the dots. Hearing the water running in the background, his mind flashed back to being naked in the shower with Kira, and he fought to push those memories aside. Now wasn't the time. She was reeling from the betrayal of her best friend and her husband, not to mention having been kidnapped. It would be wrong to prey on her while she was in such a vulnerable emotional state. Maybe someday, when they got through this, if they got through this, they could pursue something more meaningful.

Rocco was lost in his own thoughts and hadn't noticed that Kira had opened the bathroom door and was standing in the doorway, dressed in the white satin nightgown he had bought for her. "Penny for your thoughts?" She asked, crawling onto the bed next to him.

Rocco grinned. "I don't think I should tell you my thoughts."

Blushing, she sat up and crossed her legs, Indian style. "Then, how about I tell you mine?"

He rolled onto his side and propped up his head with his left hand. "All right." His interest peaked.

What came out of her mouth next was not what he had been expecting. In the dark corners of his mind, he was hoping, as any man would, but never was he consciously expecting. Kira took a deep breath and looked him directly in the eyes. "If I said I wasn't attracted to you the moment I first saw you, I'd be lying." She smiled shyly. "I don't remember everything that happened between us at The Candy Shop, mainly because I was drugged, but I know what I wanted to have happen." She gazed down and fiddled with her fingers. "I guess desiring you makes me just as guilty as Frank. I mean, lust is lust right?" Her smile faded. "I haven't been with anyone except Frank for the past twenty years. I haven't really wanted to be with anyone else. I guess I just thought that that part of me had sort of died, but then when you and I were in the shower..." her voice faded and Rocco could see her face flush. He could tell she was embarrassed to talk about it. "I felt alive again," she said quietly.

Maneuvering into a sitting position, Rocco faced her on the bed. He unknotted her hands and weaved his fingers into hers. "When I met you I told you that I would never ask anything of you that wasn't a mutual desire," he reminded her.

"Why did you request me?" Kira blurted, out of the blue and Rocco was shocked. "Why were you there in the first place?" Kira closed her eyes and scrunched up her face. "I mean, I know you told me about the flyers on your condo door, but why did you go there? Do you go to a lot of whore houses in the city? Is that like a regular thing for you?"

The conversation had taken a sudden turn and he felt unprepared for its direction. Drawing his hands away from hers, he scooted his legs off of the bed and leaned his elbows on his knees.

"I'm sorry," she whispered. "I didn't mean for it to come out like that."

It was no secret that Rocco wasn't entirely acquainted with his own emotions, that is, with the exception of anger; and he wasn't accustomed to sharing his feelings either. He wasn't exactly sure what she wanted to hear and a little afraid that telling the truth would cause more turmoil. "First of all, I never requested you. Miranda was the last woman I requested. You simply showed up when I was expecting her."

"But Lucas said you requested me..."

"He lied!" Rocco blurted, frustrated by the fact that he had to explain and re-explain every detail. "My visit to The Candy Shop was the only time in my life that I slept with a dancer, hooker or whatever you want to call her. Christine was the first woman, the only woman I've had sex with since Adrianne died." He ran his hand through his hair. "Hell, I

haven't even dated since I lost Adrianne."
Rocco sat for a moment in quiet reflection.
"Christine looked so much like my Adrianne
that I just wanted to hold onto her and never
let go. If I could have lasted longer I would
have made-love to her and never stopped." A
sense of guilt washed over him. "I never
meant to get Christine killed or any of the
others."

Scooting next to him, Kira dangled her
legs off the side of the bed. "Do you think they
brought Christine to The Candy Shop and had
her dance for you because she looked like
Adrianne? Do you think they purposefully
lured you there by putting her picture on the
flyer?"

"It crossed my mind." Rocco exhaled.
"But I've been prone to paranoia before. It
comes with the job."

"Do you think they really are setting
you up to frame you for all of the murders?"

Rocco stood up and began to pace
across the room. "It could be, but that leads
me back to the question of why?" Plagued by
the feeling that he was ultimately responsible
for the women that were killed, Rocco closed
his eyes and tried to clear his head. "I've been
checking in with Forensics every day, waiting
for them to realize that my prints are on all of
the victims," he said quietly. "But there is no
indication that they have found my prints yet."
He opened his eyes and stared at Kira. "It is
inconceivable that they wouldn't have found
my prints or any other form of my DNA."

Kira winced. "Did you wear a condom when you slept with Christine?"

"Of course," Rocco said. "But the strange thing is that I used a latex condom with a water-based lubricant, but the forensics report noted that not only were there traces of polyurethane but also the spermicidal agent, Nonoxynol-9." He glanced at Kira and noticed she had a deer-in-the-headlights expression. "Are you following?" He asked.

"I'm sorry but I haven't used a condom since before Michael and Mallory were born, so I'm a little rusty on my latex and lubricant knowledge," she retorted with a sheepish smile.

"It means someone else had sex with Christine after I did and they wore a condom made of polyurethane which contained a spermicidal lubricant," he explained. "I don't use condoms with spermicide," he added flatly.

"Should I ask why?" Kira grimaced.

"Personal preference. They can have some adverse side effects." He made it clear by his tone of voice that this wasn't a topic upon which he wanted to elaborate.

"If someone wanted to frame you for the murders, why would they have had sex with her and mask the fact that you had sex with her?" Kira puzzled.

Rocco shook his head and sank back onto the bed next to Kira. "I don't know, except that serial killers are arrogant by nature. They take pride in their craft and they don't want anyone else to get credit. My DNA on the victims might be something the killer deems unacceptable and so he's cleaning them before he kills them." His last comment was more of a question than a statement. It seemed unfathomable that the murderer could clean the women with such precision, and yet he knew that serial killers were both meticulous and patient.

"Do you think someone in forensics is covering up the fact that your prints are on the victims?" Kira posed.

"That wouldn't make sense unless the killer himself worked in forensics and is making sure all of his tracks are covered..." Rocco's voice faded as if he got distracted by his own thoughts. Leaping to his feet, he began to pace again. "Or, if he had forensics experience," he muttered. "But if that were the case, why would he remove my fingerprints as well? Removing my DNA from the women makes me believe we're dealing with a true serial mentality, a person who wants to take credit for his work; but the problem with that theory is that it doesn't fit with the idea of framing me for the murders."

"Your prints should have been on every woman except Natalie Wild, right?" Kira asked.

"Right, and except for the woman murdered last night." Rocco had forgotten that he hadn't told Kira about the latest killing. He suddenly remembered when she gasped.

"Who was it?" She questioned. "What did she look like?"

Rocco explained that he hadn't gone to the scene and that Peters said she was a medium-build brunette with blue eyes and had a geranium pinned to her blouse.

"Ginger," Kira grimaced. "Ginger was the geranium. I remember her because we were about the same height, same hair color and same eyes. Our dresses hung together on the costume rack. She was super shy, except on stage. Some of the girls said she had dance moves that put all others to shame."

This murder perplexed Rocco almost more than any other because he hadn't known Ginger. He had nothing to do with her so it stood to reason that she was killed for another purpose; and Rocco didn't think the fact that she resembled Kira was a coincidence. It was a warning. A signal. A message delivered mob style. He couldn't say that to Kira, but he believed Ginger's murder was symbolic of who they were planning on killing next.

"Can I ask you one more question?" Kira prodded and Rocco gave a nod. "After Christine was killed, why did you continue to go back to The Candy Shop?"

"I came back hoping to gain information about Christine's murder. I came back because I wanted to solve the case. I wanted to understand why my new Adrianne was ripped away from me just like the real one had been. I wanted to make it right." He shook his head. "That was where I made the greatest mistake of all. That was where I played right into their hands. It was as if they knew my ego would force me to return and each time I selected a girl, it resulted in her death. If not to publically frame me for the murders, than why?" Rocco lowered himself onto the bed with an exhausted sigh.

They sat in silence for a moment and then Kira slid her hand inside his. "I don't know what's going to happen, but I know what I want to have happen right now..." her voice tapered off and Rocco turned toward her. "I want you to make-love to me," she whispered and he didn't need to be asked twice.

CHAPTER 32

Peters knocked on the hotel door at 6:30am and darted inside the moment Rocco swung it open. He was already showered and dressed and carrying his laptop. "You won't believe this!" He blurted. Rocco yawned and walked slowly toward the coffee maker to begin brewing a pot.

"This couldn't have waited until a decent hour?" He complained.

Peters ignored him and dove right into his findings. "I did what you said," Peters began. "I started at the beginning, with the connection between Parker, Sullivan & Bates and Lucas Coronado."

"Okaaaaaay," Rocco mumbled, as in, get to the point.

"Tony Coronado, aka Iceman, was iced in prison, right?"

"Uh-huh." Rocco yawned again.

"Guess who put out the hit on him?" Peters raised his eyebrows into the top of his forehead and grinned. "Lucas Coronado."

Rocco perked up. "Lucas put out a hit on his own kid?" Peters nodded. "How do you know?"

"Because the guy who iced him is still in prison and singing like a frickin' canary, asking for a deal with the Feds. They call him Trick Malone, though his real name is Timothy."

"And you want me to believe a guy named Trick?" Rocco smirked.

"Not yet, man, I haven't told you everything." Peters followed Rocco to the couch and sat down next to him. "Shortly after Iceman was iced, Mrs. Coronado up and died. They say it was a suicide, like she couldn't bear losing her son and did herself in. According to inside FBI sources, her death caused Lucas a lot of stress and he blamed the whole thing on the fact that Parker, Sullivan & Bates lost his son's case. So he put a hit out on Landon's wife and Frank's wife. An eye-for-an-eye kind of thing."

"That's right," Kira peered over the balcony from the bedroom. "That's when the firm hired private security for our family," she added.

"Wow. I knew Tony's death was a mob hit but I wouldn't have figured Lucas would have ordered the hit on his own son," Rocco quipped.

Peters shrugged. "Obviously Lucas would rather have him dead than risk him spilling the beans on what really goes down in the mob? The point is we've got motive."

"Why wasn't a hit put out on Bates' wife too?" Rocco asked.

"Because he doesn't have one," Kira interjected from the loft. "Leon Bates is Audrey's ex-husband and Leon never had anything to do with the Coronado case. He and Audrey were in the middle of a bitter divorce at the time."

Rocco got off the couch and poured himself, Kira and Peters a cup of coffee. "Okay, let's go with this theory for a moment." He took a sip of coffee and then paced across the room. "Parker, Sullivan & Bates lose the Coronado case because of my testimony, causing Lucas' son to go to prison where Lucas has him killed so he won't talk to the Feds. This results in Lucas' wife committing suicide presumably due to grief or maybe she found out that Lucas had ordered the hit..." Rocco paused and shrugged. "So, Lucas goes back to Parker, Sullivan & Bates and threatens them?" Rocco threw up his hands. "For what purpose? What would he gain?"

"Let's go talk to the Feds who are working on the inside. Maybe they can answer that question," Peters suggested.

While Rocco showered and got dressed, Peters brought Freddie over to stay with Kira. "He likes tuna and chicken best," Peters said, handing Kira two cans of cat food.

Before leaving, Rocco set the 9mm gun and the Taser on the kitchen table and reminded Kira to keep them with her at all times, and then he shoved the .45 in his holster and the 357 magnum into the back of his pants. He jotted down the cell number for the phone he was carrying in case she needed to reach him. "I'll be back in a few hours," he told her, planting a quick kiss on her cheek. "Keep the door locked and don't go anywhere."

CHAPTER 33

Audrey heard the door creak open and then she heard several people descending the staircase. "Water?" She begged in a raspy tone, barely able to lift her head to speak.

"Get her up," a man ordered and she immediately felt two men lift her from beneath her arms. Her head fell forward and her muscles went limp. "Get her some water so she can talk. I need her to make a phone call."

"Landon?" She said almost inaudibly. "Is that Landon?" She asked the men carrying her, but her question was met with a swift smack to the face.

"You speak when you're spoken to," the man seethed. "If you were supposed to see who was talking, you wouldn't be blindfolded."

"That was uncalled for," the other man remarked.

"You got to keep these bitches in line. You got a problem with that?"

"No, but I got a problem with hitting someone who's already weak and restrained."

"Then you're in the wrong business, bro," the man clucked. "You can't turn your back, man. You of all people should know that." They dragged Audrey to the edge of the steps.

"What's that supposed to mean?" Audrey could hear indignation in the man's tone.

"It ain't no secret, bro.   You turned around for one second and got zapped." They began dragging her up the staircase. "You're the whole reason we're in this mess. If that other bitch hadn't gotten away, it'd be smooth sailing."

CHAPTER 34

Kira was looking at email on Audrey's laptop when the cell phone on the table buzzed. She jumped up expecting it to be Rocco or Michael, as they were the only ones with that number. Her heart stalled when she answered and heard Frank's voice on the other end. "Baby," he said softly. "Where are you? I've been worried sick."

Anger consumed her. "I could ask you the same question," she snapped. "I should have been asking that question for the past twenty years."

"What are you talking about? I'm in Chicago working on a case," he said. "You know that. Listen, I know I've been gone a lot but I'm going to make it up to you when..."

"Are you with Audrey?" Kira blurted, cutting his sentence short.

"Audrey? Why would I be with Audrey?"

"Because you've been screwing her."

"Kira, you don't know what you're talking about," Frank said, his tone suddenly changing.

"Yes I do," Kira barked. "I know exactly what I'm talking about. I know that you set up the interview at The Candy Shop for me and Audrey. I know all about your flirty little emails! I know that you allowed Landon to kidnap me and even called our son to tell him that he wouldn't be able to contact me for a while."

"Baby, you've got it all wrong," Frank interjected. "Landon picked you up and took you to the Adams Mark so that you would be safe and the people who were threatening us wouldn't find you."

"Then why did he steal my wallet and cell phone and leave me with nothing? Why did he have the windows blacked out and make the hotel phones inoperable?" She snapped.

"He didn't want anyone to be able to trace your phone and find you and we couldn't trust that you wouldn't contact someone and end up getting yourself killed," he explained and then paused. "Kira, you're in danger and I need you to trust me. I've never hurt you. In twenty years of marriage, I've never hurt you so you've got to trust me. The people you're with are killers and they're going to kill you too. They are police officers on the take from the Coronado family, especially Rocco Sterling. He owes the Coronado's because he was the one that put their son behind bars. You've got to get away from them," he urged and Kira's pulse suddenly quickened. Was Frank telling the truth? "I'll explain it all to you in person."

"You're lying," she said curtly. "All I want is the truth."

"I'm telling the truth," Frank rebutted. "I can't explain everything over the phone. It isn't safe. Meet me and I'll answer all of your questions. I promise."

"Where?"

"Where are you? I'll come pick you up." Frank said.

Kira paused, a prickly sensation darting up the back of her neck. "How can you come pick me up if you're in Chicago?" She said and Frank didn't answer. An eerie silence fell between them. The only sound Kira could hear was her own breathing and her heart pounding against her chest. Frank was lying. He wasn't in Chicago. The truth was he probably never even went to Chicago. He was probably with Audrey the whole time. Her stomach hollowed out and then filled back up with anger.

"I got back late last night," Frank stammered. "I'll tell you everything. I promise. You've got to believe me. You're not safe. Just tell me where you are and then we can talk."

Kira blinked slowly, a sense of numbness encasing her heart. "I hope you burn in hell, you lying son-of-a-bitch," she spat and disconnected the call.

Her adrenaline was pumping as she dialed Michael and asked him why he gave Frank her phone number. "I'm sorry, mom," Michael said. "Dad said he was really worried about you and I didn't know what else to do."

"Listen to me," she said poignantly. "Do not believe anything your father tells you right now. He's a liar."

"He's a liar?" Michael repeated, shock lacing his tone. Kira had never uttered a negative word about their father.

"Yes. No. I don't know. I'm not sure what's going on, but I know that he can't be trusted right now."

"That's a weird thing to say, mom," Michael retorted.

"I know sweetie, but do something for me, will you? Promise me that you'll stay away from your father for a while, and anyone associated with his firm."

"You've never told us to stay away from dad before." Michael sounded genuinely confused.

"It's a long story. It has something to do with the Coronado case from a couple of years ago. I know it doesn't make sense, but please, Michael, promise me you'll stay away from him until I let you know that it's safe." Kira's eyes welled with tears.

"Okay, I promise," Michael said. "Mallory wants to call you tonight after class, is that okay?"

"Yes. I'll talk to you tonight. I love you both."

As soon as she disconnected the call the phone rang again. This time it was Rocco, checking in to see how she was doing. After what Frank had said about him, she felt suddenly guarded, so she feigned that everything was fine and got off of the phone quickly.

When it rang again, Kira was tempted not to answer, but she gave in to curiosity. "Well, hello Kira," Ian's voice oozed. "I have someone here that would really like to talk to you." Kira could hear sobs in the background.

"How did you get this number?" Kira seethed.

"Kira?" Audrey's voice came through the phone and Kira wasn't sure how to feel. Audrey sounded like she was crying. Her voice was raspy and low and laced in fear. She sounded frail and afraid and compassion tugged at Kira, but anger tugged harder.

"What do you want?" Kira spat.

"I need your help," Audrey sniveled. "They're going to kill me if you don't come."

"Why don't you call Frank to help you?" Kira spewed sarcastically.

"He won't help me. He set me up."

"No, you and Frank tried to set me up and it backfired. You deserve whatever you get!" Kira screamed into the phone, rage blocking every rational thought.

"Please," Audrey wept. "You've got to believe me. I would never hurt you. Never. You know me. You know me, Kira. You've got to believe me. Please come." Audrey broke into sobs and Ian must have grabbed the phone because the next thing Kira heard was Ian's voice.

"You have exactly twelve hours to show up at The Candy Shop or Audrey dies," Ian sneered and then disconnected the call.

Kira sank onto the couch, stunned.

CHAPTER 35

It felt as if her head was going to spin clean off of her neck, as everyone's words taunted her. Audrey saying Frank had set her up. Frank claiming that Rocco was a killer, working for the Coronado family. Rocco sharing his theories on serial killers and how he believed he was being framed for the murders. Landon threatening her children and Frank's job. The longer she re-hashed their words, the more confused she became, not certain who could be trusted. All of a sudden one person came to mind. Officer Downing. Kira dialed the precinct and asked to speak with Officer Downing. When he answered she explained who she was and asked to meet with him privately. When she refused to come to the station to talk, he agreed to meet in the back of the Walgreens parking lot on Kirkwood Avenue, just a few miles from the precinct.

Kira called a cab, and then opened a can of cat food for Freddie, poured some water into a dish and set the food and water on the floor. She then slipped into a pair of blue jeans Rocco had bought her and a black V-neck sweater, carefully tucking the 9mm into the front waistband. As she grabbed the Taser from the kitchen table, she noticed there was writing on the handle. It was in tiny white lettering and it read: Property of the Federal Bureau of Investigations. Kira gasped. Did this mean that the Cher-look-alike was an undercover FBI agent?

When the cab pulled behind Walgreens, Officer Downing was already there waiting, leaning against the driver's door of his squad car with his arms crossed over his chest. Kira told the Cab driver to wait, got out of the cab and approached Officer Downing.

"Mrs. Sullivan," Officer Downing greeted her.

"I hate to ask this, but I don't have any money to pay the cab driver. My purse was, well, stolen and..."

He held his hand up, cutting her sentence short, then reached for his wallet and walked toward the cab. Kira turned to thank him when she heard the whirring sound of the first bullet as it soared across the lot and hit Officer Downing between the eyes. His body flipped backwards and hit the pavement with a thud. Kira screamed and instinctively ducked down. The Cab driver floored the gas and Kira heard two more shots before watching the cab slam headfirst into the side of the brick Walgreens building. Staying low, she scrambled toward Officer Downing's squad car and climbed in. Her hands were trembling as she reached for the keys, turned on the ignition and sped out of the lot and into traffic. She kept her head low and floored the gas, weaving dangerously around cars, unsure of where to go next. Her mind raced almost as fast as her pulse as she tried to think clearly. Who could she trust? There had to be someone. Anyone. She checked the rearview mirror but didn't see anyone tailing her. As faces flooded her mind she couldn't escape the reality that anyone she contacted would be put in danger. Officer Downing was dead because she called him. The cab driver was dead because he happened to be the one who drove her. She couldn't risk calling anyone else. There had to be a way to end this nightmare, but how? *Think, Kira! Think!*

Making her way to the highway, Kira headed toward the city. She thought to call Rocco, but Frank's words rang in her ears. Was it possible that Rocco was really on the Coronado family payroll? Her head was spinning. Digging the temporary cell phone from her pocket, she had to make a decision. Frank? Rocco? The Police? Who could she trust? All of a sudden his face popped into her mind. Leon Bates, Audrey's ex-husband. He knew about the Coronado case, even though he was never actively involved in Tony Coronado's defense. He knew about Rocco's testimony destroying Frank's case and probably knew about Adrianne's relationship with Rocco. He also had the Parker, Sullivan & Bates resources that could most likely help Kira, or at the very least, afford to hide her. She didn't know if Leon had any knowledge of The Candy Shop and Landon's business relationship with Lucas, but since Landon had never mentioned Leon's name she had a feeling he either didn't know or didn't care. At any rate, she had to believe that Leon would help her. After all, they had been friends before he and Audrey divorced and he, of all people, would understand the feeling of being betrayed.

While she drove, she pulled the 9mm from her waistband and laid it on the passenger seat and then checked her mirrors again. There was still no sign of a tail, which began to feel oddly suspicious. Why had the shooter not followed her? Why had they not taken a shot at her? Kira fought her gag reflex as the image of Officer Downing being shot filled her mind. Had the shooter followed her to the meeting location or had they followed Officer Downing?

Realizing she didn't know Leon's number by heart, Kira tossed the cell phone onto the seat next to the gun. She could drive to the offices of Parker, Sullivan & Bates, but she deemed it was probably safer to go to his house and wait for him there.

Kira found Officer Downing's sunglasses in the glove compartment and put them on. Uncertain of Leon's involvement, if any, she pulled cautiously onto his street, keeping her eyes peeled for any sign of Landon, Lucas, Ian or even Frank for that matter. Large elm trees lined the street on both sides and the red brick terrace houses, which left room for only a narrow alley between them, sat close to the sidewalk leaving little room for grass. Leon didn't have the time or the inclination toward yard work which Kira surmised was the reason he choose to move to this particular neighborhood; that, and the fact that it was a quick jaunt down the highway to the office each morning. From what she knew of Leon, he wasn't a patient man so a long commute in morning traffic would have been something he considered intolerable.

Kira purposefully passed Leon's house, pulled down the next street, made a U-turn and then parked the squad car where she could see the back of Leon's home. She thought it might be safer to knock on the back door instead of approaching the house from the busy street in front. The fewer people that saw her, the better.

Shoving the gun back into her jeans and the cell phone into her pocket, Kira gripped the Taser as she got out of the squad car and crept toward the back of the house. Leon's yard was small and surrounded by a chain linked fence. Once inside the gate, she raced up the three concrete steps that led to the back door and peered inside through the glass window in the door. The kitchen was empty but there was a newspaper opened atop the table and a clear glass mug sitting next to it. She could see that the mug was almost completely full with what looked like coffee. *Maybe he hasn't left for the office yet?* Kira wondered, ascertaining that people don't usually fill their coffee and then leave. She tapped lightly on the glass and then a little harder.

"Can I help you?"

His voice came from behind her, causing Kira to squeal and stumble off of the top step. She landed at his feet and sent the Taser hurling into the yard. Leon grinned, both dimpled cheeks proof of his amusement by Kira's reaction. "A little jumpy, are we?" He mused, extending his hands and pulling her to her feet. Retrieving the Taser, he gave Kira a one-raised-eyebrow stare. "I hope you weren't planning on using this thing on me," he quipped.

"No," Kira answered breathlessly.

"Good." Leon handed the Taser back to her. "Something tells me we should go inside and have a little chat."

After warming his coffee and getting a cup for Kira, they sat at the kitchen table and Leon listened to the whole story. Kira told him every detail she could remember. Every email she had read. Every conversation with Audrey and Frank and Rocco. Every interaction with Landon and Ian and Lucas. She held nothing back, completely bearing her soul, even to the admission of sharing Rocco's bed. Leon never interrupted and waited until she had finished before he got up, retrieved a yellow legal pad of paper and his Mont Blanc pen.

"I didn't know where else to go," Kira sighed and Leon reached across the table and gave her hand a squeeze. There was compassion in his blue eyes and she noticed for the first time that he was oddly handsome. He had a healthy glow about him, bright blue, rounded eyes, dimpled cheeks and lips that were naturally pinker than those of most men. His auburn hair was thinning and had subtle streaks of gray at the temples, but it gave him a distinguished appearance.

"Something about this whole thing bothers me," Leon said calmly, tapping the Mont Blanc against the legal pad.

"What?"

"Frank and Audrey," he said matter-of-fact with no evident emotion attached.

"I know," Kira moaned. "I can't believe it either."

"That's just it," Leon said. "I don't believe it."

"I saw the emails." Kira rolled her eyes. "Trust me, they're lovers."

Leon set his pen down and crossed his arms. He cocked his head slightly and stared up at the ceiling as if he were mulling through facts or organizing his thoughts; and then he licked his lips and returned his gaze to Kira. "Audrey caught me in bed with my assistant and it broke her heart. Now, you know Audrey, she's a hothead and when she gets pissed, watch out, right?" Kira nodded, unsure of where he was going with this story. "She barged into my office one day and punched Cheryl, my assistant, right in the nose." Leon's eyes widened and the corners of his mouth curled into a grin as he recalled the event. "I mean she cleaned Cheryl's clock!" He laughed and Kira couldn't help but smile. It was just so Audrey. "This thrust the affair out into the open, which I know is why she did it. Everyone at the office knew. Cheryl wanted to press charges for assault, of course, which made Audrey even madder."

"So, what happened?" Kira asked, as Leon had paused longer than what felt natural.

"The partners wanted to fire me, stating that my unethical, amoral behavior was a stain on the Parker, Sullivan & Bates image."

"I had no idea all of this went on." Kira said, shaking her head. It was like a daytime drama. "So, did Cheryl go through with pressing assault charges?"

"Not exactly," Leon grimaced. "Audrey retained Landon as her defense attorney, which is unethical in and of itself, and then screwed him to get back at me."

Kira could feel her eyes bulging. "Landon was the man Audrey slept with?" All this time Audrey had shrugged it off, telling Kira it was no one that she knew. "Oh my gosh, Leon, I'm so sorry."

"Don't be," he smiled. "The funny thing is her sleeping with Landon saved my career. If the partners were going to boot me for amoral behavior they would have had to boot Landon as well. Parker, Sullivan & Bates would have just become Sullivan. So, we voted to ignore the indiscretions, gave Cheryl a very nice severance package to make her go away quietly and Audrey and I divorced."

"What about Adrienne? Did she know about Landon sleeping with Audrey?" Kira asked.

Leon shrugged. "I don't think so. I think she was so wrapped up in Rocco at the time that even if she knew, she wouldn't have cared."

"Wow," Kira uttered and then took a sip of coffee. "I had no idea."

"The point in my telling you this story is that I've always had a feeling that Audrey screwed Landon on purpose, to save my career." His eyes sparkled as he spoke of Audrey. "If revenge was what she wanted she could have slept with half the men in this city. I mean, my God, look at her." Leon shook his head. "She's a lot of things, but she doesn't try to hurt people and she'll do just about anything to help the ones she loves; even when they don't deserve to be helped."

Kira studied his face. "I always thought you two hated each other."

"No," he shook his head. "She hates me but I've never hated her." Leon got up, retrieved the coffee pot and filled both of their cups. "Now, back to the issue at hand. I don't believe Audrey and Frank are having an affair."

"I read the emails myself, straight from Audrey's computer," Kira objected.

"Follow me." Leon got up, walked into the hallway and opened what looked like a regular hall closet door. He brushed some coats aside and stepped into the closet. "Are you coming?"

"Into the closet with you? No." Kira shook her head which made Leon chuckle.

"I guess this does look odd," he said as he stepped back into the hallway. "There's an old dumbwaiter shaft that I've had reconstructed and reinforced so that it now works like an elevator." He took her hand and led her into the closet. "This is one of the things that I love about old houses, all the nooks and crannies and mysteries that lie within the walls." He pressed a button and a narrow door slid open. Gesturing Kira inside, he pressed another button to close the door and then she felt the floor began to lower. "It runs slower than a normal elevator system," Leon explained. When the movement finally stopped and the door opened, Kira couldn't believe her eyes. They stepped out into what looked like an underground office. There were five-foot tall filing cabinets lining the walls, a copier/scanner/fax unit, five computer stations, a big screen television, and a shelving unit that held food supplies, water bottles, blankets, a floor heater, several guns, boxes of ammunition and a police scanner. Kira was amazed.

"What is this place?" She asked.

"My office. Well, when I'm not at the office."

"It looks like a bomb shelter," she remarked.

"That's what it was originally," he said excitedly. "This house dates way, way back and has seen some remarkable periods in history. If these walls could talk," he sighed.

Leon sat down at one of the computers and began typing. His fingers danced wildly across the keys and Kira peered over his shoulder, awestruck by how quickly he maneuvered in and out of screens. "What are you doing?" She asked.

"I'm running an investigation report on Lucas Coronado, ascertaining any link to a man named Ian within his organization. I'm also doing the same on the name Ben or Benjamin, who you said was the bartender in the Lair area, right?"

"Yes."

"And I want to see if I can pull up the names of anyone else linked to the Coronado case or family as a whole." Leon spoke without looking up or slowing down. Sliding his chair over to the next computer station, he punched in a code and brought up Audrey's email account. "Now, let's isolate all of the emails sent to Frank and received from Frank, and do a back-locator-check on the IP addresses from which those emails were derived."

Kira stared at him. "And here I thought you were just a stuffy attorney," she quipped.

"I take offense to that. Not all lawyers are stuffy." He looked up and smiled. "Nah, that's not true, most of them are stuffy. I just happen to be an enigma."

Sliding to the next computer station, Leon hacked into FBI personnel logs and began searching for the Cher-look-alike, using search parameters based on Kira's description of her. "If she's an undercover agent we'll find out who she is and why she's there."

A red flashing light in the upper corner of the room caught Kira's attention and she pointed it out to Leon, who was engulfed in running more and more investigative reports. Upon seeing the light, he rushed to a computer station adjacent to the big screen television and punched in a numeric code. The back of his house appeared on the screen. "Surveillance cameras," he said to Kira. "I've got them surrounding the house so I can see if anyone tries anything funny."

He jumped from camera angle to camera angle and then stopped, zooming the lens so that they could see that a police car had pulled up next to the squad car Kira had driven. Dashing across the room to the police scanner, he turned it on and twisted the knob until the static was gone and they could hear what was being said.

"Squad car nineteen located at the corner of Pennsylvania and Highland Avenue. Send backup to search the area."

"Search request confirmed. Back-up on their way."

Leon glanced over at Kira. "I don't suppose you were wearing gloves when you drove Officer Downing's car?"

"No, why?"

"He was shot and killed, his car stolen and your prints are on the steering wheel, not to mention it won't be difficult to pull up satellite feed that shows you driving away from the scene."

Kira's eyes widened. "I had to drive away. Someone was shooting!"

Leon shook his head. "Then why didn't they shoot at you? Why didn't they follow you and keep shooting? Why didn't you drive straight to the police station, a mere three blocks away?" Leon patted her shoulder as he made his way back to the surveillance feed. "I believe you, but you can see how bad the media is going to make this look. A good rule of thumb when leaving the scene of a crime is to think about what it will look like to a jury and then weight it in your favor." Leon grinned. "That's defense attorney rule number one."

Kira sank into a chair.

CHAPTER 36

Trick Malone wasn't as helpful as Peters and Rocco had hoped. The only thing he confirmed was that Lucas was indeed the one who put the hit out on his own son, Tony Coronado. They still didn't know why. The FBI confirmed they had undercover agents in the Coronado family but for obvious reasons wouldn't share the identity of those officers.

"Putting a hit out on your own kid, that's cold," Peters shivered as they exited the penitentiary and climbed into their rental car. Rocco surmised it would be less expensive to rent a vehicle than cab it everywhere. It was rented under an alias that Peters and his hacking skills made certain could not be traced back to either of them.

They parked the rental car a couple of blocks down from the station and walked to the precinct, instantly aware upon arriving that something terrible had happened. Several of the officers were teary-eyed, others enraged and the Captain was on a mission to tear somebody a new one. "What's going on?" Peters asked one of the officers at the front desk.

"Officer down," she said quietly and then broke into sobs. Those were words no officer wanted to hear.

"Who?" Rocco asked.

"Downing," the Captain gritted, having come down the hall and into the front area without Rocco noticing. "I want everyone in the meeting room in five," he ordered. "That includes you." He pointed at Rocco and then turned and huffed down the hall.

"Downing. Who'd wanna kill Downing, man? He was like the easiest-going guy around," Peters muttered.

Once they had all gathered in the meeting room, Captain Jameson began his debriefing. First, the facts. Downing was shot with a high-powered rifle in the forehead. Two more shots were fired, one lodging in the side of a nearby dumpster. The other bullet hit the cab driver in the neck, causing him to crash into the side of the building.

"Do we have any idea who the shooter is? Any motive behind the attack?" One officer with clenched teeth blurted. He had served on the force with Downing for the past twenty years and there was no doubt in Rocco's mind he'd be one of the first seeking revenge.

Captain Jameson shook his head. "No. Not at this time." He walked across the room and hit the light switch so the lights in the front of the room went out. Then he pulled up the satellite surveillance feed on a projector screen that lowered from the ceiling. "We know Downing received a phone call from a woman and then left, presumably to meet her."

"Who is the woman?" Someone yelled from the back.

"We're currently running facial ID recognition from the satellite feed and fingerprints from those found in both Downing's vehicle and the back seat of the cab, but results are inconclusive as of yet." Captain Jameson stepped away from the screen and played the satellite surveillance feed. Rocco's heart skipped a beat as he watched Kira get out of the cab and approach Downing. He watched as Downing took out his wallet and approached the cab, and then saw him take a bullet in the head. His mouth fell open when moments later Kira jumped into the squad car and squealed out of the parking lot. He couldn't believe his eyes. What was she doing there? Why had she left the hotel? Rocco glanced at Peters, whose mouth was hanging wide open and his eyes were bulging from their sockets.

"What time did this happen?" Rocco blurted.

"9:27am," Captain Jameson replied.

Rocco shook his head. That was only about thirty minutes after he had called Kira and she had told him everything was fine. His jaw tightened in anger. Now, a good officer was down and God only knew where Kira ended up.

"The good news is that we have located Downing's vehicle on the corner of Pennsylvania and Highland Avenue and are conducting a house-to-house search in that area for the woman," Captain Jameson explained. "I'd like to put some extra manpower on this one, so raise your hand if you're available. We don't have the funds for overtime pay, boys, so any extra work we do,

we do it for justice and we do it for Downing."
Every hand in the room flew upward and
Rocco leapt to his feet.

"Captain Jameson, sir, I'd like to
request that Peters and I be assigned to help
with the search," Rocco blurted.

"I thought you were already under-
staffed and overworked with this serial case,"
the Captain chided.

"Yes, but this is personal, sir," Rocco
rebutted. The very moment Captain Jameson
gave him the okay, he and Peters raced from
the meeting room, out the front doors and
straight to their rental car.

"What the hell is going on, man?"
Peters uttered breathlessly. "What the hell
was she doing there?"

Rocco started up the ignition and sped
into traffic. "I don't know but that's what we
need to find out. We're stopping at the hotel
to grab the computer equipment and then I'm
going to need you to put those super-hero
hacking skills to good use."

"Right on," Peters said. "Right on."

CHAPTER 37

Ian ran his index finger across Audrey's neck and then drew it up and over her chin, ending by her temples where he ripped the duct tape quickly from her eyes. She cried out and blinked rapidly as her eyes tried to adjust to the light. "What a lovely neck you have," Ian whispered. "To bad we're going to have to slice it."

"Why are you doing this?" Audrey wailed. "Ian, who are you working for? What do you want? I'll do anything."

Ian lit a cigarette and dropped the lighter back into pants pocket. "You can't give us what we want." He inhaled slowly and exhaled even slower. "Right now you're the bait and later you'll become what we like to call collateral damage."

As Audrey's eyes adjusted more and more to the light she glanced around the room, trying to take in her surroundings and figure out where she was being held. It must have been an old house because she had been brought up from what she thought was a basement. It had been colder and damper than where she sat now. Ian stood in front of what looked like an old stove and there was an empty space where she surmised a refrigerator used to fit. There was a small folding table in the corner with two chairs and a water bottle sat atop the table. Audrey lusted for the water, but she was too afraid to ask for a drink. Down the hallway which jetted to her right, two men were talking, but Audrey couldn't see who they were.

"You keep saying 'we.' Who is 'we'? Is Lucas behind this?" Audrey asked Ian and he chuckled, causing a puff of smoke to fill the air around his head.

"This is bigger than Lucas Coronado," Ian hissed. "Way bigger."

CHAPTER 38

Leon scanned the investigation reports on the Coronado family. "Come over here and tell me if you saw any of these people at The Candy Shop?" He said to Kira, who bent down and peered at the computer screen from over his shoulder.

"That's Ian," she said, pointing at the screen. "He's Lucas's right hand man."

Leon clicked on Ian's picture and a rap sheet a mile long displayed. "His real name is Issac Nader, aka the 'In Man,'" Leon read.

"Why is he called the 'In Man'?" Kira asked.

"He has multiple convictions for breaking and entering, computer hacking and a handful of charges for rape, including sodomy. It says here they call him the 'In Man' because there's no place he can't get in," Leon explained and Kira shuddered.

"No convictions for rape?" She asked.

Leon scanned the document. "Ironically, his accusers wound up dead before the trial."

"Nice guy," Kira quipped.

Leon continued to read the document. "He has mob connections with several of the families, not just the Coronado family. That's a little strange. It looks like he also has a son named Benjamin Nader."

"Ben!" Kira blurted. "The bartender from the Lair was named Ben."

Leon let his fingers glide across the keyboard. "Okay, let's see what the Nader family has to do with the Coronado family?" He mumbled more to himself than to Kira.

The red light flashed and Leon leapt up and rushed across the room to monitor the outside surveillance cameras. He clicked from camera to camera, displaying the entire exterior of the home.   "What's wrong?" Kira asked, joining him in front of the screen.

"Looks like the cops are making a door-to-door search," he mumbled. "And we've got an unmarked vehicle and two men approaching the front as we speak."

"Cops?" Kira asked and Leon maneuvered the camera angle.

"One cop, one possible undercover cop," he remarked.

Kira stared at the screen. It was Rocco and Peters and just the sight of them made her breathing quicken. "Leon, it's them," she gasped. "How did they find me?"

"Do you have a cell phone on you?"

"Only a temporary cell, not registered to my name or anything."

"Did Rocco give you that phone?" Leon peered over the computer and Kira nodded. "Then he has enough information that he can trace it and it looks like he did." Kira felt like she was going to hyperventilate. "Calm down," Leon urged. "Even if he comes in the house, he'll never find us down here."

Kira grimaced and slid the cell phone from her pocket. "How precisely can it be traced?"

Leon rolled his eyes. "Depends, but it's not a risk we should take. I don't want anyone knowing about my office down here." He checked all of the computers and made sure they were processing his data requests and then he headed for the elevator.

"Where are you going?" Kira blurted. "You can't just leave me down here."

"Give me your phone," Leon instructed. "I'll go up, answer the door and tell them that you were here, but you left; and you accidentally left your phone on the table. You stay put."

It felt like Leon had been gone forever, though she knew it had only been a few minutes. Kira decided to distract herself by reading the reports that were popping up on one of the computer screens. Scrolling through the arduous history of Ian Nader was at the very least entertaining, if not disgusting. From what she read, he was nothing more than a street thug who had made a name for himself by doing the mob's dirty work.

Making her way to the file cabinets lining the walls, Kira began to peruse the tabs, seeing if anything interesting caught her attention. Her fingers stopped on a file that bore the title: Parker, Adrienne. She felt a little guilty pulling it from the cabinet, but not guilty enough to stop. She wanted to know why Leon would have a file on Adrienne.

The first few pages were a lot of legal jargon, but the fourth page was the police report that was filed the night Adrienne was found dead. There were pictures of the front of Landon's silver Mercedes with blood caked into the grill. Kira grimaced. Flipping to the next page she closed her eyes tightly and slammed the folder shut. It was a picture of Adrienne's body, mangled from the car. Kira swallowed hard, fighting nausea. Poor Adrienne. Reopening the folder, Kira quickly flipped past the picture to the next page which was a statement from Frank wherein he reported Landon's car stolen to both the police and the insurance company. Kira skimmed Frank's statement and then started to turn the page when something caught her eye. It was the time. Frank reported that Landon's car had been stolen after lunch, while he was still at the office. The statement indicated that the thief struck somewhere between 2:00 and 5:30pm, but Kira remembered Frank talking to Landon that night on the phone and it was well after dark when he called and told Frank he had wrecked his Mercedes. Had Landon murdered Adrienne and had Frank lied to cover it up? It certainly looked that way, but she still couldn't believe that Frank would do that.

The next page sealed the deal. It was photos of the surveillance coverage of the hit and run and it was proof enough to put Landon away for life. Not only did he run Adrienne down, but he backed up and continued to hit her, at least five times, according to the report. Kira felt like she might throw up. These were the photos Rocco could never get his hands on to prove that

Adrienne was murdered. Why did Leon have them? And why hadn't he turned them over to the police?

"They're all working together," Kira mumbled to herself. Taking the surveillance photos from the file, Kira folded them up and stuffed them down the back of her jeans on the inside of her panties. She wanted to ensure they would not fall out. She then pulled the 9mm from her waistband, checked the clip like Rocco had taught her and took the safety off. Afraid Leon had already notified Landon or Frank that she was here she felt a pressing need to get upstairs and leave with Rocco and Peters as quickly as possible.

Kira started for the elevator shaft when a thought stopped her. Did Leon have a file on Frank? Rushing back to the cabinets, she found the S's and a folder labeled: Sullivan, Frank. She pulled it out and flipped it open, instantly regretting that decision. Inside were pictures of Frank with another woman. She was a brunette and she was bent over his desk being taken from behind. The next picture showed him with a blonde who was straddling him in a chair. The third picture was of Audrey. She was standing in Frank's office next to the windows and she and Frank were kissing. It felt as if Kira had swallowed a bitter pill, one so jagged as to tear her insides to shreds all the way down. Doing her best to shake off the emotion, she went back to the P's and found another file labeled: Parker, Landon. She took that one as well. Driven by curiosity, she moved to the C's and found a folder labeled: Coronado, Lucas.

She was about to head back toward the elevator when she heard the distinct humming noise of the elevator lowering in the shaft. Kira started to panic and then quickly shoved all three folders beneath her sweater, put the safety back on her gun and shoved it into her waistband. Then she grabbed the Taser from one of the desks and sat down in front of the computer screen that was showcasing the life of Ian Nader.

"Find anything interesting?" Leon asked as he stepped from the elevator.

"No," Kira stuttered, "not really." She turned to face him. "What happened upstairs?"

"Nothing," he shrugged. "I told them you had been here and you left." He handed her back her cell phone.

"And they believed you?"

"Why wouldn't they?" Leon slid into the chair next to Kira, whose heart was pounding so violently that she was amazed he couldn't hear it from where he was sitting. "Rocco wanted to take your cell phone with him, but I told him I didn't feel it was appropriate to give it to him. I told him I'd contact you and you could swing back by and pick it up."

Standing up and walking toward the screen showing the outside surveillance, Kira subtly tried to see if she could find Rocco and Peters anywhere on the screen. They were her only way out of the neighborhood which was now crawling with cops. "You know it won't take long for the police to ID you and then the entire city will be looking for you," Leon said. "Staying hidden down here might be your best bet."

Kira's nerves were shot and her options were looking bleak. Stay here locked in a bomb shelter as Leon's prisoner, get picked up by the police for stealing Officer Downing's car or worse yet, fall back into the hands of Landon, Ian and Lucas and wind up dead. Confusion toyed with her emotions and taunted her logic.

"I'll tell you what," Leon said as he slid from one computer station to the next and began keying in new search parameters. "Sleep here tonight and you and I will go together early tomorrow morning to find Audrey."

Kira stared at him. Why would he say that when she had told him about Ian's threat that if she didn't come to The Candy Shop within the next twelve hours Audrey was as good as dead? Had he forgotten? Or did he not care that the time on Audrey's life was ticking? She slowly walked behind him and peered over his shoulder at the computer screen. "You really don't think Audrey and Frank are lovers?" She asked, feigning nonchalance.

"Nope."

And that was the breaking point. "You're a liar," Kira seethed and planted the Taser against Leon's neck, holding it there until he flopped out of the chair and twitched madly onto the floor. "You're just like the rest of them!" She shrieked and then hit him with the Taser one more time. Leon's eyes rolled back into his head and his entire body convulsed as Kira ran for the elevator. Once upstairs, it didn't take her long to find his car keys hanging by the back door, make her way to his jet black BMW and drive as casually yet speedily out of the neighborhood as she could. She was cautious not to squeal out or do anything to draw attention to herself. Once she got onto the highway, the trembling set in and Kira broke down and sobbed. Had she killed Leon? Could a person be Tasered twice in a row and survive? She didn't know and it was too late to worry about it now.

CHAPTER 39

"She's on the move," Peters blurted, balancing the laptop on his knees. "Or at least her cell phone is. She's on highway 40 heading downtown."

"Call her," Rocco barked, making a U-turn and heading back toward the highway entrance. "Tell her to meet back at the hotel unless she has reason to believe that location has been compromised."

Peters punched in the number and held the phone out for Rocco to take. "She's your girlfriend, you talk to her."

"She's not my girlfriend," Rocco snipped and Peters shot him a one-eyebrow-lifted glare.

"You really wanna argue over titles right now?" Peters smirked.

"Just give me the damn phone!" Rocco muttered and snatched the phone.

When Kira answered Rocco resisted the temptation to lay into her, but only because he could tell she was in an emotionally unstable state. "We're not far behind you on the highway," Rocco told her. "It's important that you remain calm while you're driving…"

"I'm not calm!" Kira shrieked. "How the hell can I REMAIN calm when I'm not calm!"

Rocco exhaled frustration. Dealing with emotional women was not his specialty. In fact, in every life situation he had tried his best to avoid emotional women. "I want you to listen to my words and I want you to focus on your breathing..."

"What the...?" Peters snickered. "Is she in labor or somethin' man?"

"Don't tell me to breathe!" Kira yelled. "I am breathing but Leon might not be because I might have killed him."

"You might have killed him?" Rocco repeated.

"Oh, that shit don't sound good," Peters muttered.

"Wouldn't you know for a fact if you had killed him?" Rocco questioned.

"I Tasered him twice and I didn't stick around to check his pulse," Kira uttered, her voice now breaking into sobs. "I didn't mean to kill him," she cried.

Rocco lowered the phone from his lips so Kira couldn't hear what he was saying to Peters. "Send an ambulance to Leon Bate's house right away."

"Now this shit just sounds bad," Peters shook his head and pulled out his cell phone.

Rocco managed to convince Kira that the hotel hadn't been compromised and she agreed, though somewhat reluctantly, to meet him there. As soon as she pulled into the lot, Rocco rushed Kira from the car and Peters slid behind the wheel and drove off in Leon's car.

"Where is he going?" Kira asked.

"He's going to dump the car in an undisclosed location, wipe it clean and then meet us back here," Rocco explained, leading Kira into the room. "You've stolen two cars today!" As soon as the door closed, he spun around and pulled her into him. He wanted to scold her and hold her at the same time, as both anger and relief surged through his veins. Drawing back from their hug, Rocco took her face in his hands and looked deeply into her eyes. "What were you thinking? Why did you leave? You could have been killed!" His voice elevated and tears formed in Kira's eyes.

Sitting her down on the couch, Rocco draped his arm across the back and gave her shoulder a tender squeeze. "I need to know what happened."

Kira began by telling him about the call from Frank and then from Audrey and Ian's threat to kill her if Kira didn't go the The Candy Shop within twelve hours. Rocco shook his head. "Why didn't you tell me about the phone calls when I talked to you this morning?" He exhaled forcefully. "All of this could have been avoided."

"Frank said you were on Coronado's payroll." She looked down and fiddled with her fingers in her lap. "I didn't know what to think or who to trust so I called Officer Downing."

"I hope you know now that you can trust me?" Rocco said it as a question but Kira didn't answer. Instead she leapt to her feet and pulled the files from the inside of her sweater and the folded papers from the back of her panties.

"Is there anything else you have hidden in there that you'd like to show me?" He teased.

"Nothing you haven't already seen," she rebutted and sat back down, clutching the files to her chest. "I found these at Leon's and I'm sure they all contain useful information, but there's one in particular I think you'll want to see." Kira took a deep breath and exhaled slowly. "This will be hard for you to look at, but…" her voice faded. "What I mean is…it's something you…" her voice caught in her throat.

"I chase down serial killers for a living and dig bodies out of dumpsters. I think I can handle whatever is on those papers," Rocco quipped.

Unfolding the surveillance photos of Landon murdering Adrienne, Kira handed them to Rocco. "This is personal," she whispered.

Suddenly it felt as if time stood still as emotion rocked him. Rocco stared at each photograph, tortured by the evidence of a truth he knew but was never able to prove. Adrienne, his Adrienne, had been brutally murdered by Landon Parker. Rocco sifted through the photographs, feeling the agony of that night encompass him. He fought back his rage until he reached the very last photo; and then he paused. His eyes darted wildly to Kira and then back down to the picture. "Have you looked at these?" He asked.

Kira shook her head. "I accidentally saw the first one and I couldn't handle it so I didn't look at the rest. I just grabbed them and shoved them in my pants."

Rocco flipped the last picture around and held it up for Kira to view. There, next to the bloody Mercedes and Adrienne's crumbled body stood Landon, Ian and Frank. Kira gasped as if she couldn't believe her eyes. "Omigod," she uttered. "I knew Frank lied to the insurance company and I figured out today that he lied in the police report, but I never would have guessed he would have been involved in murdering Adrienne."

"He wasn't involved in her murder," Rocco clarified. "At least I don't think he was, but he was certainly an accomplice who helped cover it up."

Peter's banging on the door momentarily drew them away from the conversation, but once he was safely inside and the door was locked the three of them made coffee and began to dig through each file Kira had stolen from Leon.

"There's enough evidence here to put these cats away for life," Peters uttered. "I'm talking lock 'em up and throw away the key."

Rocco glanced at Kira, after all it was her husband they were talking about; but she appeared to be taking it in stride. He was certain after the events of today she was in a moderate state of shock and that when reality hit, her calm would crumble. He hoped to be the shoulder she leaned on whenever that time came.

Kira pushed aside the pictures of Frank screwing other women and focused on the photo of him and Audrey kissing. Rocco could see that this picture caused more brokenness than the others combined. It was the picture of a dual betrayal. He was just about to ask Kira if she was okay when Peters' cell phone rang.

"This is Peters," he answered.

"Officer Peters," the precinct switchboard operator said. "I have a man on hold that is asking to speak with Detective Sterling. I've put him through to voicemail three times already, but he insists it's urgent. I've tried Detective Sterling's cell phone but it just rings and rings and he isn't responding to my text messages. Do you know how I can reach him?"

"Yeah, I can get him a message," Peters said. "Give me the man's name and contact information and I'll make sure Roc...uh, Detective Sterling calls him back right away." Peters jotted down the name and number on a piece of paper and slid it across the table. It read:

Leon Bates 314-555-6363

"Evidentially he's still alive," Rocco said and Kira breathed an obvious sigh of relief. Rocco grabbed one of the temporary cell phones and keyed in Leon's number. "Time to get some real answers."

"Detective Sterling," Leon answered, his voice sounding raspy and weak. "Thank you for returning my call. I need to meet with you. I'm ready to come clean and I have evidence that will prove beneficial to your cause."

"Come clean about what?" Rocco posed.

"I can't discuss the matter over the phone. I've got to find Kira Sullivan before it's too late." He sounded out of breath, as if he were rapidly moving around while speaking.

"I have Mrs. Sullivan," Rocco retorted and he could sense genuine surprise in Leon's pause.

"She stole information and my car and..." Leon began but Rocco cut him off.

"If you'd like to file a report you can do that at the station."

"Listen, Sterling," Leon's voice changed and though still winded, he was seething. "The information she took is a matter of life and death."

"Yes, it is." Rocco couldn't control the sarcastic anger that crept into his tone.

"I need you to send a car to pick me up. I need you to take me into custody now. Now!" Leon hollered and Rocco could hear the sheer panic in his voice. "I'm a dead man, do you hear me? I'm a dead man!"

"Calm down, Mr. Bates. We'll send an Officer to your location immediately," Rocco responded.

"And I want you to meet me at the station. I'm not talking to anyone else. Only you."

"I'll be there." Rocco disconnected the call and instructed Peters to pick up Leon. "He's scared to death," Rocco said. "The question is why?"

CHAPTER 40

Frank paced nervously in front of his office windows. He could feel his hair graying by the second and his heart pounded like it was on the verge of exploding. This thing had spiraled out of control. He was staring down a speeding freight train with no means of stopping it or clearing the tracks. And for what? His career? A career that would be over and destroyed just like everything else in life he valued. What would his children say about their father now?

Landon strode into his office and closed the door, sank into a chair and propped his feet up on the mahogany desk. "This is all your fault," Frank uttered without turning around to face him. "You've destroyed all of our lives and for what?"

Landon chuckled and locked his fingers behind his head. "Relax, Sullivan. We're not going down today or any other day."

Frank whirled around. "You made a deal with the devil and it's costing all of us our lives!" His face was bright red and a vein protruded from the left side of his neck.

"Save that dramatic flair for the courtroom," Landon mocked. "I made a deal with Coronado, who is hardly the devil; and we're going to come out on top. You watch." He rose from the chair and headed toward the door.

"Yeah, but at what cost?"

245

Turning to face Frank, Landon's mouth drew up into a twisted grin. "Relax. I've already got a guy lined up to take the fall. Besides," he hissed, "wouldn't you give anything for your freedom?" Frank dropped his head and exhaled. "Well, wouldn't you?" Landon sneered.

"Yes," Frank uttered.

CHAPTER 41

"Six hours and counting," Ian taunted, purposefully blowing smoke into Audrey's face. She tried to blow it away and though she could dissipate the smoke, she couldn't take away the stench of Ian's words. His words strangled any hope of living through this. "Let me ask you a question," Ian said, grabbing Audrey by the hair and yanking her head back so he could look into her eyes. "Do you think you're going to go to Heaven or to Hell?" Audrey didn't answer; she just closed her eyes as reality washed over her. She was going to die. Releasing her hair, Ian took another drag from his cigarette and then dug the burning butt into Audrey's bare thigh. She jolted upward and cried out from the pain. "I'd get used to the heat if I were you," Ian seethed. "Tramp." He sauntered down the hallway, leaving Audrey alone with her thoughts.

The truth was she probably deserved to die, but not like this. No one deserved this. It wasn't as if she had been a good person all of her life. Then again, had anyone? Wasn't all of humanity flawed and sinful? With her wrists taped together behind the back of the chair, Audrey couldn't wipe her tears so they trickled down her face and dripped onto her lap, stinging as they ran over the burn and down her outer thigh. A small part of her wanted to scream, as loud as she could, but she knew it wouldn't help. In fact, she was certain it would earn her more pain. At any rate, between the lack of food, water, sleep, light deprivation and the mental and physical abuse she had endured, the fight had left her and her willingness to survive was slowly slipping away. Faces entered her mind, flashbacks of people she loved and places she missed. She thought of her mother, who had bright red hair like hers and always greeted her after school with homemade chocolate chip cookies. She had fond memories of her father, who always had a smile, even when he was dying. She wondered if...if she got the chance to go to Heaven, would she be with them again? How she had missed them.

Audrey was raised Catholic but it had been years since she attended mass or went to confession. Now, it was too late. She thought of Father Montague and how he always made her feel welcome. She'd given just about anything to see his face right now, to have the chance to jump into that confessional booth and spill her guts. Her sins filled her mind. She hadn't been a good friend or a faithful wife, though her unfaithfulness was not without motive. She did what she did to save Leon's career, but only God knew that. To everyone else she was the whore who screwed Landon Parker. The thought of being with Landon repulsed her, but her only other choice would have been Frank and she couldn't do that to Kira. She tried. She went to his office one night, acting distraught over Leon's affair with Cheryl. Frank bought her act hook, line and sinker, but when push came to shove, she couldn't go through with it. They started to kiss and all she could think about was Kira. That left Landon as the only alternative. She did it because she thought saving Leon's career would somehow save their marriage; but it backfired. She never could forgive him for sleeping with Cheryl and no matter how many one-night stands she had following his affair, the heartache of his betrayal never went away. She began to hate him but now, in the quiet of an honesty that only comes at death's door, Audrey knew that it wasn't Leon she hated, it was herself.

Closing her eyes, Audrey silently prayed. She asked God for forgiveness and salvation and for another chance at life. She prayed that Kira, whatever she had been told, would one day know the truth; and that Leon would know that she finally forgave him and always loved him. A sense of peace filled her heart and even if it only lasted a moment, it was a moment Audrey would treasure.

CHAPTER 42

Peters picked Leon up in Leon's BMW and brought him back to the hotel, making sure they weren't followed. Once inside he turned to Peters, who was carrying in several laptops and a box of Leon's files. "Were the handcuffs really necessary?" Leon quipped and then directed his attention to Rocco. "I turned myself in."

"Better safe than sorry," Peters remarked, carrying in the last box, closing and locking the door.

As soon as Leon laid eyes on Kira he narrowed his brow. "Why the hell did you Taser me?!" He hollered, moving quickly toward her.

Even though Leon's hands were cuffed behind his back, Rocco stepped between him and Kira, pushing Leon backwards. "I suggest you calm down or I'll Taser you this time."

Leon backed up and lowered himself onto the couch. "Can you at least remove the cuffs now?" He groaned and Peters obliged. Leaning forward on his knees and running his hands through his hair, Leon said, "I'm sorry. I'm in deep here and I don't know what to do." He looked up at Rocco and Kira and for the first time Kira thought she saw fear in his face. "They're gonna kill Audrey. They're gonna kill her and I don't know how to stop it."

Rocco dragged a chair from the kitchen into the living room and sat down across from the coffee table, facing Leon. "You have files of evidence against each partner in your firm. Why?"

"Job security," Leon uttered. "Life security." He shook his head. "You don't know these men. They'll do anything, so I thought I should keep a record of things in case I ever need to prove my innocence or their guilt, or to save my skin..."

"Or to blackmail them," Rocco added and Leon glared at him.

"You don't know anything," he mumbled.

"Then enlighten me." Rocco crossed his left leg over, resting his ankle on his right knee, leaned back and folded his arms over his chest.

Parading in from the kitchen with a cup of coffee, Peters said, "I don't mean to interrupt, but time is ticking on this Audrey person's life so unless you wanna be digging her out of a dumpster, I'd say we better figure out what we're gonna do now."

"Agreed," Rocco said.

Leon nodded in agreement and then turned his attention to Kira. "They want you."

"I thought they wanted to frame Rocco for the killings," Peters said. "What do they want her for?"

"You can't expect to understand unless you know the history," Leon barked.

"Okay. For the sake of time, can you give us a summation, an overview of the history?" Rocco interjected.

"I'll try," Leon said, raising himself from the couch and walking across the room, giving the appearance of organizing his thoughts. "Landon Parker was an orphan, adopted by the Nader family when he was a child, so Landon and Ian grew up as siblings, in a sense. Landon and Ian went to a private, boarding school during their teenage years but Landon met Adrienne Barkley one summer and fell for her. The story is that one night Adrienne sneaked into their dorm room to surprise Landon, but Landon wasn't there. Ian was and he raped her."

"Hold on a second," Rocco balked. "I've never heard any of this and this is something Adrienne would have told me."

"Did she tell you why she missed her senior year of high school?" Leon asked.

"Yes. She spent a year doing an internship with her aunt, who is a doctor in Connecticut. She was trying to decide if she wanted to study medicine and she said it was an opportunity she couldn't pass up." As Rocco was speaking Kira could tell that he was beginning to see the holes in Adrienne's story.

"Love is blind," Leon uttered. Reaching into the box of files and retrieving one that was labeled: Nader, Benjamin, he handed it to Rocco. "Adrienne told Landon what happened and threatened to go to the police, but the Nader family, who was more concerned about their reputation than the fact that their son was a criminal, turned to their mob connections for help." Leon pointed to the file. "Adrienne was forced to give birth to Benjamin Nader, born August 17, 1988 and the Coronado family made sure there was no record of the rape." He paced around the room. "Landon left Adrienne and the Nader family altogether and shortly thereafter, Adrienne left, leaving the baby in the Nader family's loving care," he said with sarcasm.

"What about Adrienne's family? Didn't they wonder who knocked her up? Didn't they want to see the baby?" Peters blurted. "You white people are weird about that stuff."

"Adrienne never told her parents because the Coronado family threatened to kill them if she did. She left, but the one person who knew was her brother, Richard Barkley."

"Richard, huh, I never knew his first name," Peters uttered. "Good, ol Dick. It's fitting."

"Okay, so we have our connection between Ian Nader, Landon and the Coronado family," Rocco summed up. "How does that involve Kira or Audrey?"

"Once Landon left the Nader family, he hired an attorney and attempted to seal the adoption records and any evidence that he was affiliated with them. He wanted a clean start, which worked for a long time. He legally changed his name to Parker, put himself through law school and started the practice that became Parker, Sullivan & Bates. The past appeared to be successfully behind him that is until Adrienne showed up. Still obviously in love with her, they married." Leon paused and dug through the box of files, pulling out two photos of their wedding and handing them to Rocco. "Landon thought they were in the clear, but someone was watching the whole time."

Kira leaned over Rocco's shoulder and looked at the pictures. She instantly recognized the face of the man standing in the crowd. It was bartender Ben from the Lair, aka Benjamin Nader.

Leon went on to explain that Landon began to receive letters from an unknown source, threatening to destroy his reputation by telling the world who he really was and that his wife and his brother had borne a son together, one she rejected and left. Landon turned to the only cop he knew that would be motivated to solve the case and keep it quiet, Barkley. Barkley found Ian and threatened his life if he didn't leave Adrienne alone, but the threats only pissed Ian off. Ian found Adrienne, drugged her with a syringe full of Flunitrazepam and photographed the two of them having sex. "The pictures were sent to Landon," Leon explained, reaching into the box and retrieving the photographs. "As you can imagine, he lost his mind."

Kira sighed deeply and sank onto the couch. She never thought it would be possible to feel sympathy for Landon, but it tugged at her now. "Why would Ian do that?"

Leon shrugged. "Jealousy toward Landon for marrying Adrienne. Revenge toward Barkley for his threats. Anger toward Adrienne for leaving him and Ben. Who knows?"

"Maybe the cat's just plain crazy," Peters added.

"That's why Landon started abusing her," Rocco uttered.

"That still don't make it right," Peters interjected. "I mean, there ain't no cause to hit a woman."

Leon continued to explain that in the midst of all of that, the Coronado family, knowing from Ian that Landon was now a prestigious defense attorney, came to Parker, Sullivan & Bates seeking a solid defense team for their son, Tony Coronado. Already haunted by the past, Landon didn't want anything to do with it and gave the Coronado case to Frank. "The case was in the bag," Leon said. "It was open and shut. The Coronado's had paid off an alibi and Tony was going to walk, until you came along," he said to Rocco. "Your testimony swung the jury the other way and Tony, who thought he was going to be a free man, ended up with a life sentence." Leon sat down next to Kira. "Needless to say the Coronado's were not pleased."

"Why didn't Landon give the Coronado case to you instead of Frank?" Peters posed.

"Because I had just been busted for screwing my secretary," Leon shook his head and Kira noted that regret couldn't have been etched deeper into his brow. "My marriage was in the toilet and the partners were threatening to drop me from the board. I was not in a mental place where I could focus on a high-profile case."

"So, this brings us current, right?" Rocco questioned.

Leon nodded. "It brings the motive current." He continued to explain that during the Coronado trial, Lucas Coronado sent hookers to the firm several times a week, as a gesture of gratitude for the work that was being done for his son. Landon and Frank shared the women.

Kira rolled her eyes in disgust. *And here I was at home feeling sorry for him because he had to work late every night.* She met eyes with Rocco and could tell by his expression that he was wondering if she was okay. It was her husband they were talking about and nothing about the conversation was easy. Her heart ping-ponged back and forth between sadness and anger, and the anger made her want to seek revenge. In fact, had she and Rocco been alone she might have been compelled to climb across the coffee table and straddle him right there in his chair, simply out of spite; but she knew revenge wasn't the answer. It would be enjoyable, but it wasn't the answer.

Leon continued. "I installed cameras in their offices, thereby rendering evidence of their infidelity so that I could use it as leverage to keep my position as a partner in the firm. You can imagine my surprise when my wife showed up in the pictures."

"Ooh, man, that's rough, bro," Peters shook his head. "That is rough."

"Audrey and I divorced. Tony Coronado went to prison and was murdered in prison. Shortly thereafter Mrs. Coronado wound up dead and everything spiraled out of control," Leon explained. "Coronado demanded an eye-for-an-eye."

"An eye-for-an-eye," Peters repeated and grimaced.

"His wife was dead and it was our fault," Leon said. "To even the score he wanted Landon's wife killed."

"Hold up," Peters blurted. "Hold up. That don't make no sense. I thought Mrs. Coronado killed herself."

"She did, technically," Leon responded. "But Lucas Coronado believed that she did it because she was already dying of a broken heart over the fact that her son went to prison and then died."

Peters shook his head. "Y'all think way too much."

"So Landon took it upon himself to kill Adrienne," Rocco interjected.

"With the help of Frank and the overseeing of Ian," Leon added.

"Do you see how messed up you rich, suburbanites are? You can't even kill nobody on your own without talkin' about it and overseein' it. Man, in the hood we just drive by and shoot the motherfu..." Peters noticed that Kira was watching with raised eyebrows and he stopped before using an obscenity in front of her. "You know what I'm sayin'."

"Be that as it may," Leon continued, "with Adrienne dead Coronado considered the account paid in full. He considered us even. He went his way and we went ours."

"And you buried the evidence that Adrienne was murdered," Rocco uttered, his jaw clenched and anger piercing through his eyes.

Dropping his chin downward, Leon nodded. "Yes, and for that I am sorry."

"Okay, so who is the serial killer and how is he related to all of this?" Peters blurted. "Time is ticking."

"I don't know," Leon said and Rocco flew out of his chair, grabbed Leon around the neck lifting him from the couch and thrusting him backwards against the wall. "I swear I don't know," Leon stammered.

"You're lying!" Rocco seethed.

"I ... sw...ear," Leon managed, his face turning a deep shade of purple.

Rocco dropped him and Leon drank in a deep breath.

Leon fought to catch his breath. "Ian contacted Landon and told him that Coronado was opening a gentleman's club on the Riverfront. He wanted to know if we wanted a cut of the business in the form of referral fees. Ian called it a gesture of friendship. We would refer high paying customers and Coronado would give us a percentage of what those customers spent."

"Not to mention you'd get all the free pus..." Peters caught Kira's eye again and abruptly stopped talking. "All the free prostitutes you'd want," he corrected himself and Kira rolled her eyes. *Men. It doesn't matter their age, size, color, culture, income, religion or political affiliation, when it comes to sex they're all the same, like kids in a candy shop.* All of a sudden the relevance of the name hit her and Kira burst out laughing. All three men stared at her as if she were crazy.

"Something funny?" Rocco asked, the corners of his mouth curling upward just slightly.

"The Candy Shop," she giggled. "It's so apropos. So creative and yet so obviously simple."

"I'm not following," Rocco said.

"Me neither," Peters chimed in.

"None of us are," Leon added.

"When it comes to sex, men are like kids in a candy shop." They all stared blankly as if they didn't see the irony of the name. "Kids in a candy shop run around wanting to touch everything and put all of the candy into their mouths, just like men at The Candy Shop."

Rocco gave her a cockeyed, tilted head glance while Leon shook his head as if he were lost and Peters just stared blankly.

"Moving along," Leon interjected. "Though the score was evened in Coronado's book, Ian and Landon felt jilted by Detective Sterling here." Leon motioned toward Rocco. "Since Sterling was a well-known tracker of serial killers, they decided to make you become one yourself, at least in the public eye."

"So the motive was to frame me for the murders," Rocco said in an I-knew-it-all-along tone of voice. "But then why were my fingerprints not found on any of the victims?"

Leon shook his head. "I don't know."

He went on to explain how Ian had found Christine, who shared an uncanny resemblance to Adrienne, and used her to lure Rocco to The Candy Shop. "The thing I don't understand is how these women are being killed. I mean, specifically, the manner in which they are murdered. To my knowledge, this was never discussed with Landon."

"Okay, let's come back to that. Why were Audrey and Kira sent to The Candy Shop?" Rocco questioned.

Leon got a faraway look in his eye. "Ian convinced Landon that it wasn't fair that he had to pay to even the score with Coronado and myself and Frank didn't." Leon closed his eyes. "I taped the conversation when they came to us and told us our wives needed to die." He reached into the file box and pulled out a flash drive and handed it to Rocco. "It's all on there."

"Did you and Frank just agree? Did you argue at least?" Kira chided, a lump catching in her throat.

"I pretended to hate Audrey. I told them she was a bitch and we were divorced so I didn't care whether she lived or died." Leon's voice cracked. It was obvious those things weren't true. "Frank argued but in the end his choice was to either sacrifice you or sacrifice your kids."

Tears formed instantly in Kira's eyes, not tears of sadness but of rage and injustice. *How dare they make Frank choose between my life or the lives of our children!* She leapt to her feet and screamed at the top of her lungs. "I want them dead! I want them all dead! I want them chopped into little pieces! No, that's too easy, I want them to suffer a long and terrible, awful death with pain that is unbearable and..." Rocco threw his arms around her and Kira melted into a heap of sobs against his chest. She could somehow hold it together while Downing was shot in the head, or while she was held captive by Landon, or drugged by Ian, but this piece of information was more than she could process. This involved her children.

"Should I continue?" Leon asked Rocco, obviously concerned about Kira's emotional state.

Rocco nodded. "Time doesn't allow the luxury of stopping," he said.

"Near as I can tell luring Kira to The Candy Shop became a game of sorts, one that had to involve Audrey because Frank suggested that there was no way Kira would go alone. So Frank contacted Audrey and threatened to tell Kira about what had happened in his office if she didn't persuade her to go to the interview." Kira blew her nose with toilet paper from the bathroom and then returned to her seat on the couch. "Audrey was instructed to ask to use the ladies room right after the interview because Ian had timed the interview so that your paths would cross," he said to Rocco and Kira. "I'm certain that Audrey played along only because she didn't want you to find out about that night in Frank's office."

"Yeah, I saw the picture," Kira uttered sarcastically.

"I promise you that one kiss was the only time they ever touched. Whatever was in her head when she went there....whatever revenge she was seeking against me, she didn't go through with it. Not with Frank anyway."

Confusion swept Kira's heart. Who was Frank Sullivan? He was an accomplice to murder. A doer of hookers and prostitutes. He had been willing to cheat on her with her best friend, and he was guilty of setting up his wife to be murdered and an innocent man to take the blame. Was all of that excusable by the fact that he was protecting the lives of his children?

"Ian doesn't play fair. He operates in tampering and manipulating through the use of drugs and photographs. Nothing is ever as it appears with these people." Leon swallowed hard. "When you didn't go back to The Candy Shop, they abducted Audrey to use her as leverage to bring you back. Then, when you and Rocco escaped, their plan went to pieces," Leon explained. "The deadline came and went."

"What deadline?" Rocco and Peters said simultaneously.

"October fifth," Leon answered.

"The day Adrienne died," Rocco uttered almost incoherently.

"Kira was to be the fifth death and she was supposed to be found on October fifth." Leon said it so matter-of-factly that it made Kira shudder. "This whole thing is set up symbolically, but I don't think Landon and Ian are the ones contriving the symbolic connections; at least not all of them."

"Elaborate," Rocco said. "What exactly are the symbolic connections?"

"The most obvious is the date of October fifth being the same day Adrienne died. She was hit five times and five women were slated to be murdered, Kira being the fifth and final," Leon explained.

"What about the flowers?" Kira asked. "Lucas gives every woman at The Candy Shop a flower name and you said that all of the victims had a flower pinned to their clothing."

"That's right," Rocco agreed.

"I'm not sure where the flower idea came from, other than I know that Landon used to purchase bouquets of flowers for Adrienne. She evidentially had quite the green thumb. The connection may lie in the symbolism of the flowers," Leon explained.

"Hold up," Peters interjected. "You said five women supposed to die but we've already got six ladies dead. Christine, Misty, Ilesia, Miranda, Miranda's neighbor, Natalie and Ginger."

"The last two of which I never touched," Rocco added. "That means the last two weren't part of the original plan."

"Right. It also means, now that they've already strayed from the plan, they'll have no problem killing Audrey if Kira doesn't show up."

"They're gonna kill her either way, bro," Peters quipped.

"That's why we have to find out who the killer is and stop him," Leon urged. "Landon and Ian aren't committing the murders. They're selecting the women and then handing them off to someone else.

"Is it Lucas?" Rocco posed.

Kira shook her head and blurted. "Not possible."

"Why not?" Peters asked. "It ain't like he's some upstanding citizen or nothin'."

"Lucas wouldn't degrade a woman. He loves women. He wouldn't cut off their fingers or slit their throats or even touch them in a way they didn't want to be touched." It was hard to explain.

"But you said he punished you by beating you," Rocco interjected.

"Yes, but it was more of a process of discipline, not a motive of malice. I got the feeling that he wasn't trying to hurt me, but more like he was trying to teach me a lesson." She exhaled. "I'm not making sense."

"No, you're not," Rocco said poignantly.

"I spent time alone with Lucas and I listened to him talk about his business and about his women. He talks about protecting them, as if he takes on a great personal responsibility to keep them safe and make them feel secure and ultimately meet their needs."

"Are you hearing yourself? You're defending a mob boss," Peters blurted and Kira felt the hair on the back of her neck stand on end. "Sounds like somebody's been brainwashed."

"Forget it," Kira spat. "I just know Lucas is not the one killing these women." Kira stood up and stormed into the kitchen. "In fact, I wouldn't be surprised if we found out that he doesn't even know they're being killed!"

CHAPTER 43

Audrey was sitting still with her eyes closed when she felt a tap on her leg which startled her. She opened her eyes in a panic only to see Ben standing in front of her. "I didn't mean to scare you," he said quietly. "My name's Ben. I work in the downstairs bar at The Candy Shop and I know your friend."

"Kira?" Audrey uttered, her voice raspy and her throat dry.

Benjamin retrieved a bottle of water from the table, unscrewed the cap and poured some into Audrey's mouth. She swallowed, watching his every move carefully, unsure of why he was showing her kindness after all of this time. The water was warm but it felt good as it ran down the back of her throat.

"Do you want some more?" He asked, holding up the bottle. Audrey nodded slowly and he poured another drink into her mouth. It soothed her in a way she couldn't begin to describe. Screwing the lid back on, Ben shoved the bottle into his back pocket and then took a pocket knife from his front pocket. Audrey winced at the sight of the knife. "Hold still," he instructed. "And keep quiet. I'm not going to hurt you."

Audrey obeyed and Ben sliced the tape holding her wrists together and cut her ankles free as well. Her arms felt heavy as she tried to move them forward. They had been taped behind her back for a long time. She looked at him with a puzzling gaze. "I'm gonna get you out of here. Can you walk?"

He helped her to her feet, but she could barely straighten her legs and her muscles weren't cooperating. She had been in the same curled up position for too long. Atrophy had set in. "It's okay," he told her. "I'll carry you but we have to hurry. They'll be back soon."

Ben bent down and lifted Audrey, cradling her like a baby in his arms. He carried her out of the kitchen, down the hallway and outside into what looked like an alleyway. The sun was too bright for her eyes so she buried her face in Ben's shoulder. Before long, he placed her in the backseat of a green Oldsmobile that had seen better days, hopped into the driver's seat and sped off.

"I've got to drop you somewhere and then get back and act like I was attacked by someone who came in and stole you," Ben told her. "Where should I take you?"

"Kira," Audrey said quietly. "Wait, no. Can you take me to Leon's house?" Audrey was afraid that Kira would think she had been with Frank and wouldn't talk to her or let her in. Leon would help her, despite all that had happened between them. She gave Ben the address.

Pulling onto Leon's street, Ben cursed aloud. "There's a cop right in front of the house. I can't be questioned by no cops. I've got a record. I can't go back to prison," he ranted.

"Drop me off down the street and drive away," Audrey said, her voice growing raspy again.

Ben pulled the water bottle from his pocket. "Okay, here you take this," he said and handed her the bottle. "Will you be able to get to the cop from this far away?"

It was only a couple of blocks and Audrey was certain that even if she just collapsed onto the sidewalk, someone would find her and fetch the police. Since she was still wearing her red sequined mini dress from The Candy Shop chances were pretty good that people would think she was a hooker strung out on drugs. "I'll be fine."

Ben opened the backdoor and slid Audrey from the seat to the sidewalk. She could see that he was somewhat conflicted about leaving her there, but he didn't seem to have any other options. As he set her down, Audrey touched his hand. "Thank you," she said. "You saved my life."

Ben didn't utter another word. He got back into the Oldsmobile and left.

Too afraid to attempt standing and walking on her own, Audrey began crawling toward Leon's house and the squad car that was parked out front. The Officer was coming out of Leon's front door just as she made it to his car and collapsed from exhaustion.

"Well, well, well," the Officer said. "What have we here?" He opened the backdoor to his car, lifted Audrey from the ground and placed her inside. Then he handcuffed her wrists and ran his fingers up the inside of her thigh. "You have the right to remain silent," he hissed. "And I intend to keep you that way."

Climbing behind the wheel, he started the car and sped off.

CHAPTER 44

The temporary cell phone Kira had been using was lying on the kitchen table next to the Taser and her 9mm. Peters was checking with the FBI to see if they could find out how to reach the undercover agent who was working in The Candy Shop, aka the Cher-look-alike; but it was a long shot. Undercover identities weren't easily disclosed, not even to the police.

Rocco was busy trying to assemble a team to storm The Candy Shop and rescue Audrey before it was too late. If he could convince the other officers that the people holding Audrey were the same ones that had killed Officer Downing, rallying troops would not be a problem. So far, he was having trouble making that connection.

Kira's phone rang and a man's voice whispered. "I've got Audrey, her hair is red and because of you she'll soon be dead." He disconnected the call and Kira dropped the phone, her hands trembling. She told them what he had said and Peters jotted it down on a piece of paper.

"Did you recognize the voice?" Rocco asked. "Was it Ian or Landon?"

It wasn't either of them but Kira had a feeling she had spoken to this man before. She just couldn't put a face on the voice. "He sounded older," she said, "and his voice was a little gruff, like gritty sounding."

"He was probably disguising it," Leon said. "Are you sure it wasn't Lucas?"

Kira pursed her lips and tightened her jaw. "It wasn't Lucas."

Rocco narrowed his brow, bit down on his lip and exhaled loudly. "The call makes no sense. Why would he call to tell us he had Audrey when we already knew he had her?"

"I was thinkin' the same thing, man," Peters chimed in. "He already told us we had twelve hours to get there or he'd kill her."

"Unless it was one of his men that didn't know Ian had already made the call," Leon suggested.

"Or someone else entirely," Rocco mumbled and chills darted up the back of Kira's neck.

"You mean the killer?" Kira asked and silence filled the room. That prospect was terrifying.

"Give me you phone," Leon blurted, extending his hand toward Kira.

"You gonna try to run a back-trace?" Peters asked. "'Cuz that'll be a waste of time."

Kira handed Leon the phone and Leon opened up two of the laptops he had brought with him, set them on the coffee table and went to work. "I want to see if I can get satellite coordinates."

"He's probably bouncing the call off of twenty different sites, man," Peters scoffed.

"Yeah, if he's smart, but not everybody is smart," Leon retorted. "If this was the killer, then he's already strayed from the program a couple of times. If I've learned anything, it's that panicked people make stupid mistakes."

Peters sat down next to Leon and began keying in access codes to tap into the satellite surveillance system. "If you can get me coordinates, I'll try and zoom in and see if we can get a picture of our guy."

Time was running out and Kira could feel the stress in the room intensifying. They were all on-edge. Leon's and Peters' fingers flew across their respective keyboards with lightning speed, tracing, tracking and searching for anything that would help them track down the caller.

"Could you search Ian's or Landon's phone records and get the killer's phone number that way?" Kira posed. "I mean, they've got to be keeping in touch somehow, right?"

"I already ran those searches. The records are on the on the precinct database under my key code," Rocco said. "Peters, you can pull them up."

"No need," Leon blurted. "I got him!"

Peters leaned over so he could see Leon's screen and copied the coordinates, plugging them into the surveillance database. He zoomed the feed until he could see a close up street view. "This place looks strangely familiar," Peters quipped and Rocco leapt up and rushed across the room to take a look at the screen. Kira moved in close to Rocco and peered over Peters' shoulder, while Leon leaned left to see.

"That's your street," Peters said.

"That's my street," Leon repeated.

Peters zoomed the feed again, backing up the time frame and playing it forward in fast motion. They saw the green Oldsmobile pull onto the street and stop and then watched as Ben moved Audrey to the sidewalk and left. "That's Ben!" Kira blurted. "Why would he dump Audrey on the sidewalk?"

They watched Audrey crawl down the sidewalk and encounter the police officer, who walked out of Leon's house, lifted Audrey into the squad car and drove away. "What was he doing in my house?" Leon barked.

Kira breathed a sigh of relief. "Well, at least we know now that Audrey is safe. I'm sure that cop must have taken her to a hospital so maybe we should start our search there. Barnes Jewish Hospital is not too far from Leon's neighborhood."

Peters zoomed in on the front windshield of the squad car. "Number twenty-seven," he muttered. "Same car we saw on surveillance the morning Natalie Wild was killed."

"Can you zoom in on the Officer's face?" Rocco asked and Peters searched for an optimal angle and position and then paused the feed again and zoomed in close.

"That ain't possible, man," Peters gasped. "He had a heart attack. I saw him drop like a bowl of Jell-O in your office."

Rocco's jaw clenched tighter and he swore aloud. Moving quickly past Kira, he slammed his fist into the side of the kitchen wall and grunted. "He faked the heart attack," Rocco seethed. "Son of a bitch!"

"You can't fake a heart attack, man. The EMT's took him away. I watched them wheel him out," Peters rebutted.

"Check his hospital release date," Rocco ordered and Peters quickly switched screens, tapping into the St. Anthony's Hospital patient database and searching medical records for Richard Barkley.

"He had motive, opportunity and was able to stay one step ahead of us because he was one of us," Rocco muttered. "Somehow he must have altered the forensic lab results which is why he complained about my requesting more DNA analysis. It was more work for him to cover his tracks." Rocco's jaw tightened. "I should have seen it." He shook his head. "I should have known."

"How would Barkley have gotten mixed up with the Coronado's? Kira questioned.

"Not the Coronados," Leon interjected. "His connection was through Landon. Remember, they were brother-in-laws."

"That's right," Rocco added. "And Landon convinced Barkley that had I not been involved with Adrienne, she would never have gone out to meet me the night she was killed."

"She was going to meet you?" Kira spun around to face Rocco. "Is that true?"

Rocco momentarily closed his eyes and the opened them with a sigh. "Yes, we were supposed to meet, but she obviously never showed up."

"Holy cow, man," Peters interrupted. "It says here that Barkley was released less than two hours after he arrived in Emergency. It says the patient suffered a bout of indigestion."

Rocco paced the floor. "Just before he collapsed in my office we were discussing the fact that Miranda's neighbor had given a statement to the police. He faked a heart attack so we would think he was out of commission and he could easily kill her."

"He also knew about The Candy Shop!" Peters snapped his fingers.

"Put out a city-wide APB right away on car number twenty-seven and on Officer Barkley. List him as armed and dangerous," Rocco told Peters, who jumped up, taking his cell phone into the kitchen to make the call.

"Don't you want a state-wide search?" Peters asked.

"He won't leave the city," Rocco responded confidently. "He's already planned Audrey's murder and Kira's for that matter. He won't stray from his plan." Rocco checked the clip on his .45 and the 357 Magnum and then slid on one of the Kevlar vests and covered it with his black jacket. "Leon, I need to know where he's taking her and I need to know now!"

Leon picked up the laptop Peters had been using and fast forwarded the feed, watching as Barkley drove up Pennsylvania and headed toward the freeway. "He took the highway into the city," Leon said.

"I'm gonna need more than that," Rocco quipped. "I'll head that way. Call me with specifics." Before Kira could open her mouth to speak, Rocco was gone and her heart sank.

CHAPTER 45

While Peters and Leon were busily tracking Officer Barkley and relaying directions to Rocco, Kira shoved the 9mm into the back of her jeans, hooked the Taser onto a belt loop and took her temporary cell phone into the bathroom. She wasn't convinced that they were safe at the hotel and she felt better having a weapon on her.

Turing on the fan, Kira dialed The Candy Shop. She had subconsciously committed the number to memory when she had called in sick several days in a row. The first time she called, it rang and rang and no one answered. The second time it rang only three times and then she heard a voice.

"How may I help you?" Lucas asked and Kira grew suddenly nervous. She hadn't expected him to answer, then again, she didn't know what she had been expecting.

"Lucas?" Kira said sheepishly. "This is..."

"I know who you are," he interrupted. "What I don't know is why you are calling."

"Audrey's in trouble," she blurted, uncertain of why that particular phrase flew from her lips.

"Ah," he exhaled. "How ironic that it is the demure one who makes a daring move to help the one who appears most bold. Perhaps you are the strong one after all?"

He was talking in riddles again and this time, stone cold sober, Kira didn't find it poetic. "You said that you protect your girls, but..."

"I was under the impression that you and your friend were not still in my employ," Lucas interrupted. "Have I been misinformed?"

"No, we're not."

"Then I fail to see how it is my responsibility to provide protection," he rebutted.

"Do you know that Landon Parker and Ian Nader are murdering your girls?" Kira blurted forcefully. "Christine, Misty, Ilesia, Miranda and Ginger are all dead and Audrey is next!" Emotion caught in her throat and her voice cracked. "They say you're behind it and that you want me dead too. Is that true?"

Lucas didn't answer.

"Is that true?!" Kira demanded and her gut told her that Lucas wasn't responding because he was shocked by what she had told him.

"I will look into this matter immediately," he uttered, his tone not nearly as smooth as it had been before. "Thank you for bringing this to my attention."

Lucas disconnected the call and Kira stood frozen for several seconds, staring at her reflection in the bathroom mirror. Was calling him the right move? Would it somehow help save Audrey? She didn't know, but of one thing she was certain, calling Lucas couldn't make the situation any worse.

CHAPTER 46

Barkley led Audrey from the squad car, down an alley and through a door into an empty warehouse. She gimped handcuffed and helplessly along, surrendering to the fact that she would not live through the night. She didn't speak, despite the fact that Barkley never shut up. He gave her a play by play of every move, and Audrey wasn't sure at times if he was talking to her or to himself.

"When we get inside I'll make you nice and comfortable on the bed," he told her. "My ladies are usually not delivered to me conscious so this is a little different. It's exciting actually." He led Audrey through the dark, to the back of the warehouse and toward a yellowish glow that came from a lamp sitting atop a cardboard box.

He sat her down atop a queen sized bed with an un-sheeted mattress that had seen better days. Audrey surveyed her surroundings. Chains with locked cuffs were attached to the metal legs of the bed frame and positioned eerily atop the mattress awaiting the next victim. "Don't mind the restraints," Barkley said. "I've never had to use them." The warehouse was damp and cold and looked as if it had been abandoned for years; but it smelled of flowers.

"I have to tell ya," Barkley began, taking off his police belt. "You're not the one I was supposed to do, but like I always say, beggars can't be choosers." He dragged a folding chair over to the bed and sat down in front of Audrey. "You were the back-up, the understudy, if you will." Pulling a pack of cigarettes from his shirt pocket, he slid one out and lit it. "But tonight, you get to be the star of the show." He took a long drag from his cigarette and blew the smoke up in the air. "Tonight, it's all about you." He ran his fingers across the burn mark on Audrey's thigh, as if he were studying the wound. "Somebody wasn't very nice to you, were they?"

Audrey didn't answer. She just stared at him, certain that he was crazy and uncertain of what might set him off. She thought she saw a spark of anger in his eyes as he studied her burn and she didn't know if that anger was directed at her or the person who had hurt her.

Making a clicking noise with his tongue, Barkley's shoulders slumped forward. "It isn't nice to mistreat a lady like that," he said, running his fingers over the burn mark again. This time Audrey winced. "Oh," his eyes widened and he withdrew his hand, "does it hurt when I touch it?"

She nodded.

"Then I won't touch it anymore." He ran his fingers up the inside of her left thigh and down the inside of her right thigh. "That didn't hurt, did it?"

Audrey stared at him, her mind racing and fear growing in her gut. "My name is Audrey," she said quietly, remembering from an episode of CSI that abductees who connect with their abductors statistically live longer and have a higher rate of survival. "May I have a drink of water?"

A grin spread across Barkley's face, as if he enjoyed the fact that she was conversing with him. "Anything for a pretty lady," he said, retrieving a bottle of water from a small refrigerator that sat in the corner next to the bed, dually serving as a nightstand. Unscrewing the lid, he poured the water into her mouth. It was cold as it ran down her throat.

"Thank you," she uttered.

"You know I wasn't always the bad guy," Barkley said as he screwed the lid back on the water bottle and set it on the floor by the bed. "I used to be a damn good cop; but then I realized that even as a cop I couldn't stop shitty things from happening to good people. You know what I mean?" He took another drag and then dropped the cigarette butt to the floor and put it out with his shoe.

"How long have you been a cop?" Audrey asked, figuring every second she kept him talking was a second longer she would be alive.

"Long time," he said. "Too long." Barkley's eyes appeared to gloss over. "I worked my ass off at first, but I just didn't have the instincts that some of the others had. It was frustrating to work so hard for something other people just took for granted." Barkley rose from the chair and walked toward a steel cabinet, opening the door and retrieving a pair of latex gloves. "You're not allergic to latex are you?" He asked and fear gripped her. Why was he putting on gloves? Was he going to kill her right now? He slid his hands into the gloves, closed the cabinet and then approached her. "We should get this show on the road."

"I smell flowers," Audrey blurted, trying desperately to keep the conversation going.

Barkley's face lit up. "Do you want to see my garden?" He pulled her up and walked her across the warehouse, through a doorway and into a room that looked like a greenhouse. Temperature controlled lights hung low over all different types of flowers. "Let me see," he said, tapping his finger against his lips. "I'm going to need a camellia flower for you."

Audrey was shocked that he knew her name from The Candy Shop. "Did Lucas tell you that?" She asked. "Is Lucas paying you to kill me?" Tears formed in Audrey's eyes and spilled onto her cheeks and Barkley reached over and wiped them without missing a beat. "Why does he want me dead?"

"There's no need to cry," Barkley soothed. "It's business. It's nothing personal. I'm sure Lucas likes you very much."

"Why do you have to kill me?" Audrey sniveled as he led her back to the bed. "Why can't you just let me go? No one will know."

"That's not possible. See, I have to slit your throat and chop off your left ring finger and then leave you to be found in a dumpster. But don't worry, you're not gonna feel any pain. I promise." A smile filled his face. "I'm not an animal."

Audrey started to cry harder.

"I know it sounds bad, but it's necessary symbolism." He held her head against his stomach and stroked her hair. "See, the left ring finger represents the bond of marriage and the commitment one enters into with holy matrimony. When that bond is broken by infidelity, well, it is severed forever. So, the finger must be severed, but don't worry, I'll sedate you so you won't even know it happened," he assured her.

Insanity oozed from him as he spoke, and Audrey knew that her only hope was to keep him talking. *Just keep him talking.* "What do you do with the fingers you sever?" She asked and she could tell by the way he drew away from her and sat back down in the folding chair that he was excited to talk about it. It was as if he wanted to tell someone about his methods and reasoning.

"I throw them in the dumpster with the body, but away from the body, to symbolize that the marriage was thrown away. Do you get it?" Audrey could now see the wild excitement in his eyes. He was completely insane. Before she could answer his question, he continued talking. "You see, I burn the prints off of all the fingers except the one I sever. Do you know why?"

Audrey shook her head to indicate that she didn't know the answer.

"Because even if we try to hide who we are and what we've done by severing our marriage vows, the evidence of our infidelity still exists with God. It still exists on our commitment finger." Barkley's eyes widened as he pointed upward.

Omigod, he's not only insane, he's an insane religious fanatic! The most dangerous combination on the planet. Audrey cleared her throat. "Can I ask you a personal question?"

"Absolutely," Barkley beamed. "I'm really enjoying our conversation. Like I said, all of the other ladies were delivered to me sedated so I haven't had a chance to talk to anyone." Barkley's grin spread from ear-to-ear and Audrey forced herself to smile back at him. "So, what's your question?"

"Was someone unfaithful to you? Is that why you do this?"

The smile quickly left his face and Barkley sank back into the chair. *Oh no! That was a bad question to ask. You need to keep him smiling!* Audrey berated herself.

"No. It was my sister that was forced to betray her own body and she wound up dead because she broke the bonds of holy matrimony."

"Did you kill her?" Audrey hesitantly asked.

"No. Her lover did." Hatred filled Barkley's face and Audrey could see his jaw tighten with rage.

"That must have been hard to lose her," Audrey feigned sympathy. "You must have loved her a lot."

"I did." Barkley smiled again. In fact, the first woman I killed resembled my sister and it was really hard, but I did it for Adrienne. I did it to honor her and to cleanse her from her sinful ways, but mostly I did it to punish the man who violated her." Barkley's eyes lit with a gleam of insanity. "You want to hear something ironic?" He asked but didn't wait for her to respond. "The man who violated my sister and is ultimately responsible for her death is going to be blamed for all of the murders." He let out a sinister chuckle. "The ironic thing is he's a detective who specializes in finding serial killers." Barkley laughed so hard his eyes began to water. "Is that the best thing you've ever heard or what? It's brilliant, right!"

Audrey pretended to appreciate the irony, but she wasn't sure that Barkley was buying it. "Well," Barkley slapped both hands down on his knees and raised himself out of the chair. "This has sure been fun. I've really enjoyed our little chat." He walked to the cabinet and retrieved a syringe. "But, it's time to get down to business." As he approached her, Audrey began to kick her feet and scream. She thrust her body upward to try and run but she was still weak and no match for his girth. "Don't fight it. It'll just be a little stick in the neck and then you won't feel a thing."

"No!" Audrey screamed with a deep, raspy tone.

"Relax. I'll give you love before you leave this world." He pushed her backwards on the bed and climbed on top of her.

"No!" Audrey yelled. "Please! I don't want to die! I don't want to die...please...pl..." her screams faded into sobs and then the stinging sensation in the side of her neck made her body go limp.

CHAPTER 47

"Damnit! I lost him," Leon spewed and Peters dashed across the room to stare at the screen.

"Back up the time frame to the last place you saw him and roll forward again," Peters instructed.

"I've done that three times already, but I lose him on the highway," Leon groaned.

Rocco, who was on speaker phone, hollered and his voice filled the room. "C'mon guys, get it together! We're running out of time. I need to know which exit he took!"

Peters snatched the laptop from Leon and started analyzing the feed. "This don't make no sense man. He just disappears on the highway."

"He can't just disappear!" Rocco barked.

Running the feed back again, Peters noticed a gap in the time frame. "Holy shit!" He belted. "Somebody put a stop-drop in the feed."

"What does that tech-jargon mean, Peters?" Rocco huffed.

"The surveillance feed has been tampered with," Peters explained. "They erased a small block of time to create a gap which was just long enough for us to lose him."

"Can you jump the gap and find him again?" Rocco asked, but Peters didn't answer. He looked up to see a .45 aimed at his head. Leon disconnected the call and instructed Peters to put the laptop down, stand up and face the wall.

"What the hell, man?" Peters said, lifting both hands in the air as Leon pulled the 9mm from his holster and slid it into his waistband.   "You're one of them?"

"Shut up and turn around," Leon ordered and then cuffed Peters' hands behind his back. "Now, I'm going to dial Rocco and you're going to tell him you accidentally disconnected the call and then you're going to send him to this location." Leon held up a piece of paper where he had scribbled down directions.

"That's in East St. Louis, man," Peters grimaced.

"I know," Leon smirked.

"You can't send a white boy alone into East St. Louis after dark," Peters huffed.

"He won't be alone." Leon aimed the .45 at Peters' head. "Are we going to have a problem?"

"No problem," Peters mumbled as Leon redialed Rocco's number and put the call on speaker.

"What the hell happened?" Rocco barked.

"Change of plans, man," Peters spoke slowly. "You need to stay on the highway until you cross over the river into East St. Louis. As soon as you cross, take your first left on North Front Street. Pass Bloody Island

and take your next available left. There should be some barges there."

Rocco didn't respond for several seconds. "That's where Adrienne's body was found," he uttered. "I'll call back when I get closer."

"Bravo," Leon sneered.

"Man, I pegged you all wrong," Peters shook his head. "I thought you really cared about your ex-wife. I bought your whole sad sob story."

Kira sneaked quietly out of the bathroom and peered down from the balcony. She saw Peters handcuffed and Leon holding a gun and it didn't take a genius to figure out what was going on. The question was what was she going to do about it?

"You came here acting all righteous and shit, but they sent you here to stop me from being able to track down the killer," Peters huffed.

"I didn't have a choice," Leon rebutted. "None of us has a choice."

"That ain't true, man. In life that's the one thing we always got. A choice." Peters pursed his lips together and shook his head. "You can choose to do the right thing, man. You can save Audrey and end this whole thing right here and now."

The sound of the gun shot made Kira jump completely out of her skin. Leon had shot Peters in cold-blood. Pulling the 9mm from her waistband, Kira crouched down on the side of the bed, took the safety off and held the gun out in front of her. She knew

Leon would come looking for her and she knew she was going to have to kill him.

The steps creaked under Leon's weight and Kira felt as if she might vomit. Pressing her back against the wall she waited for him to reach the balcony and turn the corner.

"K...i...r...a," he called out her name in elongated, sing-song fashion. "Come out, come out wherever you are."

Kira's heart beat wildly in her chest.

"Come on out. I'm not going to hurt you. You can trust me. Peters and Rocco are working for the Coronado family. They were going to kill you."

He's lying. He's lying. He's lying. She repeated in her head over and over.

"Come on. I'll take you to see Frank. He's worried about you."

The sound of his voice grew closer and Kira's hands trembled. Would she be able to shoot him if she had to? She had never shot anyone before, then again, she had never Tasered anyone before and she seemed to be a natural at that. Her breathing quickened and she tightened her grasp on the gun.

"Michael and Mallory are worried too," Leon uttered. "Don't you want to see them again? To make sure they're safe?"

At the mention of her children's names, a defensive rage that only a mother could understand filled Kira and empowered her to leap upward from her crouching position and unload her clip into Leon's chest. The shots were rapid fire and Kira didn't stop until the

9mm chamber clicked empty and Leon lay motionless on the bedroom floor.

Bending down over the body, Kira wrapped her hands around Leon's right hand that was still clutching his gun, raised it up and fired two shots; and then she let his arm fall back down.   The fact that Leon's weapon had been fired in her general direction was enough to substantiate self-defense. "Defense attorney rule number one," she panted sarcastically.

Leaping over his body, Kira ran down the stairs toward Peters. He had taken a bullet to the chest, but he was breathing. Kira dialed 9-1-1, grabbed the duffle bag that had Rocco's extra guns and ammo, the keys to Leon's BMW and the paper with the directions to where Rocco had been sent and raced out of the hotel.

CHAPTER 48

Barkley stroked the inside of Audrey's thighs as she lay motionless on the bed. "First, I will give you love and then we'll move to the shower so it won't be messy when I kill you," he told her, as if he thought they were still actively involved in a conversation. "I'll slit your throat, cut off your finger and then burn off your prints. Then I'll wash you off nice and good." Arching back to slide on a condom, Barkley prepared to violate Audrey when all of a sudden the warehouse door burst open and two men wearing black ski masks and dressed in all black, stormed inside. The man on the right fired off a single shot, which hit Barkley just below the ribs and sent him hurling off the side of the bed. While he walked around the bed and finished Barkley off, the other man lifted Audrey over his shoulder and headed for the door. They never spoke a word and left as quickly as they had arrived.

CHAPTER 49

Kira sped down the highway, weaving in and out of traffic. Rocco wasn't answering his phone and she feared he had already walked into a trap. She crossed the Mississippi River, heading toward East St. Louis with red flags waving. This was not a part of town in which a woman should be wandering around by herself, night or day. Kira followed the instructions, turning left onto North Front Street and began scanning the road for the next opportunity to make another left. It wasn't long before she saw several barges along the riverbank and Rocco's rental car. She killed the lights, pulled to the side of the gravely dirt road and made sure her doors were locked.

She dialed Rocco's phone one more time but there was no answer. Reaching into the duffle bag, Kira retrieved a box of ammunition and reloaded the 9mm clip. She then took out the .22 pistol, loaded the chamber and slid it into her waistband. She didn't have a plan; in fact, she had no idea what she was going to do except find Rocco.

Sliding out of the BMW as quietly as possible, Kira stayed low and made a dash for Rocco's car, which was parked approximately fifty yards away. She hadn't wanted to pull too close and risk being seen but now, making the jaunt on foot in the dark made her wish she had parked a little closer. Rocco wasn't in his car and she ducked down by the back tire to catch her breath and decide what to do next. Part of her thought to call the police, but after what happened to Downing and learning that Barkley was a killer, she didn't trust them. For all she knew, there were several cops on Landon and Ian's payroll.

Kira surveyed the layout. Straight ahead on the riverbank were several barges connected to a towboat. Since this was the only structure within eyesight, she surmised that it must have been where Rocco headed. Tightly clutching the 9mm, Kira began her trek down toward the river. When she got within thirty feet of the towboat, she saw a figure pass one of the towboat windows. She couldn't tell whether it was Rocco or someone else, so she crouched low to the ground and quietly inched closer. The figure passed by the window again and this time she could make out his silhouette. It was Landon.

As she got closer she could hear voices coming from inside the towboat. It was Ian, Landon and Frank. They were all there, but where was Rocco? Had they killed him? Kira crept closer so she could eavesdrop.

"The great Detective Sterling," Landon seethed. "Not so mighty now are you? Seems ironic that you should die in this place, a short distance from where Adrienne died."

"How romantic," Ian spewed and then chuckled.

Kira climbed onto the towboat and leaned against the outer wall. "I'm gonna give you one more chance to tell me where Audrey and Kira are," Landon uttered.

Rocco didn't respond, at least not that Kira could hear.

"Just kill him and get it over with," Frank blurted and Kira could barely believe her ears. When had her husband become a murderous monster? Anger boiled in her veins and Kira clutched the 9mm tighter. The element of surprise was on her side, so if she could get a couple of shots off before they shot back, she might be able to give Rocco a fighting chance. Then again, she couldn't guarantee that she wouldn't accidentally shoot him too.

"We're not gonna kill him," Landon chided. "We're going to make sure he goes to prison for the rest of his life, labeled a serial killer, bunking with all of the killers he's put behind bars." Landon passed by the window again. "I don't want to take his life," he hissed. "I want to ruin his life."

Kira's heart was pounding. She wished she had a real cell phone that would record video or audio instead of the stupid temporary one with no apps. "You already destroyed my life the night you killed Adrienne," Rocco said sternly and Kira's breathing quickened as she strained to hear every word. "There's nothing else you can do to me. If you want to frame me, then frame me, but end this now. You've already murdered innocent women, seven counting Adrienne...."

"Innocent? Ha!" Landon clucked. "They were whores. They were all whores!"

"Audrey and Kira aren't whores," Rocco said. "Let them live. Leave them alone and you do whatever you want to me."

No! Kira felt enraged. *No sacrifices! No deals! This ends now!* She was smart enough to know that men like Landon and Ian and evidentially even Frank, weren't honorable. They would never keep their word. She knew That she and Audrey would be hunted down, if Audrey was still alive, which seemed like a long shot at this point, and killed out of spite.

"Audrey's the biggest ho going," Ian sneered. "She screwed Landon, she screwed Frank, she screwed me and she even had her claws into Lucas."

You liar! Kira gritted her teeth and inched her way closer to the door. She was mentally preparing herself to attack, when she heard something that sounded like a footstep. Kira peeled her eyes, scanning the ground between Leon's car and the towboat. She couldn't see anyone, but she distinctly heard footsteps against the ground.

Turning back to face the towboat door, Kira took a deep breath. It was now or never. Just as she raised her gun to burst through the door, a black leather glove smacked over her mouth, followed by hands that gripped her feet and her shoulders, lifting her off of the ground and carrying her quickly away from the riverbank. Kira tried to kick and squeal and even bite as she looked at the ski masked faces, one at her feet and one at her head. She kicked and thrashed, but to no avail. They took the 9mm and the .22 from her, and threw her in the back of a black, unmarked van, where the driver, whose face was also covered by a black ski mask, held her at gunpoint.

From inside the van she heard gunfire, but she didn't know what was happening. "Let me out," she begged the driver. "Please let me go," she said again, but he didn't acknowledge. Moments later, the two men returned to the van, released Kira, handing her the 9mm and the .22; and then they climbed in the van and slid the door closed. The driver stuck his left arm out the window, pointed toward the towboat and then sped off.

Kira rushed toward the towboat, stopping abruptly in the doorway. Nothing could have prepared her for the sight she beheld. Landon and Ian had been shot in the head and their brains were splattered all over the walls. Frank had been hit in the chest and blood was gurgling in the back of his throat. Rocco was taped to a chair, stained with blood from all three men, but otherwise unscathed. Kira started toward Rocco when she heard Frank trying to speak. Sobs rose in her throat and she froze. He was a monster but she had loved him for twenty years. He was Michael and Mallory's father and as much as she hated him for what he had done, she didn't want him to die. Kira felt her pocket for her phone, intending to call for an ambulance, but it must have fallen out when she was carried to the van.

"Go to him," Rocco said quietly and Kira dropped to her knees next to Frank.

Placing his hand in hers, she brought it to her lips and kissed it. "Don't die," she whispered. "Please don't die."

A tear escaped from his right eye and rolled down the side of his jaw. "I don't...deserve...to live," he mouthed, the words barely audible.

"Don't say that," Kira wept.

"I'm so...sor...sorry," he managed and then Frank was gone.

CHAPTER 50

Rocco got off the phone with Captain Jameson and turned to Kira. "The Captain says Peters is in stable condition," he told her and she breathed a sigh of relief. She had felt guilty leaving him. They retrieved the duffel bag from Leon's BMW and then left his car parked by the river with the keys in the ignition. "In this neck of the woods, it'll be stolen and stripped down before dawn," Rocco remarked.

After driving back across the Mississippi, they had one stop to make before heading to the station to meet with the Captain and begin re-hashing everything that had occurred. Formal statements and a barrage of questioning lay ahead; but Kira needed to do something first.

Rocco pulled up in front of The Candy Shop and a new valet greeted them. "Keep it running," Rocco quipped. "We won't be long."

"Mr. Coronado has been expecting you," the new valet said, taking the keys from Rocco and ushering them inside. "He asked me to tell you to meet him in the living room."

Kira knew Rocco was not happy about stopping at The Candy Shop, but she felt strongly about meeting with Lucas. Rocco made it clear that he agreed to stop only because he didn't want Kira to meet with Lucas alone. "We still don't know the depth of his involvement," Rocco warned as they entered the building. "And he's a very powerful mob Boss." Kira appreciated his concern, but oddly enough, she was no longer afraid of Lucas Coronado.

They walked straight back through the double doors and into the room where her nightmare had begun. Kira instinctively approached the stained glass windows and peered down at the stage. It felt like eons ago that she had stood gazing down at the stage, tempted by the curiosity of whether or not she was young enough or sexy enough to still dance. When the side door opened she whirled around expecting to see Lucas, and was shocked to find Audrey standing in the doorway. She looked pale and thinner than normal, but alive. Kira rushed toward her and they embraced in a tearful reunion. "I'm so sorry," Audrey cried, gripping onto Kira. "I'm so sorry."

Kira stroked her hair and held her tightly. "It's okay," she uttered softly. "Everything's okay now." She closed her eyes and fought the urge to crumble beneath the weight of her own emotions. She and Audrey had a lot to discuss but this wasn't the time or the place. When she opened her eyes again, Lucas was standing by the bar. Kira released Audrey and slowly approached him.

"The bold and the demure," he said, but this time he looked at Kira when he said the word bold and at Audrey when he said the word demure. "Indeed an irony."

Kira licked her lips and tried to keep her emotions in check. "Thank you," she said, her voice cracking.

Lucas held out his arms, palms up and shrugged. "I did nothing," he said and then subtly gave a quick wink of his right eye.

Kira understood his reason for denial, especially in front of Rocco. He could not admit to sending his men to kill Barkley or in taking out Landon, Ian and Frank; even if his motive was to save her and Audrey. Kira threw her arms around his neck and hugged him. "I know it was you," she whispered. "You kept your promise. You protected your girls."

"You will always be one of my girls," Lucas said softly and then released Kira and quickly cleared his throat. Turning his attention to Rocco, Lucas said, "Detective Sterling, or shall I call you Mr. Green?" His lips stretched into a Joker-esque grin. "I believe your work here is done?"

Rocco nodded. "We're even."

"I am happy to hear it. Now, if you three will excuse me, I have a business to run." Lucas escorted them toward the living room doors. "One more thing," he said, stopping in front of the doors. "Take Agent Collier with you. I think her work here is done as well."

"Agent Collier?" Rocco feigned innocence, as if he wasn't privy to the fact that an undercover FBI agent was at The Candy Shop.

Lucas opened the doors and they stepped into the foyer to find the Cher-look-alike sitting in one of the red velvet armed chairs, waiting. She stood up as Kira approached her.

"You saved my life," Kira said. "Thank you."

Agent Collier raised her eyebrows. "All I did was give you the tool. You saved your own ass."

CHAPTER 51

Frank's funeral was beautiful and his murderous actions and sexual sins remained a secret. Kira thought it best to let Michael and Mallory believe that their father had died standing against mafia crime. In their minds he would always be a hero.

Leon had written a clause into his Will that left everything to Audrey, despite the fact that they had divorced. She was financially set for life. After baking a batch of her mother's special chocolate chip cookies, Audrey took them to Father Montague, promising to attend mass every Sunday and to go to confession regularly.

Captain Jameson promoted Officer Reginald Peters to Special Detective and he became Rocco Sterling's new partner.

Strangely enough, the entire Nader family was found dead. Benjamin was found floating in the Mississippi with a bag over his head. The rest of the family blew up when their house exploded due to a nasty gas leak. Kira imagined that it was the ski-masked men who wiped out the Naders, though no one would ever know for sure.

With Michael and Mallory back at school, Kira gave herself permission to break down. She mourned the loss of Frank and with some professional help, came to terms with the fact that she had killed Leon albeit in self-defense. She couldn't get the images of his body out of her mind, but the therapist assured her that those too would fade in time. "Stay busy," the therapist advised, which was often easier said than done.

A day never passed without Kira thinking about Rocco. A part of her wished he would call but the night Frank was killed, she had asked Rocco to stay away. She didn't know how to cope with what had happened. At that time, she didn't know what she was going to tell Michael and Mallory and the last thing she wanted was more confusion in her heart. She needed time to process and to heal. Still, there were days and especially nights when loneliness engulfed her and she would have given anything to lie in his arms.

In the weeks that followed, Audrey and Kira met for coffee, every Tuesday morning at the Starbucks on the corner. Although it was Tuesday, Kira didn't feel like going. Teary-eyed and feeling sorry for herself, she dialed Audrey's cell phone and cancelled.

Fifteen minutes later the doorbell rang. Kira exhaled and shuffled toward the door in her oversized, white, terrycloth robe and bulky slippers. She knew when she opened the door she would find Audrey standing there, holding two cups of coffee and lecturing her on how to fight depression. Sure enough, she opened the door and there stood Audrey with two cups of coffee. "You're predictable," Kira moaned.

"Right back atcha," Audrey rebutted. "I was already in the drive-thru line to get our to-go coffees when you called to cancel."

Audrey stuck her tongue out at Kira and strode passed her, heading for the kitchen.

Kira was about to close the door when something caught her eye. It was a car that had turned onto her street and stopped in front of her house. Her heart started racing and although she wanted to yell for Audrey, she stood frozen.

Stepping out of the Hummer carrying a giant box of chocolates was Rocco, who abruptly stopped when he saw Kira standing in the doorway. Their eyes met and everything slipped into slow motion.

Butterflies fluttered in her stomach as he approached.

"You asked me to stay away," he began and Kira's eyes welled up. He drew closer. "But I was hoping, over the past several weeks that you might have had a change of heart." A single tear ran down her cheek and Rocco inched closer to wipe it away.

"I don't know how to do this," Kira whispered, emotion rising in her throat. "I don't know how to get through this."

"One day at a time," Rocco answered quietly, taking her hand in his and squeezing it tenderly. "Sometimes, one minute at a time."

Kira fell into his arms and clung to him. In that moment she knew she was going to be okay. His arms wrapped tightly around her provided the security she needed to let everything else go.

Peering around the corner Audrey met eyes with Rocco. She gave him a smile and a thumbs up and he blinked his eyes slowly and mouthed the words, "thank you." They had made a secret pact that, when the time was right, and Audrey believed Kira needed him, she would call and he would come. Audrey had made that call this morning.

Leaning forward, Kira brushed her lips against his and Rocco took it as his cue to surrender to the passion between them. He pulled her into a deep and tender kiss. A kiss that told Kira growing older didn't mean she had lost her sexiness. A kiss that let her know she didn't have to be alone. It was a kiss of healing, a kiss of truth, and one that soothed her soul. It was a new beginning.

Suddenly remembering the chocolates, Rocco handed the box to Kira. "Don't eat it all at once," he teased.

"Bite size pieces," Kira said quietly, remembering Lucas' words. "Bite size pieces."

ABOUT THE AUTHOR

S.R.Claridge, nominated for the 2010 Molly Award, 2013 Pushcart Prize and awarded the 2011 Rocky Mountain Fiction Writers Pen Award, writes full-time and lives in Colorado. She loves autumn, moonlight and Grey Goose martinis with bleu cheese or jalapeno stuffed olives. She believes Friday nights are for indulging in Mexican food and margaritas and Sunday mornings warrant an extra-spicy Bloody Mary. Growing up in St. Louis, Missouri and earning her BA in Psychology from the University of Missouri, Columbia, S.R.Claridge is a mixture of mid-western family values and western wild nights. She loves Jesus, believes in the power of prayer, in the freedom of forgiveness and that life is a gift that should be enjoyed to the fullest. With a background in theatre, S.R.Claridge creates characters with dramatic flair and is known for her intense plot twists and engaging humor. S.R.Claridge would rather walk dangerously where there's a view than sit in idle safety and let life pass her by. Her spirited outlook comes shining through in her novels, as she takes readers to the edge of their seats with bone-chilling suspense.

OTHER BOOKS BY S.R.CLARIDGE

Tetterbaum's Truth (book 1 in the Just Call Me Angel series)

Traitors Among Us (book 2 in the Just Call Me Angel series)

Russian Uprising (book 3 in the Just Call Me Angel series)

Death Trap (book 4 in the Just Call Me Angel series)

Loose Ends (book 5 in the Just Call Me Angel series)

Divine Intervention (book 6 in the Just Call Me Angel series)

Petals of Blood (short story Ebook; Pushcart Prize Nomination 2013)

Spouse in My House (short story Ebook; a la Dr. Seuss style)

House of Lies (Political cult suspense)

No Easy Way (debut novel; nominated for The Molly Award from the HODRW 2010)